COLLATERAL
CRIMES

FOR MORE INFORMATION ABOUT JEFFREY YOCHIM, GO TO

JEFFREYYOCHIM.COM

COLLATERAL CRIMES

THE FIRST RULE OF MURDER:
KEEP IT SIMPLE

JEFFREY YOCHIM

WEST WAVE PUBLISHING, LTD

Remember to sign up for the Jeffrey Yochim reader list at

JeffreyYochim.com
West Wave Publishing, LTD
2306 E. Commonwealth Ave
Chandler, AZ 85225
www.WestWavePublishing.com

Book and Cover design by 3rd St. Web

ISBN: 978-0-9975395-1-6
First Edition: April 2016

10 9 8 7 6 5 4 3 2 1

For my little sister, Missy

Acknowledgements

I want to thank:

Larry Barnes. Your hard-nosed critique of my early efforts and your guidance throughout the long process were invaluable.

Andrew Walters for contributing key story concepts.

Hickok45 and Clinton Armer for their technical firearms reviews.

My beta readers and proofreaders:

Michelle Yochim, Melissa Howell, Susan Walters, Elizabeth Yochim, Susan Hickman, Ken Franke, Melissa Carey, Tom Caswell, Brian Metro, Joni Brown, Laurel Hostetler, Glen Cantrell, Debbie Sheahan, Michael Westlake, Bill Appel, Laura Frear Stahlecker and Jeff Leonard.

Thank you all for assisting me in creating this story.

Jeffrey Yochim

ONE

VALDO ESPOSITO walked into the restaurant. The door swung shut behind him, and after his eyes adjusted to the darkness he was able to take in the familiar surroundings at the Song Tree Inn. It was late afternoon so it was quiet, except for the subtle tones of an exotic instrument drifting in the background creating an atmosphere of serenity which was wasted on him. He had no time to relax. He had a job to do.

He proceeded past the register and into the dining area, searching, not turning his head but scanning the empty tables with his eyes. A young woman in a red silk gown scooted into his path and cut him off with the cheerful greeting, "Welcome to Song Tree. Come this way, please."

He looked her over. She was small and pretty with long black hair put up in a fancy bun. Probably Korean. They own all these places.

A man called out, "Valdo," and he spotted Doc Marley seated in the corner by the window. Doc was animated, motioning for him to come over. Valdo stepped around the hostess and marched over to the table. Doc sprang out of his chair, beaming, extending his hand. "Mr. Esposito, so good to see you."

Valdo kept his hand by his side and said, "Sit down. You know why I'm here." They sat down and soon a man appeared with a menu. Valdo waved him off.

Doc said, "You really should try the spring rolls. There's nothing like them anywhere."

Valdo's stomach growled, but he said, "No thank you."

Doc picked one up, dipped it in tamarind sauce, and held it out, offering it to Valdo. "Seriously. Try one."

Valdo grabbed Doc by the wrist, bending his hand backwards. "I said no thank you."

Doc's face twisted up. "Ow, that hurts. You're hyper-extend-ing—"

"Stop talking."

"But you're—"

"Stop talking."

"Okay, okay."

"Now listen to me. Cause this is important. For you."

"I'm, I'm listening."

"Good." He let go of Doc's wrist and said, "Jimmy wants his money. Now."

Doc hesitated, opening and closing his hand.

"Do you have it?"

"No."

Valdo shook his head in disgust.

Doc said, "That's what I was trying to tell you. I have something better."

"Better than money?"

"Yes."

Valdo folded his arms.

Grinning, Doc leaned in close and said, "You know Angel Tor-rez?"

"The baseball player? What about him?"

"He's injured."

"Yeah, what's wrong with him?"

"He sprained his wrist." Doc rubbed his own wrist. "Like you almost did to me." He looked at Valdo but Valdo showed no sympathy. Doc continued, "The dummy was clowning around, sliding into second base head first—in practice!" He chuckled. "Man, are they pissed off at him."

Valdo said, "How bad is it?"

Smiling wide now, Doc said, "Torrez won't be starting tonight."

Valdo shook his head in approval as the gears turned. "Who knows about it?"

"Just me. And the Dodger management, of course. They're keeping a lid on it until game time."

"You think you can get out of paying Jimmy by giving him this information?"

"I was hoping."

"Well, this don't make the payment. Consider this your late fee."

"Okay. Thank you."

"So when can Jimmy expect his money?"

Valdo said the words in unison with Doc, "I just need a few days."

Doc's smile vanished. Valdo said, "Oh, and Jimmy's gonna want more tips like this."

"Okay. When I get some information I'll pass it along." Thinking now, he said, "For how long?"

"For how long what?"

"I have to give you guys some tips, but, you know, how long do I have to do that?"

"From now on."

Doc looked depressed.

Valdo stood up and said, "Enjoy your meal." He took a step away from the table, turned back, picked up the plate of spring rolls, and walked off saying, "On second thought, I will try them."

* * *

By the time Valdo arrived at Jimmy's, a crowd was lined up along the sidewalk. Valdo parked his car and bypassed the line, heading straight to the entrance which was blocked by an intimidating man in a black suit. Valdo said to him, "You ready to go, Daniel?"

Daniel said, "I'm ready for anything."

Valdo said, "Yeah, well, don't get too pumped," and entered the club, hurrying up the steps to the security control room. One of his guys was there and Valdo told him to leave. The control room windows overlooked the main floor and under them was a bank of monitors, recently installed to help Valdo keep an eye on things. There were cameras everywhere.

Valdo moved over to the monitor at the end of the board and punched a button he hoped was the right one. Technology was not his strong suit. The image switched from the back alley camera to the Dodger pre-game show, so that was good.

Nick, one of his guys out on the floor, yelled out, "Hey, Valdo," and Valdo looked up.

Everyone had stopped working and all eyes were on Valdo. Nick pointed to his headset. Valdo put on his own headset and heard Vin Scully hawking Farmer John sausage over the com devices. He pressed the button on the microphone, said, "Sorry," and flipped a switch on the board.

Nick said, "That's better," and everyone went back to work.

Valdo focused on the show. Ten minutes had passed without anybody saying anything about Torrez. He picked up the phone, selected an outside line, and called his bookie, Bernie. Bernie informed him the Dodgers were playing Arizona and the Diamondbacks were having a bad year so the Dodgers were favored. The spread was two-and-a-half runs. Valdo was about to place his bet when Jimmy called him on his headset. "Come see me."

Valdo spoke to his team through the head mic. "Nick's got the floor."
Nick said, "Okay, boss."

The staircase shook as Valdo trotted up to Jimmy's office. He stopped at the door and knocked. Jimmy said to come in and Valdo opened the door. Jimmy Deguardia was sitting in front of a laptop, comparing the screen with a stack of documents in his hand. He looked up and said, "Valdo, come on in, sit down a minute." He set the papers on the desk and took off his reading glasses.

Valdo said, "It's almost show time."

"That's okay. Sit."

There was an antique armchair in front of Jimmy's cherry wood desk. Valdo hesitated before sitting down on the fragile piece. Jimmy stared at him as if he were about to say something but after a long period of silence said, "Nah, never mind."

Standing up, Valdo said, "Okay. Is that all?"

Jimmy said, "No, it isn't."

Valdo settled back onto the chair. He thought he felt it crack.

Jimmy opened his desktop humidor and took out a cigar. He clipped the end of it and held a butane lighter under the other end, turning it until it was lighted, puffing it, drawing in the smoke, releasing it slowly. Valdo looked at his watch. Jimmy said, "The mayor called. He's paying us a visit tonight. I told him we could ensure his privacy."

"I understand."

"He doesn't want his wife going on Instagram and seeing pictures of him with Yvonne."

Valdo had no idea what "Instagram" was, but he got the point. "No problem. I'll give him the side booth upstairs, bring them in through the kitchen."

"Yeah, I figured you would. I already told him to go to the back. He's going to call me when he gets here. I'll give you a buzz."

"Okay."

"You know what, give him the whole room up there."

"Okay. We done?"

Jimmy examined his cigar. It was burning evenly, the ash line a perfect circle. He took another puff, blew out a smoke ring and said, "I heard that Rolf quit yesterday."

"Yeah."

"Without giving his notice?"

"Yeah. He was gonna leave in the middle of his shift. I convinced him it would be in his best interest if he stayed till closing."

"You got a replacement?"

"I'm working on it. I wanna put Daniel out there."

"The kid? He's been here what, a week?"

"This ain't his first security gig."

"Yeah, but—"

"He's a smart guy, and tough. He used to play tackle for SC."

"Yeah?"

"Yeah, he was gonna turn pro, the Raiders were looking at him, but he blew his shoulder out body surfing."

"So he's tough. You think he's ready?"

"Almost. I need to go over the rules with him, how we deal with the public."

"You make sure he doesn't do anything stupid. I don't need some young bull busting heads, bringing me lawsuits."

"Don't worry." Valdo looked at this watch again. "Is that it?"

Jimmy wasn't finished. "Did you get a chance to talk to Marley?"

"Yeah, I talked to him this afternoon."

"And?"

"Doc gave us some interesting information."

"Why do you call him that?"

"Call him what?"

"Doc. He's not a doctor."

"I thought he fixed up the baseball players."

"He does physical therapy, training, that sort of thing."

"Everybody calls him Doc. He don't seem to mind."

"No he doesn't. He didn't make the payment?"

"He gave me a tip on the game."

"Yeah?"

"Torrez ain't playing tonight. He busted his arm."

"Let me guess, they haven't told anybody."

"Yeah. I called Bernie, and the odds haven't changed."

"Did you tell Bernie about Torrez?"

"No."

"Good. He doesn't need to know. Did you let Marley slide on the payment?"

"No way." Valdo smiled. "The little weasel was shittin' his pants. I told him he still had to pay and he had to keep the tips coming."

"Very good."

"Can I go?"

"Go."

Valdo hurried down the stairs and into the control room. He called Bernie and Bernie said, "The game's about to start. You gonna place a bet or what?"

Valdo said, "Yeah, five grand on the D-Backs."

"Five on Arizona."

"No, ten."

"Ten. On Arizona?"

"Yeah, ten. Wait. Make it twenty."

"You know something, don't you?"

"I got a hunch."

"Yeah, right."

"You gonna take my bet, or I gotta call someone else?"

"It just seems peculiar, that's all."

"You been taking my money for years, now all of a sudden it's peculiar."

"Have you talked to Jimmy about this?"

"Never mind." Valdo hung up. Screw Bernie. He punched in a set of numbers and a woman answered.

"Miriam."

"Hey, Mimi."

"Valdo, it's so nice to hear your voice. What can I do for you?"

"I wanna put some money down on tonight's game."

"Which one?"

"The Dodger game."

"How come you're not going with Bernie?"

"I got my reasons."

"I don't want to step on Jimmy's toes."

"He don't care."

"Okay then. How much?"

"Twenty." Valdo hesitated before saying, "No, Twenty-five."

"You sure? That's a chunk."

"Yeah, I'm sure."

"Okay, twenty five on the Boys in Blue."

"No, on Arizona."

"Really?"

"Yeah."

"What's going on, Valdo?"

Now Mimi was starting in.

"Nothing's going on. I got a hunch."

"You got a hunch. You know, Bernie's made a fortune on your hunches."

"So this is your chance to get a piece of me."

"Oh, I love it when you talk dirty."

"You gonna take my money?"

"I don't want to take advantage of you. Well, I do, but not that way. Why don't you just bet a few dollars, then come on over and watch the game with me. Either team wins, you'll get lucky."

"I gotta work tonight."

"I've got champagne."

"I don't drink."

"I do."

Valdo knew she wouldn't give up. Might as well give her what she wants. "How about next Wednesday? I don't work Wednesday."

"You're going to make me wait that long?"

"Ain't I worth waiting for?"

"Yes you are."

"So put me down for twenty-five grand on Arizona, and I'll be there Wednesday to collect."

"You know I don't give points."

"Don't matter."

"All right, Valdo. Oh, It's going to be so much fun collecting from you."

Valdo hung up and stepped outside for one last talk with Daniel before they opened the club. Valdo, towering over him, leaned in and said, "Remember what I told you. This is a good crowd, but there's always somebody. You run into a drunk or some asshole don't want to behave, don't let him get to you. Just keep your cool and don't put your hands on nobody."

"I won't."

"Things get too hot, you call for backup."

"Don't worry, I can take care of things. I've dealt with trouble-makers before."

"I'm sure you have, but for now, you call us. We'll show you how we do things at Jimmy's. Once you been here a while, you can handle things on your own."

"Got it."

"Okay. It's time."

Valdo went back inside and Daniel went to work screening the line.

Valdo hurried to the monitor showing the Dodger game. The music in the night club had started so he put his headset on, just in time to hear Vinny announce that Torrez wasn't starting the game. A groan spread through the crowd at Chavez Ravine.

Valdo kept a close watch on the game. By the time the mayor arrived at the club, it was the top of the ninth and neither team had scored. He went to the back door and escorted the mayor's party through the kitchen, stopping them at the swinging doors while his crew secured the hallway and the edge of the floor area that was within view. He waited to hear Nick on the headphone say it was clear before he led them down the hall and up the stairs. Valdo said, "Please be seated. Monica will be here shortly to take your orders. If you need anything else, ask for me. My name is Valdo."

Back at the monitor, Valdo saw the Dodgers were coming up to bat and were two runs behind. He watched the first two Dodgers strike out swinging. One more out was all he needed. But they weren't ready to surrender.

They got a bloop single, followed by a double. An intentional walk loaded the bases. Then sonofabitch, there he was: Torrez—wrist covered in sports tape—walking out of the dugout with a bat in his hand. The stadium erupted but quieted down as the umpire called timeout so a girl could retrieve a beach ball some fan had thrown onto the field.

Up to the plate now, the injured star watched the first two pitches go by—strikes. A single strike stood between Valdo and twenty-five thousand dollars. Torrez fouled the next three pitches down the left field line before knocking a grand slam home run into the center field parking lot.

TWO

EARLY SUNDAY MORNING just after closing Valdo came to Jimmy's office and sat down on the leather sofa next to the window. He stayed quiet for a while before he said, "The club was packed last night. The receipts good?"

"Very." Jimmy looked up from his work. "I heard you lost a bundle on the game."

"Word gets around, huh?"

"So why'd you go with Mimi? What's wrong with Bernie?"

"It ain't against you. I don't want to mix my hobby with my job."

"I can respect that. What happened? Was Marley BS-ing us?"

"No, the tip was good. I just got greedy, bet more than I should've."

"You should've gone with Bernie, taken the points."

"Yeah, I know."

"All right, we'll give Marley the VIP treatment when he comes in. He's a good contact, could make us some money."

"Yeah."

"If we don't get greedy."

"Yeah."

"So how are you doing for cash?"

Valdo didn't say anything.

Jimmy said, "I know it's none of my business. I just don't want you going to the sharks, not even my guys."

Still no reply from Valdo.

Jimmy turned his hands up and raised his eyebrows as if to say, "Well?"

Valdo said, "There's a lotta month left."

Jimmy nodded. "Look, I know this guy, this FBI agent. We did some business with him after the rag heads hit the towers on 9-11."

"You worked with the feds?"

"No big thing, just kept our ears open, passed along information when we got it. Same as we did in World War II."

Valdo smirked and said, "I knew you were old, but World War II?"

"We—the organization, smart ass. Anyway, I hadn't heard from the guy in a long time. Now he calls, says he's with the ATF."

"Yeah?"

"And he's looking for a shooter."

"How much?"

"I didn't ask. I wasn't sure it was a good idea."

"Why not?"

"I don't know. The guy seemed a little queer."

"There's a lot of that goin' around."

"No, not that. He seemed odd. Flaky."

"Flaky."

"Yeah. When I knew him before, he was this all-American boy, a real straight arrow. Dark suit, buzz cut, really fit the mold. You know, I could tell he didn't like working with us, acted like it was beneath his dignity to associate with criminals."

"And now?"

"I don't know. It's like he has another personality that takes over from the boring one. He's calm and professional one minute, then suddenly he gets loud and aggressive." Jimmy thought for a moment and said, "He seems very angry. It made me nervous, so I did some checking. It turns out he had some kind of meltdown a while back. Started drinking and wore out his welcome at the Bureau. That's why he got on with the ATF. They stuck him in a field office out in Phoenix."

Valdo said, "So he's gone loco and wants me to hit someone?"

"He said it's for the government."

"You were gonna tell me earlier, weren't you?"

"I was, but I changed my mind. I'm just telling you now because I know you're broke."

"And then some."

"You know what? If you're interested, you can take some time off with pay. I'll even front you the money you get for the job."

"At how much?"

"No no, straight up. Hold you over until you get paid."

"Thanks, Boss."

"So you're taking the contract?"

"I'll talk to him, find out what the job is about."

"That's smart. I'll give him your number and you two can work things out. His name is Agent Roberts."

VALDO WAS HOME in his South Gate apartment when the call came in. On the fourth ring, he picked it up and said, "Yeah?"

The voice on the phone said, "Valdo Esposito?"

"Yeah."

"Agent Roberts. Jimmy said you're in."

"Maybe."

"You have experience driving a truck. That will be a key component to this operation."

Valdo had driven trucks for his uncle down in Mexico. Jimmy must have told him about it.

"Yeah, that's right."

"Semis?"

"Yeah. Long boxes. I never drove no doubles."

"That's fine. After you take care of the driver, you will be required to relocate the vehicle with its cargo from point A to point B."

So it was more than just a hit. Now it was a hit and a hijacking.

Valdo said, "Point A to point B?"

"Both the point of origin and your destination are located within the State of Arizona. My estimate of your total time of travel is one hour."

That was some math. Yeah, an hour from A to B, but how long from California to Arizona? And he'd have to hire a guy to drive his car when he grabs the truck. The fee had better cover all that. "What's it pay?"

"You tell me."

Valdo had never killed for anyone besides Jimmy. Jimmy always paid him ten grand, but that was a kind of bonus on top of his salary. Better double it, throw that out there and see the guy's reaction. "Twenty."

Roberts didn't hesitate. "Twenty's good. Look, I want to bring you up to speed on the operational details, but I will need to secure our communications. I'm sending you a cell phone to use."

"I don't need no cell phone."

"Well, there is a unit en route. It's a prepaid phone. Utilize it for this job and dispose of it afterward."

Valdo planned to dispose of it sooner than that.

IT WAS EARLY MONDAY MORNING when Roberts called again. Valdo picked up the phone and said, "Yeah?"

"Check your mailbox. I'll call you later."

"The mail ain't here yet."

Roberts repeated, "Check your mailbox," and hung up.

Valdo slipped a .45 into his bath robe pocket and walked to the mailboxes where a woman with blue hair was standing in the alcove smoking a cigarette. She must have been a new tenant because she actually spoke to him. She said in a smoker's voice, "The manager told me the mailman comes in the afternoon."

Ignoring her, he opened his mailbox and took out a large envelope. The woman raised her penciled eyebrows. She fished a jangly key ring out of her purse, walked over to her own mailbox and opened it, frowning when she saw it was empty. By then Valdo was halfway back to his apartment. Once inside, he went to his bedroom and grabbed a knife off the table next to his bed. Moving to the living room, he slit the top of the envelope and turned it over. A cell phone covered in bubble wrap plopped down onto the coffee table. He reached inside the envelope, snagged some papers that were still in there and pulled them out. It was a bill of lading in carbonless triplicate. The information typed on it specified a shipper in Riverside, California and a receiver in Maricopa, Arizona. The freight was listed as 38,000 lbs used machinery parts in crates, class 50, and the spaces where the date and the seal number went were empty. Valdo dropped the bill of lading on top of the phone, got dressed, and left the apartment. He was hungry, and he wanted to think.

He drove down to the Casa Buena Café and ordered breakfast: two orders of huevos rancheros with refried beans and flour tortillas. They knew him there and the waitress left a carafe of coffee on the table. While he was waiting for his food, he went over the situation. Roberts had warned him he was sending a phone, so that was expected. But why did he send the bill of lading? For the addresses? He could have written those on a scrap of paper. Roberts had something more in mind. When the food arrived Valdo devoured it, dropped a twenty on the table, and left the restaurant.

Back at the apartment, he called Jimmy and asked if he had anything for him to do today. Jimmy told him to go ahead and take care of his other business, so he settled down in front of the television and waited for Roberts to call. Walker Texas Ranger had just come on when the ball of bubble wrap on the table started to ring. Valdo ignored it. Roberts was going to have to get a few things straight, and the first thing was, Valdo didn't use cell phones. It rang three more times during the episode. Finally, his home phone rang.

Valdo picked up the phone and said, "Yeah?"

"Did you get the envelope?"

"Yeah."

"Did the phone ring? I just called you on it."

"It rang."

"Why didn't you answer it?"

"I told you I don't need no cell phone. This phone works fine."

Roberts was loud. "And I told you this operation requires secure communications."

There was a long pause.

Roberts said, "Look, Poncho, no cell phone, no twenty grand. I'm hanging up now and calling you on that phone. If you're still interested in the job, you'll answer it."

The line went dead and a moment later the cell phone rang. Valdo unwrapped it and punched Accept Call. He held it up to his ear and said, "Yeah?"

"Okay. Did you get the B-O-L?"

"Bee oh ell?"

"Bill of lading. It's in the envelope."

"Yeah, I got the bee oh ell. What's that about?"

"You're going to give it to the driver."

Valdo paused.

Roberts said, "You still there?"

"You want me to give the papers you sent me to the guy I'm doin?"

"Yes."

"That don't make no sense. The driver shouldn't even see me. Maybe once, the last thing he sees."

"You have to give it to him. Otherwise he won't proceed to the proper destination."

"It don't matter where he's going. He ain't gonna get there. I'll find a place to do it along the way."

"No no no no no. Every detail has been planned out. Your part at that stage of the operation is to execute the documentation switch at the shipping point."

"At … at the shipper? That's the worst place to do it. It should be someplace I can slip in and out without being noticed."

"You won't have to slip in. You'll be working there."

"Work? What?"

"I have arranged for you to be employed at the shipping location. That way you will be in a position to facilitate the diversion when the shipment departs. I need you to switch the bills of lading. You will also be available to report on any unexpected complications."

"I'm working there and the guy picking up the freight gets popped? Gee, I wonder who the cops are gonna suspect?"

"Relax. I have prepared a cover for you. You will need to see a man in Downey who will photograph you and produce an official looking identification. The entire process should take no more than ten minutes."

Valdo said, "Cover or no cover, I can't work in no warehouse."

"Why not? Jimmy indicated that you're a qualified lift truck operator and you know your way around a freight dock."

"That was a long time ago. I don't hump freight no more."

"It's only for a few days."

"A few days is too long. Everybody who works there is gonna see my face. I don't need that kind of exposure."

"It won't be a problem. Just blend in. Put on some work clothes."

"Listen, you're doing this all wrong. Let me do it my way."

"Look, Buddy, I'm running the show here."

Jimmy had said the guy worked for the government, and he sure sounded like it. Valdo tried to get through to him.

"I know you're running the show, but you gotta listen."

"All right, I'm listening."

"Okay. Are you gonna know when the shipment goes out?"

"Affirmative."

"Good. When you find out, you tell me."

"I tell you." Roberts sounded bored.

Valdo tried to be patient. "That's right. You tell me when the shipment goes out, then I follow the truck. I watch where it goes and wait for an opportunity."

"An opportunity?"

"Yeah, some place like a truck stop, or an off ramp in the middle of nowhere, or something. A place where I can pop the driver without no witnesses. Then I get in the truck, and I drive the truck to you, and you pay me the money."

Roberts started out calm, his voice rising as he talked. "Well, that's a nice little story, but I have a better one. In my story, you take the job that I arranged for you, and you do it the way I tell you. The difference is my story has a happy ending that includes your fee."

Valdo said, "Then my fee is fifty"

"Fifty? We agreed on twenty."

"That was for the driver. I gotta do what you say, work on a dock, do the driver where you say to, it's fifty."

Roberts exhaled. Calm again, he said, "All right, fifty. Now, as soon as we're done here, you go get your photo ID. I will text you the address. Your interview at the warehouse is scheduled for 2 PM tomorrow. Be there. Your contact's name is Glen Cornwall."

"Contact?"

"He's your immediate supervisor at the warehouse."

"He knows what's going down?"

"No, just you and me."

Roberts hung up, and a minute later the cell phone vibrated. It took a while for Valdo to figure out how to bring up the text message. He wrote the information down on a pad of paper and walked out to his car.

The address brought him to a house in an older but well kept residential area near the 605 freeway. He knocked on the door and when it opened, a man appeared in a cloud of pot smoke. He was in his late fifties, lanky. He was bald in front, but he made up for it with a long gray ponytail, and he had a large diamond stuck to his earlobe. With a tilt of his head, he invited Valdo inside. The house was well kept, but the furniture didn't fit the guy's appearance. It was old fashioned, the kind an elderly woman might own. Valdo followed the guy to a back room where he weighed and measured Valdo before taking his picture. The guy sat down at a computer and edited the photo. A special printer spat out a California driver's license which he handed to Valdo, saying, "There ya go."

Valdo examined the license. It looked authentic and his picture wasn't bad. When he saw his identity, he said it out loud, "Pancho Lopez?"

He glared at the guy and the guy said, "Hey, buddy, that's the name they said to give you."

TUESDAY AFTERNOON Valdo drove to the address typed on the bill of lading. It was a warehouse out in Riverside with a small yard and twelve dock doors, two of them with trailers and the rest empty. The asphalt in the yard was old and cracked, dotted with potholes. He parked and entered the front office. Behind the desk in the reception area sat a pale, red-haired girl with a ring in her nose who was playing a game on the computer. Valdo told her he had an appointment to see Glen Cornwall and she informed him Mr. Cornwall was busy and he could have a seat if he wanted to wait.

There were three chairs along the wall. Valdo picked the one in the middle. The door to an adjoining office was open and he could see a man inside talking on the phone. Valdo couldn't help overhearing the conversation and it became clear it was Glen Cornwall in the next room. He was talking to someone named "Wayne" and their conversation was about a cruise ship—the date of departure, the accommodations, the entertainment, etc. Personal stuff. They talked for fifteen minutes before Cornwall hung up and reclined in his executive chair.

Cornwall made Valdo wait for another half hour before yelling out to him, "All right, Lopez, come on in."

When Valdo got a closer look at Cornwall he saw a tiny man in a cheap suit and a purple shirt. Cornwall looked Valdo over and seemed disgusted with him.

Cornwall said, "Sit down."

"Yes, sir."

"I've been going over your resume." He picked up a stack of papers, holding them out for Valdo to see. "You know, I've got a box full of applications, all better than yours." He dropped the papers back down on the desk. "Unfortunately, corporate says I have to hire you. Unless there's something really bad on your record. Is there?"

Valdo said, "No, sir. It's clean."

"I know it is. I ran a background check on you. It says here you worked the dock at Behringer Trucking in La Mirada."

"Yes, sir."

"Well, they went out of business ten years ago, so I can't check with them to see if you're worth a shit." Cornwall leafed through the other resumes, lifted them up, and slammed them down on his desk. Frowning, he said, "All right, since I don't have any choice, I'm going to hire you. But I don't have to keep you." He leaned over the desk and jabbed his finger at Valdo's face. "If you're late for work, you're fired. If you're as lazy as you look, you're fired. If you have an accident, you're fired. Do you understand what I'm telling you?"

Valdo had run into his type before, at the club and in bars. Strutting little banty rooster, puffing himself up, picking fights with big men. Probably sat behind a computer in a room full of women before some relative in corporate decided it would be a good idea to give him power over other people. Valdo figured, Well I can put up with him for a few days.

"You're telling me not to screw up or I'm fired."

"I'm telling you I have you by the balls." He waited for a reaction, and seemed disappointed when he didn't get one. He continued, "You start tomorrow. Be here at 6 AM ready to work. I'll have Omar the Tentmaker put together some uniforms for you. Here, fill out these papers and give them to the girl at the front desk."

Valdo took the papers and headed out of the office. At the door, he turned around and said, "Can I ask you something?"

"What?"

"What did you do before you became a freight manager?"

Cornwall picked up his pen and started writing on a piece of paper. Without looking up he said, "None of your business."

Valdo shook his head and left.

That night Valdo was at the club coaching one of his crew when the cell phone started to ring. He said, "Excuse me," and took the call. He couldn't hear over the music so he went to the control room and closed the door.

Valdo said, "Yeah?"

Roberts said, "How'd it go?"

"What?"

"How did it go?"

"You have to talk louder."

Screaming now, Roberts said, "How did it go?"

"It went like I saw the guy and filled out the forms."

"Why didn't you call me after the interview?"

"What for?"

"This is a tight operation. You should have called to report the outcome of your meeting."

"I'll call when I have something to say."

"You will report to me at every phase of the operation."

Valdo said, "I can't talk right now, I'm busy," and hung up.

VALDO WAS GLAD to see Wednesday arrive. Roberts had called back five times. Driving a forklift would be a relief. He left early in case of traffic and to try on his uniform, arriving at 5:30. The uniform fit loosely but close enough. Since he wouldn't be wearing his suit, he couldn't carry his .45 unless he stuck it in his belt, and he figured it would dig into his back when he drove the forklift, so he left it in the car. He still had a Beretta Bobcat in his ankle holster—his backup gun.

Six o'clock rolled around and he went to work. The time clock was computerized and the forklifts were made in Japan, but other than that everything looked familiar. He thought back to the last time he had stood on a freight dock. That was the day Jimmy sent a man over to collect from Valdo. Big dumb guy with slick black hair, thought he was going to push Valdo around. Instead of the money, Valdo gave the guy a busted shoulder, threw him right off the dock. Jimmy was so impressed he hired Valdo to take the guy's place.

Back in the day, Valdo could pick up a dime with a forklift, but this morning he felt awkward climbing up onto the seat. He hadn't gotten any smaller over the years. By lunchtime he felt his skills coming back and he knew he was doing a good job, even though Cornwall kept bitching about his work.

When he got home he turned his cell phone on. There were seven missed calls from Roberts. He punched in the pre-programmed speed dial number and called him.

"Roberts."

"You called?"

"Yes I did. Why didn't you have your phone on?"

"I was either working or driving."

"You need to keep that phone on at all times."

"Look, maybe you never had no real job, but you can't take personal calls at work."

"You don't have a choice. You will keep that phone on."

"Fine. But if you get me canned, I'm collecting my money anyway. You got it?"

"Calm down. You're not getting fired."

Valdo kept the phone on after that. Roberts called him two or three times a day to tell him things or ask him questions. It was never anything that couldn't have waited, it was just Roberts keeping him on a leash, yanking the chain. At least once a day Cornwall would catch Valdo talking on the phone, and every time he responded with threats and insults and comments about Valdo's mother. This went on for a week-and-a-half.

LATE SATURDAY MORNING, Valdo got an angry call from Cornwall.

"I need you down at the warehouse."

"What's going on?"

"Corporate called. They've got a special shipment."

"Yeah?"

"Yeah. It has to go out today, so get your fat ass in here."

Why did he have to talk like that?

Valdo drove out to Riverside to find Cornwall brooding in the dispatch office. The warehouse was quiet; they were the only ones there. Cornwall handed Valdo a bill of lading and told him to find the crates and load them to go. He didn't say which door to load them in, but there was only one trailer backed up to the dock—a 53 foot Wabash that looked brand new. Valdo walked out onto the dock and looked at the bill: 38,000 lbs used machinery parts in crates, class 50, the same thing printed on the bill of lading Roberts had sent him, but instead of going to Maricopa, the load was shipping to Nogales, Arizona.

He found some crates in the back of the warehouse and checked their PRO number labels. They matched the number on the bill, so he jumped on a forklift and started to load them, driving back and forth from one end of the building to the other. He was bringing one of the last crates into the trailer when his cell phone rang. He struggled to fish it out of his pants pocket. His entire focus was on the cell phone and he almost had it when the forklift jarred to a halt.

He had rammed the forks into the stack of crates.

Maybe he could ease them out without causing any damage. He put the forklift in reverse and pulled back an inch at a time, but at three inches, one of the crates popped open and spilled its contents onto the trailer floor. Strewn across the smooth laminated hardwood was a jumbled pile of military weapons: AK47s and M16s.

Okay. This was the freight Roberts was hijacking.

His cell phone rang a few more times before his pocket went silent. He scanned the rifles, covered with cosmoline grease, poking out here and there through a chaotic nest of excelsior packing material. It looked like the Easter basket from Hell. He backed the forklift up, moving the intact crates out of the way and lowering the broken one to the trailer floor. He climbed down off the forklift, grabbed an armful of rifles, and as he was putting the guns back into the crate, he heard Cornwall screaming from behind the forklift.

"What the hell is going on here?"

Squeezing past Valdo into the trailer, Cornwall looked at the broken crate and said, "Son-of-a-bitch. Big ape can't do …" His eyes grew wide and all the color ran from his face. He opened his mouth, gaping like a fish, and turned to leave but collided with Valdo, who was now standing right behind him. He tried to push his way past, but Valdo stopped him with his hand. He tried again. This time Valdo just cocked his head a little and gave him a hard look. Cornwall's face changed from shock to understanding, then to fear. He began to tremble. He said, "We, uh, we should call the police." There was desperation in his voice. He looked at the guns, looked at Valdo, and looked back at the guns. "Maybe the FBI. This is really bad." By now he was squeaking.

Valdo was matter-of-fact. He said, "No. We're not gonna call nobody."

Cornwall said, "I mean it. We're in a lot of trouble."

Valdo said, "We?"

Cornwall paused, straightened his tie, cleared his throat, and in his best manager voice said, "Why don't I call the driver and tell him the shipment's been canceled. Then we can figure a way out of this mess. Whatever trouble you're in, you don't want to make it worse. Look Pancho, I can help you. I can tell them that you didn't know anything about it."

Valdo said, "You gonna help me? Well thanks, but I don't need no help. You do."

Cornwall's eyes darted left and right, twitching, and beads of sweat appeared on his forehead. Was he having a heart attack? That would make things a lot easier.

Cornwall looked up and said, "I won't tell anybody, I swear."

Valdo said, "I'll make sure of it." He looked at his watch and said, "Well, —"

Valdo's cell phone rang and Cornwall shrieked, his voice sounding like a little girl's. Valdo worked the phone out of his pocket and looked at the screen. It was Roberts. Who else would it be? He shrugged and said, "I gotta take this."

Cornwall edged towards the door and said, "No problem."

Valdo held up a finger and said, "Just a minute."

Cornwall stopped. He looked resigned to his fate, his shoulders slumping.

Valdo put the phone to his ear and said, "Yeah?"

"Why didn't you answer your phone?"

"I was in the middle of something."

"Is everything all right there?"

"… Everything's fine."

"You sure? You hesitated."

"Well, we had a little problem, but it's under control."

Cornwall started to whimper and Valdo waved his hand to hush him up.

Roberts said, "What kind of problem?"

"I really can't go into it right now. So what do you want?"

"The shipment is going out tonight."

"Yeah, I can see that."

"What do you mean?"

"I just loaded a bunch of crates for Nogales. I figured it was them."

"Do you remember what I told you?"

"I know what to do."

"Are you sure everything is okay?"

"Everything's fine. Just a couple loose ends to take care of."

"Well, take care of them. Things are moving fast."

"Don't worry about it."

Valdo put the phone into his pocket and said to Cornwall, "I'm really sorry, Boss. I know you don't like me taking no personal calls while I'm on the clock."

By now Cornwall had composed himself again. He said, "That's okay. It sounded important." He sniffled and wiped his nose with his shirt sleeve.

After they stood there for a moment, Valdo said, "Now, where was I? Oh, yeah." He reached down, drew the Beretta, and pressed the barrel up to Cornwall's forehead.

THREE

JONATHAN STARKER FOCUSED on the high definition TV display attached to his Woodway treadmill. He wasn't supposed to see the movie showing at the Convention Center in Mesa, Arizona, at least not from his home. The event wasn't being broadcast, but it was being recorded and there was a live feed available for the promoters in New York to keep track of their investment. One of the engineers at the Center had told him how to hack into the feed, so Jonathan was able to exercise and enjoy the entertainment at the same time.

The movie was the premiere of West Wave I, the first installment of the West Wave Trilogy. It was an action-adventure fantasy set in a hybrid world, a combination of Ancient Rome and the Old West. An aqueduct carried water from an alpine lake to the sleepy town of Ovest, a Roman village on the far edge of the empire, where it filled the communal bath inside the rowdy saloon, as well as the horse trough outside. In Ovest, citizen homesteaders wore togas with cowboy boots and Stetson hats, and Gladiators entered the arena ready to draw their six shooters.

West Wave focused on a particularly bizarre cast of characters. One such character was Angelini, known as "Angel". She was tall and blue-eyed, with long blond hair that swept down across her impossibly round breasts, which were so colossal they could barely be constrained behind her skimpy leather breastplate. Another character was Tamara, known as "Mara", who was taller, her breasts even larger, but with eyes, hair and skin a deep, rich ebony hue. Their bodies swelled with an armor of bulging muscles which quivered with the slightest movement; their clear, smooth skin glistened with oil. Then there was Giovani—Geo, the movie's hero, who was built like a Russian weight lifter. He was a tremendous mass of sinew and flesh, a human monument to anabolic steroids.

As strange as the story's concept and characters were, the people who came to see them were even stranger. They were devoted fans, fully immersed in the West Wave experience. Many of them came dressed as their favorite characters, and the quality of the costumes ranged from the professional to the pathetic. The promoters were anxious to see how these true believers accepted the film. Science fantasy freaks were notoriously critical about how closely film adaptations followed their favorite book or television show. So far, audience reaction was positive, but the final scene would be the real test.

Jonathan stopped running and picked up his iPad. He navigated to the West Wave Internet forum and scrolled through the posts.

> awesome
> perfect ;)
> just like the novels
> makes L.O.T.R. look like sesame street

Jonathan smiled. He turned on a pedestal fan, aimed it towards the treadmill, and went back to his running. The rip-roaring tale played out on the screen with the good guys hanging on the edge of certain destruction. One predicament led to another and all appeared lost until Our Hero came through at the last possible moment to save the Roman village through strength, determination, and massive firepower.

As the velvet curtains closed in from the sides of the stage and the overhead lights blinked and fluttered to life, the room filled with applause which turned into a standing ovation.

A man with a wireless microphone walked onto the stage. The applause got louder.

The announcer egged them on. "Ladies and gentlemen, citizens of Ovest, wasn't that a-maz-ing?"

The convention crowd whistled and cheered.

Backstage, the director screamed into his walkie-talkie, "What do you mean, you can't find him?"

The announcer continued. "The exclusive, world premiere of West Wave I, presented to you by the first annual West Con International."

More applause.

"And now, the moment you've all been waiting for, live and in person, the creator of the West Wave Trilogy, Jonathan Starker." He turned to his right with his arm outstretched but nobody came onto the stage. He looked confused.

The audience started to chant, "Jon-a-than, Jon-a-than, Jon-a-than …"

A woman came from the side of the stage and whispered in his ear. He mouthed something obscene and stormed off the stage.

After a while the chanting faded, giving way to grumbling.

Jonathan stopped the treadmill and picked up the iPad. The forum posts had turned ugly.

> "movie was great but no js"
> "where the h3ll is he?"
> "Sht. Stiffed us again"
> "200 bks for no show. rip off"

He put down the iPad and went back to his treadmill.

When Jonathan stopped taking his Zoloft several months earlier, these workouts had become his coping mechanism. His office/bedroom was spacious at seven hundred square feet and he had a comprehensive assortment of professional exercise equipment. His mother had encouraged him to add them to his collection of high-end video arcade and virtual reality games. She said it was more appropriate for a man his age. He was twenty-eight.

The MacBook on his desk started to beep, indicating he had an incoming video call. When the treadmill slowed, he hopped off and went over to the desk. He clicked the icon to accept, and a face appeared in the video chat window: an attractive woman in her mid-fifties with hazel eyes and auburn hair. It was Jonathan's agent, Debrah Schwartz, calling from New York. She did not look happy.

"Jonathan?"

"Yes, Deb?"

"Where are you?"

"In my office."

She took off her glasses and moved in close to the screen to see the room behind Jonathan. "Oh no, not again. Jonathan, why aren't you in Arizona?"

What could he say? "I can't. I just can't."

"First you pull your disappearing act in San Diego, now you don't even bother to show up. You get a reputation, Jonathan, and your fans will turn on you."

"I'm sorry, Deb." He looked at his iPad. There were at least 40 more angry posts on the forum.

Debrah said, "Hey, Jonathan, over here."

He turned back to the laptop.

Debrah said, "I swear, in the 30 years I've been doing this, I've never had a client who didn't love going on stage."

Jonathan shrugged.

"I don't know what you're afraid of, Jonathan. Those people

aren't going to hurt you. They adore you."

"I know."

Her face contorted and her voice became stern. "I've coddled you as long as I can. I went along with letting you video conference your appearances, but they want you, Jonathan, not your face on a video screen. You have to go there, you have to be there for them."

Jonathan shook his head no.

"You can't stay holed up in your mother's basement forever. You have to stop hiding from the world."

"It's not a basement. It's my home office."

Debrah sighed. The emotion left her voice. "Okay. Okay, we can fix this. Pack your bags, Jonathan. I'm sending a car over to pick you up and take you to the airport." She fiddled with her iPhone. "Let me see. I can get you on a Southwest flight from John Wayne to Phoenix Sky Harbor. Done. Your boarding pass will be waiting for you at the ticket counter. We'll have you on that stage tomorrow. Sunday's a bigger deal, anyway. They'll be happy to get you on Sunday. Okay, Jonathan? Jonathan? Okay?"

"You know I can't do that."

"Look, it'll be all right. You can handle a one hour flight, I know you can, you'll be just fine. I'll get you something to calm your nerves. The driver will pick it up on the way over."

"Deb?"

"What, Jonathan?"

"Who in their right mind schedules a convention in Phoenix in July?"

"Just be ready to go."

JONATHAN WALKED out of his room, turned, and started down the hallway. His mother was sitting in the living room, gossiping with her friend, Rita Talmeier. Jonathan tried to be stealthy but Rita locked on to him as he was passing by.

"Oh hi, Johnny. Your mother was just telling me how they made your comic book into a movie. How exciting!"

Jonathan's mother said, "Graphic novel, Rita. Johnny doesn't write comic books. He's an artist. You know, he's won awards for his work. Go get them, Johnny. Show Rita your trophies."

"Maybe later, Mom. Can I talk to you?"

"Sure, Johnny, of course."

They stepped into the kitchen.

"Mom, I need you to drive me to Phoenix."

"Okay. When?"

"Now."

"Oh, you've got to be kidding. I have to go to work tomorrow."

"Why do you keep working, Mom? I can pay the bills. I've got plenty of money."

"I love my job."

"Then just take a few days off. I'll pay you to take me."

"Oh, no. The last time I did that, you left me sitting there by myself with all those strange people."

Jonathan shuddered. That was Comic Con, and it was a nightmare. Thousands of fans swarming him, trying to get his autograph and take pictures with him. It made him feel as if he were suffocating. He had stayed as long as he could before he made an excuse and fled the convention center. He ended up viewing the ceremony on the hotel room TV, watching as the camera zoomed in on the empty seat next to his mother when Debrah accepted the Eisner Award for him.

His mother put her hand on his arm and said, "Johnny, you really should make another appointment with Dr. Shakoor."

Jonathan turned away and said, "Never mind." He wasn't going to waste any more money on that quack. He walked over to the refrigerator and looked inside. Out of the corner of his eye he saw his mother frowning as she returned to the living room. He overheard Rita say, "What was that all about?"

"Johnny wants me to drive him to Phoenix."

"Oh?"

"I can't do that. I have to go to work. Now, what was that about Mark?"

Jonathan tuned them out and rummaged through the fridge. The yogurt looked good but they were out of cherry. Maybe the leftover meatloaf? He was reaching for an apple when he caught something Rita said about her son's new truck.

"Mark is so proud of it. He was scheduled to go to Colorado, but he traded another driver for Riverside just so he could come down here and show it to me. I was hoping he could stay and visit, but he has to go back to Arizona."

Jonathan edged into the living room. He said to Rita, "Arizona?"

"Yes. Some place called 'Nogales.'"

"Nogales, Arizona?"

"Yes." Rita Talmeier was old and frail, not as sharp as she used to be, and she wasn't taking the hint.

The thought of hitching a ride on a big rig did not appeal to Jonathan, but it sounded better than dealing with the anxiety attack he would face on a crowded bus or, God forbid, a plane. He persisted.

"Your son, Mark, is driving to Arizona tonight?"

Rita said, "Yes," and her face showed a flash of inspiration. "Oh, you know, you could ride along with him. He's going right through Phoenix."

Finally.

"You sure he wouldn't mind?"

"Oh, no. He's all alone in that truck. I'm sure he'd love to have some company." She looked at the clock and said, "Oh, we'd better go. I want to fix Mark a nice dinner before he leaves."

Jonathan threw some clothes into a bag and followed Rita out to her car. It was a battery-powered two seater about the size of a golf cart. Jonathan looked it over and said, "What happened to your Buick?"

"I traded it in. The man said this one is better for the polar bears."

"Polar bears?"

"Oh yes. All their ice is melting. That's why I bought this car. To help the polar bears."

"That's um, admirable. Where should I put my suitcase?"

"Oh dear, I have some clothes for Goodwill in the back. I'm afraid you'll have to hold your bag on your lap."

Jonathan got in the passenger seat and yanked on his suitcase, wedging it sideways so he could close the door. He couldn't keep it from bumping against Rita's arm, but she said it was fine and they took off down the street with the suitcase blocking Jonathan's view.

Rita drove Jonathan to her house, and as they approached it she pointed to the semi tractor parked out front. "That's Mark's new truck," she said. "Isn't it beautiful?"

Jonathan peeked around the suitcase and had to agree it was an impressive machine. It had a long hood in the front and a huge cab that extended far to the back. The finish was a deep red color, polished and shining. The hood was open, swung forward and hanging over, exposing the engine. Front and center on the hood was a red and chrome emblem with 'Peterbilt' in chrome script. There was a man leaning over the engine doing maintenance. Mark, he supposed. Rita honked and Mark turned around. Tall and athletic, he was a match for the truck. With his tanned skin, his wrinkled face, and his long hair, he looked like an aging surfer.

Rita pulled into the driveway and parked. They got out of the car and Rita called to Mark that dinner would be ready in 20 minutes. Mark called back he was sorry but they didn't have time, they had to leave right away, so Rita walked down to the truck and hugged Mark goodbye and told him to have a safe trip. Mark thanked her and lowered the hood.

Jonathan carried his suitcase down to the truck. He said, "Hi, I'm Jonathan," and they shook hands.

Mark said, "You can put that in the sleeper cab," and stepped up into the driver's seat.

Jonathan climbed up into the passenger seat and looked around. The truck was not what Jonathan had expected. Everything was plush and cozy; the passenger seat was as comfortable as the twelve hundred dollar Herman Miller chair he had in his office; the area behind the seats looked like the sleeping quarters of a motor home, with a bed, a television, and a refrigerator. When Mark started the engine, Jonathan could sense the power, but the cab was so well insulated it wasn't at all noisy. It reminded him of a luxury car.

Jonathan said, "You have a nice truck."

Mark said, "Thanks," and opened up a laptop computer.

"Hey, why do you have two brake pedals?"

"What?" He didn't look up.

"The brake pedals, you have two of them."

Mark looked down at pedals and started to laugh. "That one's the clutch."

Jonathan blushed and said, "Oh, yeah, like on a motorcycle."

"You ride bikes?"

"Well, actually—"

"—Dirt bikes, right? Mom said you didn't have a driver's license."

"A simulator. It's very realistic. I had it flown in from Japan."

Mark laughed even harder.

When he gained his composure, he said, "I'm sorry, Dude. Look, you ever want to ride a real motorcycle, come with me. I'll take you out to the dunes. I mean it."

"Dunes?"

"Sand dunes, out in Glamis, right outside of Yuma. Me and some guys from the force like to head out there, putzy around in the sand. Between all of us we've got every kind of bike and quad you could imagine. Anything you want. We'll set you up."

Guys from the force. Jonathan remembered hearing Rita tell his mother that Mark used to be a cop.

Mark said, "You'll have fun, I promise. We ride until the sun goes down, then we boil up some shrimp, build a campfire, pass the bottle. Someone always brings a guitar. Oh man, the singing is brutal. But you can't beat the company."

Jonathan said, "Sure," but didn't sound convincing.

"Well, you don't have to decide right now. Just think about it. The offer's always there." He folded the laptop and tossed it into the sleeper cab. "We'd better hit the road. I've got a load in Riverside, have to be in Nogales by morning. I can drop you off when we pass through Phoenix."

"I really appreciate this."

"No problem. It's always nice to have someone to talk to." He pulled the gearshift lever towards himself and back, pushed a couple buttons on the dashboard—a red one and a yellow one—and the wheels hissed. The truck jerked a little, rolling forward an inch.

Jonathan said, "Air brakes?"

Mark said, "Uh huh." He pulled the truck away from the curb and headed for the freeway. "Once we pick up the trailer I'd like to put some miles behind us before we stop to eat. That okay with you?"

"That's fine."

"Hey, you like to be called John, or Jonathan?"

"Jonathan."

When they got to Riverside, they exited at Columbia and worked their way over to the warehouse. There was a trailer backed up to the dock.

Jonathan said, "Is that yours?"

"Yeah." Mark pulled into the yard and backed up to the trailer. He set the brakes, said, "Stay here. I'll be right back," and climbed out of the truck.

Jonathan watched him in the mirror as he walked towards a ramp leading into the warehouse. He was limping.

FOUR

Glen Cornwall's crumpled body lay silent next to an AK47 as a pool of blood spread across the trailer floor, soaking the excelsior and seeping under the crates. Valdo walked to the maintenance supply cage and came back with a broom, a dustpan, a sack of absorbent clay, and a large black cleanup bag. He rolled the body into the bag and sprinkled the clay over the blood. He swept up the clay and poured it into the bag, which he propped against the sidewall of the trailer.

Working fast now, he nailed the broken crate back together, stacking the rifles inside before hammering down the lid. He removed the dock plate, pulled down the rollup door, and secured the latch with a heavy-duty seal, the kind that has to be cut off with bolt cutters, and realized he needed to record the seal number. He went to his car and came back to the trailer with the bill of lading Roberts had sent. Squatting low and holding the seal at an angle so he could read it, he wrote the seal number in the space provided.

He hurried to the dispatch office and fed the real bill of lading into the shredder, which chewed it up and stopped, the job completed. It was then he heard the semi pulling into the yard.

Valdo picked up the phone. He talked to the dial tone—play

acting the dispatcher—when the driver came walking up the ramp, swinging his leg with each step. Valdo hadn't been there when the trailer was dropped off, and he was surprised how tall the driver was. He could almost look Valdo straight in the eye. Valdo concluded his imaginary conversation and turned to the driver.

"What can I do for you?"

The driver pointed his thumb towards the trailer. "I'm picking up the load for Nogales."

"Oh, yeah." He walked over to a stack of papers. The fake bill of lading was on the top. "There's been a change. This shipment ain't going to Nogales."

"Where's it going?"

"Maricopa." He handed the document to the driver.

The driver looked it over and said, "Maricopa? That's a lot closer."

"Yeah. The shipper wants to save money, have it go to Maricopa instead. They got a place there." Valdo making it up, acting natural.

"Well, the agreement was for Nogales. I'll have to charge the same whether it goes to Nogales or Maricopa. That was the deal."

"Don't matter to me. I ain't paying it."

"What time does it have to be there?"

"Same time, eight in the morning."

Valdo's cell phone rang. He let it ring until it didn't.

The driver said, "That's a lot of wait time. Any chance they'll take it early?"

"They said eight. Be there at eight."

"Doesn't hurt to ask." The driver signed the papers and handed them back to Valdo.

Valdo pulled out the driver's copy and gave it to him, saying, "Have a safe trip."

"Thanks."

Valdo watched the driver hobble back down the ramp. When he was out of earshot, he opened his cell phone and called Roberts.

Roberts said, "Why didn't you answer?"

"I was talking to the driver. He just picked up the load."

"Are you following him? You're supposed to tail him to Maricopa."

"Relax. He's just hooking up to it now."

"Then say that. Don't tell me he just picked it up."

"You know, I could take care of him right now and drive the truck the whole way, make sure it gets there."

"No good. If he gets stopped for an inspection along the way, it's their sack of shit. If you get stopped, it's mine."

Valdo wondered who 'they' were, and what they would think of the sack of shit bleeding in the back of the trailer. He heard footsteps and turned around to see the driver coming back up the ramp. He said to Roberts, "Hold on."

The driver said, "Hey, there's a lock on the fifth wheel pin."

Valdo put the phone down and walked out of the office. The driver followed him over to a greasy cardboard box full of pin locks. They all had keys in them. Valdo found a key without a lock and grabbed it. He walked down the ramp, stooped under the front of the trailer, and removed the lock from the pin, getting grease on his bare hands. The driver said thank you, but Valdo walked silently up the ramp. He went to the men's room and scrubbed the grease off before it could spread and get all over him the way fifth wheel grease does. When he was sure he was clean, he returned to his phone.

"I'm back."

"What was that all about?"

"Nothing. I had to take the lock off the trailer."

"What lock."

"It don't matter. Hey, are you sure you don't want me to take care of things here?"

Roberts became angry. "No. Just wait for him to depart the premises, and follow him—discretely. And don't forget to check in."

* * *

MARK CLIMBED BACK into the truck and pushed in the red and yellow buttons, put the truck in gear and backed the tractor under the trailer. Jonathan felt the trailer pushing down on the truck, and heard them latch together as the truck bumped solid up against it. Mark shifted gears and pulled forward a bit, dragging the trailer. He got out of the cab and Jonathan heard him work on the rig, getting it ready to go. Mark got back in the cab and opened his laptop, saying to Jonathan, "Change of plans. We're not going to Nogales."

"What?"

"Yeah, they want me to take it to Maricopa instead."

"They do? Can you still drop me off in Phoenix?"

"Oh, yeah, don't worry."

Mark closed the laptop, released the brakes, and pulled the rig out of the yard. He worked his way back to the freeway, and brought the truck up to 55 miles an hour. Ten miles later, Jonathan got a call from Debrah.

"Hi, Deb."

"I just got off the phone with your mother, Jonathan. She says you hitched a ride on a truck."

"Yes, I did."

"You're not just making up a story?"

Jonathan put the phone on speaker, turned to Mark, and said, "Honk your horn."

"What?"

"Honk your horn."

Mark pressed the center of the steering wheel and the horn beeped.

"No, the loud one. The truck horn."

Mark grabbed the cable and gave it a good, long blast.

Jonathan said to Debrah, "Now do you believe me?"

Debrah said, "All right, Jonathan. You know you could have at least texted me."

"I'm sorry, I forgot. I was in a hurry."

"Well, I was able to get the promoters to reschedule your appearance for Sunday evening. You will be there, right?"

"Yes, Deb."

"I'll text you the details."

After the call, Jonathan turned to Mark and said, "I don't have to get to the Mesa Convention Center until tomorrow evening."

"Mesa? I thought you were going to Phoenix."

"I meant Phoenix in the general sense. Google Maps showed it right next to Phoenix."

"It is."

"Is that a problem?"

"It could have been if I was going to Nogales, but we have time to kill now that I don't have to drive through the whole darn state. Let's see, if I drop you off on the way through, you'll be there about one or two in the morning."

Jonathan's phone vibrated and he pulled up the incoming text message. He read it and said, "Damn."

"What's the matter?"

"Debrah booked me into the Marriott."

"So?"

"That's where all the fans are staying. The promoters worked out a special rate."

"Fans? Your fans?"

"Yes."

"You have fans."

"Yes."

"So you're like what, a celebrity?"

"I guess so."

"That sounds pretty cool."

"No, it's not cool."

"Why not?"

"Those people will be all over me."

"Let me get this straight. You get the rock star treatment because you write comic books?"

"I don't write comic books."

"I thought you were going to a comic book convention."

"I create graphic novels."

"Graphic novels?"

"Yes. Besides being artistically superior, my novels contain a sophisticated story line beyond the limited restrictions of a comic book."

Mark laughed. "I didn't know that. Well, I'll tell you what. I wouldn't mind being a star."

"It's not all that great."

"Are you kidding? When you're a star, you can have pretty much any woman you want. Uh, you do like women, don't you? I don't mean to get personal."

"Of course I like women. It's just that I never …"

"Never?"

There was a long period of silence until Mark said, "Well, I could drop you off somewhere else. Do you know anybody in the valley?"

"I don't know anybody in Arizona."

More silence, again broken by Mark. "Tell you what. This is my last load till Monday. Why don't you come on over, hang out at my place. It's down in Arizona City, a couple hours from Phoenix. I'll call my girlfriend, Cathy, have her bring her sister with her. They're real nice girls, cute too. Her sister's a little young but probably just right for you."

"I don't know."

"Come on. We'll throw some rib-eyes on the grill, blend up some margaritas, relax by the pool. Give you a chance to decompress before your gig. And, you won't have to deal with the fans."

Jonathan said, "How am I going to get to Phoenix?"

"Cathy can drive you. Don't worry, she doesn't drink, used to be Mormon. Clean living kind of stuck with her, I guess."

They both laughed. Jonathan wasn't sure what he was getting into, but Mark seemed okay. "All right, that sounds good. Thank you."

"No problem, my friend."

They were almost to Beaumont when Mark said, "There's a Pilot truck stop in Palm Springs, has a Wendy's."

"They don't have a restaurant? I like truck stop food."

"You eat at truck stops?"

"I used to. I always took the Greyhound on my book signing tours."

"A lot of them have switched to fast food. Man, it's a shame."

"It sure is."

When they got to the Wendy's, Jonathan got another call from Debrah, so Mark took Jonathan's order and left him in the truck while he went inside.

VALDO FOLLOWED the truck off the freeway at Indian Canyon Drive to the Pilot station, driving past it so the driver wouldn't see him. He turned around and came back, parking his car in the lot a short distance from the truck. From there he watched the driver climb out of the cab and walk over to the Wendy's. Valdo looked around and saw the truck was in the perfect place for him to hijack it. It was farther back than the other trucks, so the cab was hidden, and if he used his suppressed Ruger MK II, nobody would hear him pop the guy. It wouldn't be a problem getting someone to pick up the car, either. Jimmy had people in Palm Springs. It would be so easy.

The Pelican case he used to transport his handguns was on the back seat. Valdo grabbed it, opened it, and removed the Ruger along with the suppressor which he screwed onto the barrel. He stepped out of the car and moved behind the row of trucks, entering the gap between his target and the truck next to it. He stalked along the trailer until he reached the back of the tractor, where he could watch for the driver without being spotted. Ten minutes went by before he saw the driver leaving Wendy's with bags in his hands. When the driver was half-way to the truck, Valdo raised the pistol and sighted him in. Valdo waited, hanging back in the shadows with his finger on the trigger.

The truck parked next to his target released its brakes and drove away, leaving Valdo exposed.

He tried to squeeze into the space between the tractor and the trailer, but there wasn't enough room. He hid the pistol behind his back and watched the driver come closer and closer. Twenty feet from the truck, the driver stopped to look into one of the bags and Valdo slipped away. By the time Valdo returned to his car, the driver was back in his truck.

Hungry and forced to wait, Valdo walked over to the Wendy's and went inside. He scanned the room. The place was packed—not a single open table. After he used the restroom, he waited in line to order his dinner, keeping an eye on the truck outside. When his food arrived, he carried it back to the car, and on his way he noticed the dome light glowing in the truck cab, but he couldn't see inside.

Valdo had just bitten into his cheeseburger when his phone rang. He opened the phone and said, "Yeah?"

"Where are you?"

"I'm in Palm Springs. Our boy got hungry."

"He's not supposed to stop. They always drive straight through, dammit, that was the deal with the ATF. Well, keep me informed, let me know if he makes any more stops."

Roberts had let it slip, and it made Valdo wonder: If the ATF— the Bureau of Alcohol, Tobacco, Firearms, and Explosives—was using this guy, why would Roberts be hijacking the load? And why was the ATF shipping guns in the first place? Was this a sting operation?"

Roberts said, "You still there?"

"Yeah, I'm still here."

"Good. Do you have the Eloy address?"

"Yeah. I mapped it out two days ago."

"Good."

Valdo looked up just in time to see the truck leaving the parking lot. He dropped the phone and said, "Shit," yanking the gear selector, putting the car in Drive. He rushed out of the lot and as he approached the intersection, the light turned yellow, so he stomped on the accelerator and made a hard left. His cheeseburger rolled off his lap, bounced onto the floor and fell apart, cheese and meat and lettuce and tomato all spread out and covered with lint and shoe grime.

THE SUN WAS SETTING as the big truck rumbled down Interstate 10 past Desert Center. Nobody had said a word since dinner. Finally Mark broke the silence.

"I gotta ask."

"Ask what?"

"Don't be offended."

"Just say it."

"I heard you were living in your mother's basement."

Here we go. Rita Talmeier and her big mouth.

"I am not living in my mother's basement."

"See, now you're offended. I didn't mean anything by it. I just wondered—"

"I live in a family room that my father built on to the house. At ground level."

"Well that makes more sense. I didn't think houses in La Mirada had basements."

"It's more like an apartment."

"Yeah?"

"It's big. I use it as a combination office/bedroom. It has its own full bathroom."

"That doesn't sound too bad."

"It's not. I can do my work in there without being disturbed."

"Have you ever thought about getting a place of your own?"

"I've thought about it. I've just never done it."

They crossed over the Colorado River and passed the sign: Arizona, The Grand Canyon State Welcomes You. A few moments later, they saw the sign for the truck scales.

Jonathan said, "Do we have to stop?"

Mark pointed to small black electronic device near the top of the windshield and said, "See that green light? That means we don't have to. That's the beauty of the PrePass system." He kept driving and they were a little way past the scales when he pulled into a rest area and parked.

"What are we stopping here for?"

"I need to get something." Mark unlocked a cabinet in the sleeper cab.

"What are you looking for?"

"My Python."

Jonathan's voice rose. "Your what?"

Mark held up a large revolver. "My Python." He closed the cabinet door, unlocked another cabinet, and pulled out a box of ammo. He opened the cylinder, loaded six rounds from the box into the chambers, and closed the cylinder.

"What do you need a gun for?"

"Insurance. In case we have to stop in the middle of nowhere, I don't want to get jacked. The desert is full of predators, my friend, some of them animals, some of them human." He was trying to sound like a movie character, but Jonathan couldn't tell which one.

"Well, if you think you need it, why lock it up?"

"It's not legal for me to carry a firearm in California." He smiled and said, "But this is Arizona, Johnny." Jonathan was pretty sure that one was Jack Nicholson.

Mark slid the pistol into a holster attached to the driver's door, shifted the transmission into gear, and released the brakes. A minute later they were going 75 miles an hour along the steadily climbing highway.

After a while they came upon Quartzite, a tiny outpost of civilization surrounded by desert wilderness. The street lights and signs revealed a truck stop and some fast food restaurants.

Mark said, "In the winter, this place is packed with recreational vehicles."

They passed through the town quickly, and were once again traveling in darkness. They rolled along behind a long red string of eastbound tail lights, while in the opposite lanes, a long white string of westbound headlights flowed towards them, an endless parade of trucks in both directions.

Jonathan said, "There's a lot of traffic out here."

"Oh yeah. Truckers pick up and deliver during the day, then the freight moves between the cities at night."

"It looks like it's just one big machine. The highway, the trucks in motion."

"And right now, we're a part of that machine." Mark turned and smiled.

Jonathan said, "I wouldn't mind making this drive in the daytime, when I can see what's around us."

"It's the clouds. On a clear night the sky is plastered with stars, and during a full moon, you can see for miles, every rock, every bush. But when the monsoon clouds move in, it's like driving in a tunnel."

"Monsoon?"

"The summer storms, up from Mexico. Look." He pointed towards the southeast. A cloud flashed bright for an instant on the far horizon.

* * *

VALDO KEPT THE TRUCK in sight, always staying several cars back so he wouldn't be noticed. Soon after crossing the border, he saw a sign for a weigh station, so he moved into the right lane, knowing the truck would have to stop, but the truck didn't stop, it just blew right by the scales. As Valdo started to work his way back to the center lane, the truck pulled into a rest area. Valdo tried to follow, but a car was in the way. He slowed down and the car slowed down, too, matching his speed. Valdo sped up and cut the car off, but by then it was too late, he had missed the turnoff. He kept his speed under 45 miles an hour and waited for the truck to catch up with him. When it finally did, he allowed it to pass, and resumed following from a distance.

Valdo wondered when it was going to cool down. It was too hot for this time of night. The air conditioner on his old Crown Vic had always done its job in L.A., but out here in the desert it couldn't seem to keep up. Sweat built up on his forehead and was trickling down his face.

This is supposed to be a dry heat?

Finally after he passed through Quartzite the air cooled down a little, but pretty soon it started getting warm again. He opened the window, but that was worse, a lot worse. He rolled the window back up and grabbed his Fanta orange soda. He took a swig and spat it back out. It was lukewarm.

AROUND MIDNIGHT, the sky to the east became a little brighter as they approached Phoenix.

Jonathan said, "So where's the shipment going to?"

"Maricopa, a couple hours from here. Google maps shows it out in the desert west of the Ak Chin Reservation."

"In the desert?"

"Yeah. I know the area. We go target shooting out there. I don't recall seeing any industry, just a few homes and a lot of wilderness, but that's where they want me to go."

"Are you sure you can find it?"

"I always do."

They were approaching Phoenix when Mark pointed to a billboard and said, "Look, it's you."

It was an artistic rendition but it looked just like him: long blond hair, skinny chin-strap beard, John Lennon glasses. The artist had depicted him as Geo from West Wave so he was buff too. His promotional self was being embraced by Mara and Angel.

Mark said, "Wow, you really are a celebrity, aren't you?" and gave Jonathan a fist bump.

As they passed through Phoenix, they saw Jonathan's face on two more billboards. Mark noted how aggressively they were promoting the convention, and Jonathan agreed. They exited the interstate at Queen Creek Road and turned right. There was a sign telling them they were entering the Gila River Indian Community, and the landscape changed from suburbs to desert. Mark said they were on the John Wayne Parkway, which made Jonathan smile. The reason he was there was to avoid the John Wayne Airport.

When they got to Maricopa, Mark made a right, then a few miles down made a left and drove across some railroad tracks onto a narrow two-lane. "Almost there," he said.

It seemed to Jonathan they were going deep into the desert. They had only seen a few cars since leaving the interstate, and every road they turned on seemed more remote than the last. At one point, he thought he smelled cows. They drove through some rolling hills, and when they cleared the last one, an oasis of brightly lighted buildings rose in the east.

Mark said, "That's the Ak Chin Casino."

Jonathan nodded.

Mark downshifted and they slowed to a crawl. He pointed off into the desert. "That's where we go shooting. The road we need to turn on is up ahead, not too far. On the satellite view it didn't look paved." They crept along past a hill and stopped in front of a dirt road. Mark said, "That's not it," and they moved on. A little farther was another road, but that wasn't it, either. After they crossed an arroyo, they came upon a street sign. Mark said, "Can you read that?"

Jonathan said, "Saguaro Lane."

Mark turned and eased the truck off the pavement onto a desert road—a trail, really—barely wide enough to fit the truck. Creosote bushes and palo verde trees scraped the sides as the wheels bumped over the sandy ruts and sharp granite. Mark wasn't happy about taking his new truck into the desert. He looked up into the sky. "Man, if it rains while we're out here, we're screwed."

Three hundred yards in, a large steel shed appeared, the road winding around it in a loop. They followed the road past the shed and back into the cloud of dust they had raised on the way in. When the tail of the trailer was about even with the shed, Mark stopped the truck and tugged on the brake valve buttons. They popped out, and the air brakes hissed, raising more dust.

Mark said, "Now we wait." He turned the key and the big diesel engine shut off. He pushed a button on the dashboard and a small engine started.

Jonathan said, "What's that?"

"Auxiliary engine. So we can keep the AC on." He reached down and grabbed his revolver, setting it on his lap. He pointed to the sleeper cab with his thumb. "You can crash back there."

"I'm okay up here."

"Look, I'm gonna stay awake, keep an eye on things. There's no point in both of us doing that. You get some sleep."

"Are you sure?"

"Yeah, go ahead, just take your shoes off first."

Jonathan said, "All right. Hey, look." He pointed towards the south. More flashes of light.

"Dammit."

"What's wrong?"

"We're overdue for some rain. I really don't wanna get stuck out here. Those monsoon rains can be a bitch." He looked around in the darkness. "This is the first time I've taken this truck off the pavement. I'm getting on the phone tomorrow and letting them know that it's the last."

Jonathan took his shoes off, pushed the curtain aside and climbed into the bed. It was soft. He said, "This is nice."

Mark said, "Help yourself to the fridge."

WHEN THE TRUCK turned at the narrow two-lane road leading out into the desert, Valdo maneuvered onto the shoulder and parked. The old car had a push-pull switch with a round handle that controlled the car lights, and when he pushed it in, all the lights went off: headlights, running lights, everything. He waited until the truck was almost out of view before pulling back onto the pavement, turning left, and driving over the railroad tracks, leaving the switch pushed in so he could run dark as he crept along. He followed the truck over several rises and watched as it stopped, drove a bit farther, and stopped again. When it turned off the road and headed into the desert, Valdo looked around for a vantage point—some place to stop and observe the truck. He found a clearing to the right and drove onto it, where he watched the truck's headlights fan out into the desert, revealing bushes and cacti ahead of it, the rest of the truck outlined by the running lights. It bumped along slowly, turned around and stopped. The squeal of the air brakes echoed off the nearby mountains. Valdo looked around at the vast emptiness, and he knew: this was where he would kill the driver.

FIVE

It was obvious to Valdo. They were far away from any houses so there would be no one to witness the crime. It was pitch black so he could sneak up on the driver. Hell, out here he wouldn't even need a suppressor. The only problem was finding somebody to move his car out of the area when he hijacked the truck. Jimmy didn't run any operations in Arizona—it was outside his turf—but he had connections here, so Valdo opened the cell phone and punched in Jimmy's home phone number. He held the phone up to his ear, looked at the screen and said, "Shit."

He was in a dead zone.

It figured. The one time he actually needed a cell phone and there was no service. It was another missed opportunity, a big one, out here in the desert in the middle of the night. If only Roberts had listened. Valdo made a u-turn and headed towards Eloy.

Roberts was right about the travel time. It took a little over an hour to get to the warehouse. When he arrived, a young Hispanic man in a white, sweat-stained athletic shirt met him in the driveway. Tattoos covered the man's arms and neck, and his left hand rested on a Glock 19 which he kept in a holster on his belt. He was definitely a gangster, which didn't concern Valdo, organized crime being his own chosen profession. But he was probably a cartel member, he had that look about him, so Valdo stayed extra alert.

The guy said in Spanish, "Are you Esposito?"

"Yeah."

"Roberts wants you to wait for him here."

Valdo looked around. "There a Seven-Eleven around here?"

"Circle K."

Valdo got directions and drove two blocks to the convenience store. He filled a large cup with coffee and brought it to the check-out counter where he waited behind a scraggly old man who reeked of tobacco and body odor. The man asked for six lottery tickets and a pack of generic cigarettes, and waited until the clerk had totaled them up before searching his pockets for cash. He counted out the exact amount down to the penny so the change back would come to a quarter, and the clerk handed him his purchase. Grandpa stayed there, blocking the counter until he had scratched all his tickets with the quarter. One of the tickets was a ten-dollar winner, and when the clerk handed him his winnings, he immediately bought ten more tickets which he proceeded to scratch. None of them paid off so he picked up his cigarettes and turned around, bumping into Valdo, wincing, flashing him a toothless smile before wandering out of the store.

When Valdo got back to the warehouse, he drove to the far end of the yard by the fence, turned around, and parked facing the driveway. He turned off the motor and took a sip of coffee.

After several hours he watched the first glint of sunrise appear in the rear-view mirror, a subtle pink glow reaching out over the top of a distant mountain. It was almost time. He got out and took a leak on the side of the building. Up close, he could see the warehouse was old and built with corrugated steel, rusting now through the white paint. His bladder empty, he walked behind the car and popped the trunk. The air had never really cooled down during the night and his clothes were soaked, sticking to his skin. Hidden behind the raised trunk lid, he took off his dock worker uniform, folded it carefully and set it in the trunk. He reached for a leather suitcase and opened it, took out his suit clothes, still in their dry cleaner bags, and hung them up from the trunk latch. After he dressed himself, he closed the trunk and walked back to the driver's door. He opened the door and leaned in, grabbing the Pelican case from the back. He swung the lid open and removed his .45, putting it in the shoulder holster under his coat before climbing into the car.

The sun was shining brightly by the time Valdo saw the red Dodge Charger roaring into the yard. The back end spun around, threw some gravel, and skidded to a stop. Out stepped a man in Tommy Bahama shirt and shorts. He was a thin man in his forties, about six-one, his weak jaw shaded with a five o'clock shadow. A pair of Mephisto sandals rounded out the 'gringo in paradise' look.

Valdo got out of his car. Surprised, the man said, "Wow. You're a big one, aren't you? Not exactly inconspicuous."

Valdo said, "You mean like your ride? That thing is a cop magnet."

"This?" He smiled. "You know, this used to belong to a meth cook. The agency confiscated this vehicle when they apprehended the owner running a contraband cigarette operation up in New River. When I transferred to Phoenix, this magnificent beast was sitting in the impound yard gathering dust." He caressed the fender. "She seemed so lonely." He glanced at his watch and said, "Get in the car, Poncho. We have a schedule to keep."

Valdo didn't move.

The man said, "Hello, my name is Agent Roberts. How do you do? Get in the car."

Valdo climbed into the Charger and they took off, tires squealing as they left the gravel and hit the pavement.

Roberts said, "Did you experience any difficulty locating the warehouse?"

"I'm here."

"Yes you are, and you're about to earn fifty grand."

"This place where the truck is, it was dark last night. Does anybody live there?"

"Nah, it's perfect. It adjoins BLM land."

"Bee ell em?"

"Bureau of Land Management. Wilderness. The only people around there are the gun nuts. They all come to play army. Hell, you could blast a Howitzer and nobody would even flinch."

Roberts took the 10 west to the 8 towards San Diego. It was a different route than Valdo had taken.

Valdo said, "You're going the long way."

"How would you know? You're not from around here."

"I can read a map. It's quicker through Casa Grande."

"I am aware of that. I prefer to take the freeway. Besides, I have everything timed perfectly."

"Timed perfectly? Well, this ain't no bank robbery where you gotta time it for the safe to open or the Brinks truck or something. This kind of job, you gotta be flexible."

"Flexible, huh? Look pal, I've got fifteen years with the FBI. I know what I'm doing."

Valdo shook his head. "You don't know shit."

Roberts scowled at Valdo and said, "Who the hell are you to talk to me like that?"

"You talk about perfect. Well I've already passed up a perfect opportunity to do the job. Two, really. Now who knows what we're walking into?"

"Jeez, Pancho, it's not exactly rocket science. All you have to do is tell the driver you're there to receive the load. When he turns around to open the trailer, you put one behind his ear."

"Just like that?"

"Yes, just like that. I've investigated enough homicides to know how it's done."

"You don't know shit."

"I'll put one behind your ear, you keep saying that."

"You think that driver is going to be that easy? You think because he's a truck driver he's stupid or something?"

"You mean like your Tio Manny?"

It took Valdo by surprise.

Roberts said, "Oh yeah, I know about your uncle, how he taught you how to drive his truck, so he could sit on his ass and drink his tequila. I know all about you and Manny."

"This ain't about Manny."

"What were you, sixteen? Just a kid and driving a truck. Well, that's Mexico for you."

"This ain't about me, this ain't about Manny and this ain't about Mexico."

Roberts smirked. "That's what you think."

Valdo, trying to keep Roberts focused, said, "Hey, I could've taken him at the truck stop or the rest stop. I could've taken him last night in the desert. It would've been easy because he wouldn't be expecting it. Now he's sitting in the middle of nowhere waiting for us. Your perfect timing ain't got no element of surprise."

"He'll be surprised as hell when you put his lights out."

"Listen to me. It's daytime. The driver seen me before, because you made me work at the warehouse. He's gonna be wary. And he's probably gonna be carrying a piece."

"Is that what Manny does, carry a piece?"

"Damn right he does. But I thought you knew everything about him."

JONATHAN WOKE UP. It took him a moment to remember where he was and for his surroundings to make sense. It was morning and Mark was still awake, sitting in the driver's seat. Jonathan looked out the window on the side of the sleeper cab. There was nothing but sand and desert bushes and cacti as far as he could see. He pushed the curtains back and looked through the windshield. He could see the dirt road they drove up last night, Saguaro Lane. He thought he could see some buildings, miles away. Maybe they weren't as far into the desert as he thought. As the sleep cleared from his head, he became aware of popping sounds in the distance. It reminded him of fireworks. "What is that?" he said.

Mark said, "Gunfire. People go target shooting out here, remember?"

"This early?"

"It's summer. They want to fire off some rounds before the sun gets too high."

"Is it safe with them shooting like that?"

Mark said, "They're on the other side of that hill."

Jonathan needed to go to the bathroom, but he decided to wait. He felt safer in the truck. He reached into his pocket, pulled out his iPhone, and navigated to the West Con forum. He scanned the posts. Good, the mood at the convention had improved.

JB here tonight
Excellent!
I went yesterday. Gotta buy another ticket.
Promoters are comping, go to the website.

Jonathan opened his Safari browser and navigated to the West Con website. Sure enough, the promoters were giving free Sunday tickets to convention goers who had bought tickets for Saturday. Jonathan knew Debrah must have arranged it. She would have arranged for it to come out of his royalties, too.

Mark said, "Heads up. We're not alone."

A red car had turned onto Saguaro Lane and was speeding towards them, bouncing and fish-tailing down the dirt road.

Mark's demeanor changed. He had been relaxed and easy going the whole trip. Now he seemed intense as he said, "This doesn't feel right."

Jonathan said, "What do you mean?"

"The way they changed the address on the bill of lading, sending us to this remote location."

"What are you going to do?"

"I'm going to be careful. He picked up the revolver, flipped the cylinder open, spun it, and flipped it closed. "I want you to stay down behind the seat. Don't go sticking your head up." Jonathan hesitated and Mark said, "Did you hear what I said? Get down and don't get up until I tell you."

"Okay." Jonathan made himself as small as he could behind the driver's seat. Mark pulled the curtains closed, shutting off the sleeper cab from view. Jonathan heard the car skid to a halt not far from the truck. A car door opened.

Mark said, "I know him. That's the guy from Riverside, the dispatcher. Stay down." He opened the door and climbed out, pistol in hand.

Jonathan opened the video app on his phone, slid to the edge of the driver's seat and held the phone up to the crack between the curtains, trying to aim the camera towards the windshield.

When Roberts and Valdo reached the truck, the driver was standing next to it. He was holding a revolver—a big one. Roberts looked at Valdo and Valdo shook his head. Valdo said, "Stay in the car."

"Why?"

"Let me talk to him. I'll strike up a conversation, put him at ease." Valdo stepped out of the car. A slight breeze blew across the desert and his sweat-soaked back felt almost cool for a moment. He walked towards the driver.

The driver held up the palm of his free hand and said, "Stop right there."

Valdo stopped.

The driver said, "What are you doing here?"

"I'm here to receive the shipment."

"So you're the shipping clerk and the receiver?"

"I know it looks weird. I can explain."

"Explain."

"The guy who was supposed to receive the shipment quit and they didn't have nobody to take his place, so they sent me."

"All the way from California?"

"I know. But hey, I'm making a shitload of overtime on this deal, so I ain't gonna complain."

There was silence for few moments until the driver said, "Aren't you a bit overdressed for receiving freight in the middle of nowhere?"

"I was going to my sister's wedding when they called. They said I had to be here right away, so I didn't change, I just left. Look, can we unload the trailer, or do you got any more questions?"

"Just one. Why are you carrying a piece inside your coat?"

How did he know?

"Same reason you got that wheel gun. I ain't coming way out here without no protection." The driver stared at Valdo, thinking. Valdo said, "So we gonna unload this? I want to get home."

The driver said, "Give it to me."

"What?"

"Give me your weapon. I'll hold on to it while I call the broker and make sure this is legitimate."

"You don't trust me?"

"Trust but verify. In the meantime, hand it over."

"Why should I give you my weapon, so you can shoot me?"

"Why would I shoot you, so I can steal my own freight?"

Valdo said, "Okay," and reached inside his coat.

The driver said, "Slowly," and raised the revolver, holding it with both hands now.

Valdo said, "Easy. Don't get excited," and drew the .45 from its holster. He held it up for the driver to see. With his free hand, he pointed to the driver's handgun and said, "I see you carry a .357, old school."

The driver said, "Put your weapon down."

Valdo said, "I'm old school, too." He showed his pistol. "1911."

"Put it down."

Valdo kept talking, looking for an opportunity. "You know, people argue, which is better, a .357, or a .45. What do you think?"

"I think you should leave."

Valdo said, "Every man has his preference. Me? I like the way the .45 feels in my hand."

"You're not going to like the feel of a slug in your chest."

"Easy, brother."

"This is your last chance. Put your weapon away, turn your car around, and leave."

Roberts flung the car door open and stepped out. He said, "Federal Agent, ATF."

The driver said, "Show me your badge. Move slowly or I start shooting. I can kill you both before you can get a shot off."

Roberts reached into his back pocket, retrieved a wallet, and held it open for the driver to see. There was a badge inside.

The driver said, "Throw it over here."

He tossed it at the driver's feet. The driver kept his eyes on Valdo and Roberts as he lowered himself and reached for the wallet.

Valdo raised his .45 and aimed it at the driver, but before he could shoot, the driver squeezed the trigger on his revolver. A bright yellow flame erupted from the barrel with a roar, the blast echoing across the desert. Valdo felt the slug slamming into his chest, the pain knocking him to the ground. He turned and raised his pistol and fired a shot at the driver.

SIX

THE SMOKE CLEARED and the echoes died away and there were two big men lying on the ground. A puddle of blood was forming around the driver, soaking into the sandy granite road. Valdo was covered with dust, but he wasn't bleeding. He picked himself up, smacking his pants and coat with his hand, trying to rid himself of the dirt.

Roberts looked at Valdo with disgust and said, "Do you always engage in conversations with your victims before you kill them?"

"Do you have a problem with my work methods?"

Roberts paused before saying, "No. You got the job done."

"Because we can discuss it if you like."

Roberts gave him a look and said, "Hey, you're lucky I was there to distract him."

"Yeah, well I had things under control. You should've stayed in the car like I told you."

"If I had, you'd be dead."

Roberts grabbed the front of Valdo's coat and felt the fabric. He said, "Built-in body armor. Nice."

Valdo said, "Custom made," and removed Roberts' hand.

"Who made it, Omar the Tentmaker?"

"Gee, I never heard that joke before. You're a funny man."

Roberts smirked.

They walked over to the driver's body and Roberts started going through the pockets.

Valdo said, "What are you looking for?"

"This." Roberts held up a cell phone.

"You really like those things, don't you."

"No, pendejo, it has a GPS."

"Gee pee ess?"

"Yeah, the telephone company tracks everyone who has a cell phone."

Valdo shook his head and said, "So if we take that with us the police will find the warehouse."

Roberts smirked again and said, "Oh, he gets it."

"So we leave it here."

"Exactly. I wanted to make sure it was on him and not in the truck. But there's more than just the phone." Roberts climbed into the truck cab, ripped the PrePass module off the windshield, tossed it out of the truck, turned around, and reached between the curtains to the sleeper area. He grabbed a laptop, climbed back out of the tractor with it, and said, "Pop the hood."

Valdo unhitched the latches on the fiberglass hood and pulled it open.

Roberts said, "Look on the frame. Inside the rails."

When Valdo climbed up into the engine compartment, he was impressed with what he saw. The engine was so new, so modern, he had no idea what half the tubes and cables and boxes did. And it was tight, not a speck of oil on it. Blow off the layer of tan colored dust and it could be on the showroom floor.

Roberts said, "You find it yet, Pancho?"

Valdo looked along the frame rail and found nothing. He climbed down and went to the other side where he found a black electrical device that was hidden from view. He said, "What should

I do with it?"

Roberts said, "Unhook the connector and pull it off the frame."

Valdo did what Roberts said, took one last look at the engine, and closed the hood, latching it down.

They tossed the electronic devices on top of the body and grabbed the limbs. Valdo held the legs and Roberts held the arms.

As they lifted, Roberts grunted and said, "Jeez, couldn't they hire a normal size person? Between you and Dirty Harry here, I feel like I'm living in the land of the giants."

"He carried a .44 Magnum."

"What?"

"Dirty Harry carried a .44, not a .357."

"Shut up."

They carried the body straight west, out into the desert, leaving it behind a rocky hill a hundred yards from the truck. They walked back to the shed and were about to leave when Valdo said, "One more thing." He went to the back of the trailer, pulled out his .45, and shot the seal off the door. He opened the door, rolled it up a little, and reached in. He grabbed the bag with Cornwall in it and dragged it out. It made a thump when it landed.

Roberts glared at Valdo and said, "Who is that?"

Valdo said, "That's Glen Cornwall."

"And who, exactly, is Glen Cornwall?"

"Don't you remember? He's the warehouse manager. Used to be."

"Oh, yeah. Why is he dead? And in my trailer?"

Valdo had to be careful. Roberts didn't know about the broken crate, and didn't have to know. Valdo said, "Mr. Cornwall here started getting suspicious. He said he was going to call the cops."

Roberts said, "Suspicious about what? A bunch of crates going to Nogales? What are you not telling me?"

Valdo said, "Hey, it's getting late. If we don't hurry with the body, we'll get behind schedule."

Roberts looked at his watch and said, "Damn."

Valdo said, "Well?"

Roberts said, "You killed him, you get rid of him. I'll meet you at the warehouse," and headed towards the car.

Valdo gripped the bag, and tossing it over his shoulder he walked back out into the desert. Standing next to the driver's body, he dropped the bag and looked around. When he was sure nobody could see him, he began to take off his coat. The slug from the driver's revolver had passed almost completely through the body armor and had actually indented his chest. The slug and some of the Kevlar material was stuck in him like a cork between two ribs, and he was pretty sure one of the ribs was cracked. Although his skin was intact, the entire area felt as if it were on fire. He tugged gently on the coat and yelled in pain as it pulled out of the wound. He stuck his hand inside his shirt to assess the damage, and satisfied, started back towards the truck.

ROBERTS SPED BACK TO THE PAVED ROAD and stomped on the accelerator, painting a long black patch on the asphalt. He picked up his phone and held it a moment before putting it back in his pocket. What was he going to do with this guy, goes and kills a man on his own? It wasn't that Roberts had a problem with killing. Everything about this operation involved killers and killing. But all the murder and double crossing and hijacking made this an exceptionally dangerous operation. Every aspect had to be carefully managed, or he'd be the one rotting in the desert, food for the buzzards. Finally, he punched in the numbers on his phone.

A man answered, "Yes?"

Roberts said, "De Guardia? Agent Roberts."

Jimmy De Guardia said, "How may I help you, Agent Roberts?"

"It's about Valdo."

"What about him?"

"He's become a problem."

"I've never had a problem with him."

"He killed the manager at the warehouse."

"I'm sure he had his reasons."

"He didn't have permission to do that."

"Well, the way it works with Valdo, you tell him what you want to accomplish and let him work out the details."

"That is not acceptable. I have too much riding on this. The details have already been carefully worked out and there is no margin for error."

"What can I say? You do things your way, I do things mine. But get to the point. Or did you just call to complain?"

"Yeah, well I might need to take care of this problem, but I thought I'd call you first—as a courtesy."

"The answer is no."

"But he's an idiot. He's going to screw everything up."

"I will tell you this once. Valdo is on loan to you, but he still works for me. When he is finished with this job, he is to be returned to me—alive. Do you understand?"

Roberts felt his blood pressure rising. He was being disrespected by a stupid, wretched criminal. He wanted to tell Jimmy to go to hell and kill Valdo anyway, but he knew from his time at the bureau that people who defied Jimmy usually ended up disappearing. He would swallow his pride—for now.

Jimmy said, "Tell me you understand what I am saying."

Roberts said, "I understand," and slammed the phone down on the floorboard. He reached under the seat and found the fifth of Stolichnaya he had stashed there. He popped a Xanax and washed it down with the vodka.

JONATHAN SAT THERE in shock, his heart racing. He waited until he was sure the car had left before viewing the video on his iPhone.

The angle of the recording wasn't perfect, but he could clearly see the man shoot Mark, and caught a glimpse of the other man as he threw his wallet with the badge. When the video ended, he pulled the curtains open wide enough to get a better look out of the truck, but he could only see in three directions. If he knew it was clear, he could get out of there and run away. He still had to go to the bathroom, but he decided if he got the chance to run, he wouldn't stop until he found somebody who could help him, even if it meant peeing his pants.

He climbed out of the sleeping area and sat down in the driver's seat where he could use the side mirrors to check behind the truck. When he looked at the left mirror, all he could see was the side of the trailer, so he moved his head a little to the right and saw the enormous man in the dark suit walking out of the desert straight towards the truck. He sprang back into the sleeping area and scrunched down behind the driver's seat. A second later he came out again to pull the curtains shut before returning to his hiding place.

VALDO CLIMBED INTO THE TRUCK CAB and his jaw dropped. It was the most beautiful truck interior he had ever seen: the leather, the digital readouts, the air conditioning. Of course, the only trucks he had ever been in belonged to his Uncle Manny and his friends, and the contrast could not have been greater. He wasn't expecting such luxury in a truck. Jimmy's S-Class Mercedes, maybe, but not in a truck. When Valdo pulled the curtains to the sleeper cab back a little, he let out a low whistle. Manny would go crazy over this.

It had been a long time since he had driven Manny's smoky old White Freightliner. It was a cab-over, and even at sixteen, Valdo's feet were cramped by the way the engine shroud stuck into the cab area. But this truck was a conventional, and with the engine mounted in front of the cab, Valdo was able to stretch his legs. He looked over the controls and found the ignition switch. When he started the engine he thought, "Wow". He might have said it out loud.

Now he had to drive this truck. Manny's truck had ten speeds— five gears and a splitter. He looked over the diagram on the shifter knob, and saw that it had thirteen. On Manny's truck, first gear was a granny gear—a real low gear you only used when you started out going uphill, and he assumed it was the same on this truck, so he pushed in the clutch and slid the gear shift into second. He released the brakes and eased the clutch out. The truck rolled forward. He kept it in second until he got onto the pavement where he wound the engine out and shifted into third. He missed the shift and ground the gears, so he slid it back into second and wound it out again. This time he found third, and fourth, and on up through the gears.

He kept his speed down a little below the speed limit, but not too much below. He didn't want to arouse suspicion and get pulled over by the cops.

JONATHAN REMAINED FROZEN, his mind working on a way to escape. Eventually somebody would look far enough into the sleeper cab to see him and that person would kill him. His plan was to wait until the killer got out of the cab, then sneak out and run like hell, run to the police. But when they shot Mark, he heard a man say he was a cop. No, a federal agent. A federal agent who stood there and watched that man shoot Mark to death, even helped him do it? Was he really working for the government? Was the federal government in on the killing? If so, whom could he trust? If he went to the police, he could end up dead anyway.

He needed a strategy. He needed to get in touch with someone who could help him escape this nightmare. Calling the police was out. He couldn't call his mother. She wouldn't know what to do. Finally it occurred to him: contact Debrah. Deb was the one person he knew who was smart enough and knew enough people to save him. Maybe. He pulled out his iPhone and set it to silent mode, shuddering at the thought it could have rung or vibrated at any time and alerted the killer to his presence. He pulled up messaging and typed in TRUCK DRIVER KILLED, attached the video, put Deb's address in and hit SEND.

The phone went into its shut down sequence.

He forgot to charge the batteries. He always forgot to recharge the batteries, and now he might die because of it.

The truck bounced over some railroad tracks and turned, pulled off the road and stopped. He got ready. This could be his chance.

VALDO HADN'T THOUGHT about Manny for a long time, but now he couldn't get him off his mind. He remembered the way he had taken Valdo in when his Nana died, raised him, taught him to be a man. Manny loved to talk about buying a fleet of trucks and making some good money. Of course, Valdo would manage the business for him. But Valdo had moved to the States and as time went on, he had lost touch with his family in Mexico.

Valdo drove down West Farrell Road past the Ak Chin Casino and turned left onto the John Wayne Parkway. A couple miles up he crossed some railroad tracks and turned right at the Maricopa-Casa Grande Highway. On display at the corner was a shiny old rail car marked The California Zephyr, and just past the exhibit was an open lot where Valdo parked the truck and pulled out his cell phone. He sat thinking for a minute and when he remembered the phone number he punched it in. Manny's wife, Tia Carina, answered. She immediately recognized his voice and started to cry. She asked how he was and he said he was fine but that he couldn't talk for long. He asked about Manny. Carina told him Manny was still driving the same old truck, but maintenance and repairs seemed to eat up all the profits. She said Manny was on a run and would be sorry he missed his call but he would be back from Guaymas tomorrow. Valdo said he had to go and they said goodbye.

Valdo released the brakes and returned to the highway. He looked ahead and noticed something strange about the sky. It was a hazy blue, but to the east it was an odd shade of gray—a dark greenish gray. It reminded him of the sky down in the southern areas of Mexico right before a big chubasco storm. The sky never looked like that in Los Angeles.

JONATHAN WAITED FOR THE KILLER to get out of the truck, but he stayed in the cab and made a phone call. He talked to somebody in Spanish for a while before he started back down the road.

By this time Jonathan had to pee so bad he was in pain. He was glad the road was smooth, or maybe it was the truck that made it seem smooth. He wanted to find out where he was. All he could see from behind the seat was the sky. He decided to take a chance and try to spot some landmarks, edging over and up a little until he could see out of the tiny window on the side of the sleeper cab. There was not much to see, mostly sand and scrub and dry hills in the distance. Through the window on the other side of the cab, he thought he saw some railroad crossing gates. He figured the road they were on ran next to the tracks. After a while he saw some kind of factory or warehouse, a big red building with cars parked around it. There were smaller buildings with solar panels on the roofs, and he saw a sign that said Frito Lay. A short distance from there he spotted a tall white building with an A on it. After that the truck slowed down and he hoped it would stop, but it didn't. It was maneuvering through a developed area. A few minutes later it sped up again. He had the idea of checking his phone's GPS to see where he was but remembered the dead batteries. At this point he wondered if he were going to die.

SEVEN

VALDO TURNED RIGHT onto Sunshine Blvd and crossed the railroad tracks. He drove a short distance and turned left, pulling into the driveway next to the warehouse building where he had left his car. He drove close to the building and turned sharply right. He stopped and put it in reverse, backing up to the lone dock door on the side of the building. He stopped just an inch too late and the building shuttered as the rear of the trailer slammed into it. Manny had always been on him about that. He would say, "Go slow, and your mistakes will be small ones." Valdo set the brakes and left the engine running. He had climbed out of the truck and started up the steps leading into the warehouse when a man burst through the door near the top. They collided, the man smacking into Valdo's injured ribs, spinning around Valdo, and stumbling down the steps. The man didn't say oops or that he was sorry. He seemed oblivious to the fact he had run into somebody. Valdo didn't let on that he was in pain, didn't even grimace. He continued up the steps and through the door into the building.

* * *

It seemed like an hour before the truck had slowed down and turned, but since Jonathan didn't have use of his phone, he couldn't be sure how long they had been driving. He saw a sign that read Sunshine Blvd; a minute later, the truck pulled into a gravel drive-way and backed up to a building, hitting it hard. When the killer left the cab, Jonathan was ready to make his move. He raised his head up and peered out the corner of the sleeper cab window. It was clear. When it was clear on the other side, he moved into the main cab for one last look before making a run for it, but he had to stop when he realized he wasn't wearing his shoes. He moved quickly into the sleeper cab and slipped his shoes on. When he got back into the driver's seat, a skinny white guy with a red baseball cap had come out of the building. Jonathan spotted him in the side mirror. The guy walked into the center of the yard and stood there. He seemed nervous and kept looking around. When he turned, Jonathan could see a pistol sticking out of his pocket. He would have to wait.

Valdo looked around the warehouse. It was abandoned except for a forklift and three propane tanks sitting in the corner by the door. Above, dust covered the windows inside and out, block-ing the light passing through the glass. Below, the cracked concrete floor showed signs of the rodents that long ago crept in the shad-ows, back when there was food to attract them.

Roberts was standing by the dock door. The guy with the tat-toos had already opened it and was rolling up the trailer door. As it opened, he made a face and stepped back as if he were getting out of the way of something. He said, "Esta cabrón. It smells like somebody died in there."

Valdo and Roberts exchanged glances. The guy set a small steel plate across the gap between the dock and the trailer, shook his head and said, "Shit, man." He walked over to a forklift, climbed into the seat, started the engine, and drove into the trailer.

Roberts called Valdo into a small office in the back of the warehouse. The only signs that business had once taken place there were a gray metal desk and several piles of yellowing paper in overstuffed bankers boxes. Worn out asbestos tile partially covered the floor, and spiders with their webs occupied all the corners of the room. There was a black leather briefcase on top of the desk. Roberts opened it and pulled out a manila envelope. He dumped the contents of the envelope onto the table: stacks of U.S. dollar bills.

"There you go," he said. "Count it."

Valdo stood silent.

"Or don't."

Valdo said, "I want the truck."

He had it worked out in his head by the time he reached the warehouse. He would wait for Roberts' men to unload the trailer and he would drive the truck to San Diego. Jimmy had people there who could go over the truck, change all the identifying markings, paint it a different color, give it a whole new life. It seemed a shame to change the finish, though. Manny liked red.

It took Roberts by surprise. "You want the truck?"

"Yeah."

"What, fifty grand isn't enough?"

"Keep the fifty grand."

"Keep the ... Oh, I know what this is about. You want the truck for poor old Uncle Manny. Well, Manny can't have it."

"Why not?"

"Because I don't want the damn thing traced back to me."

"It won't be traced."

"I know it won't, because once those crates are off, that entire truck is going to disappear."

"Jimmy can disappear it better than your people."

Roberts stood with a blank expression.

Valdo said, "Look, you get to keep the fifty grand, and you don't need to pay nobody to get rid of the truck. It's money in your pocket."

Valdo waited for Roberts to reply. Finally Roberts said, "Okay, Pancho. You've got a deal. The truck is yours."

JONATHAN FELT THE TRUCK pitch and roll, and heard something going on in the trailer. They must be unloading it. He couldn't wait any longer to pee. He was cramping up and was bent over in agony. He opened the tiny refrigerator, found a nearly empty two-liter bottle of Pepsi and emptied his bladder into it. With that problem solved, he peeked outside again. The guy was still there but now he was facing away from the truck, holding his hand against his forehead and shielding his eyes as he gazed into the distance. Jonathan strained to see what he was looking at, but from that angle his view was limited. The guy seemed agitated and kept looking back towards the steps. He paced back and forth a few times, turned and jogged up the steps into the building.

Jonathan's heart pounded in his chest. He stood up, climbed into the driver's seat, and looked out the side window. Nobody was there. He moved to the passenger seat and looked out that window. Nobody was guarding that side, either. He pulled the door handle, but the door wouldn't budge. It was locked. He found the door lock button and pressed it, but nothing happened. He pressed it again and realized there must be a master locking mechanism on the driver's side. He scooted back to the driver's door and pulled on the handle. The door opened, but a sudden gust of wind slammed it shut. He pushed it back open just a crack and stuck his foot out, feeling for the step.

VALDO HAD LEFT ROBERTS in the office and was waiting by the exit, watching the tattooed guy unload the crates. The guy was staging them on the dock in pairs of two. At this rate, there would be around twenty pairs of crates. Valdo figured it would come to less than 900 kilos per pair. That meant they intended to smuggle these arms in small trucks, probably in vans, which was smart. If they did it right, made sure the van drivers didn't know each other, there would be no connection between loads, so if customs caught one of the vans going into Mexico, only part of the shipment would be lost. Valdo tried to remember the word for that method of keeping everything separate. He had heard Jimmy use it. It sounded like 'compartment'.

Valdo thought, Why am I daydreaming?

He slapped the back of his neck the way Tio Manny used to on long drives and pulled himself out of the fog his mind had fallen into. He needed sleep. He was thinking about getting some coffee when the guy who had bumped into him on the steps bolted through the door. Valdo stepped aside just in time to avoid a repeat of their earlier collision. The guy was frantic. He looked around the warehouse and called out for Agent Roberts.

The office door opened and Roberts stepped out. He said, "Zac, what are you doing in here? You were supposed to secure the yard."

Catching his breath, Zac said, "There's a big ass dust storm coming, bigger than shit."

Roberts turned to Valdo. "This is your lucky day. You're about to witness your first haboob."

"Ha-what?"

"Haboob. That's an Arabic word."

"What does it mean?"

"It means big ass dust storm."

Valdo stepped outside to see the haboob. The sky to the east was dark, the sun blotted out by a cloud of brown dust rising up incredibly high—thousands of feet, roiling and billowy, reaching from as far as he could see to the north to as far as he could see to the south. It was magnificent. He couldn't take his eyes off it.

But it was moving. Fast. In his direction.

Before he could turn away, a wall of dust and sand enveloped him and everything around him. A continuous blast of hot wind was blowing debris at almost freeway speed. Tumbleweeds and plastic bags were flying past him, catching on the truck and sticking to it before peeling off and blowing away. It was smothering him, so he covered his face with his coat sleeve and stepped back into the doorway. Just before he closed the door, out of the corner of his eye, he spotted something on the truck: the driver's door was partway open and a man's leg was sticking out. Valdo yelled, "Somebody's stealing the truck," and jumped to the ground.

As JONATHAN'S FOOT found the step, dust engulfed the truck. He had gotten lucky. He could hide in the dust storm and nobody would see him running away. He looked at the side mirror, a last check before he made his escape, and he saw a man emerging from the brown cloud. It was the killer, and he was running this way, closer now, close enough to shoot Jonathan if he wanted. He slid back into the cab and pressed the door lock button.

His mind raced as he analyzed his situation. In a fraction of a second he knew what he had to do.

Since he couldn't get away from the truck, he had to get away with the truck.

Okay. How would he do it? He looked down. Mark had told him about the pedals. There was the clutch, the brake, and the accelerator. He scanned the dashboard, searching the array of switches for the lights, the audio system, the air conditioning and yes, the two brake release buttons, one red and one yellow. He pushed down on both buttons and the brakes let out a hiss.

The ground in the yard had a slight incline away from the building, and when Jonathan released the brakes, the truck inched forward. Somebody in the trailer yelled something in Spanish. The truck settled to a stop and the killer appeared at the driver's window. He had climbed up onto the step and was yanking on the door handle. Jonathan read the shift pattern printed on the gearshift knob. First gear was towards him and back. He stepped down on the clutch pedal and jammed the transmission into first. The killer stuck his hand under his coat, drew his pistol, and slammed it against the window. The window held. The killer hit it again, and it shattered. He reached in and grabbed Jonathan by the hair. Jonathan released the clutch and stomped on the accelerator. The tractor crept forward, and Jonathan heard a terrible crash behind the trailer. When the killer turned to see what happened, Jonathan smashed him in the face with his elbow. It caught the killer off guard and he fell backwards, but still hung on, dropping his pistol, grabbing on to Jonathan's hair with both hands now, yanking Jonathan's head out the window. Jonathan thrust his arm through the window, swung it around and hammer-fisted the killer in the face. The killer held on tight.

ROBERTS HAD REACHED THE EXIT when he heard a metallic clanking like a steel bell over by the trailer, followed by somebody cursing in Spanish. He turned around in time to see the forklift suspended in mid-air. The truck had moved forward, leaving the front of the forklift hanging on the tail of the trailer, with the back of the forklift hanging on the edge of the dock. The man driving it scrambled to jump off, but when the truck started moving again the forklift twisted sideways and the safety cage struck him in the head, dragging him along as it fell to the ground. Roberts ran to the dock door and examined the gruesome sight below. The machine had landed on its side, crushing the man's head against the dock plate. This could mean trouble. The dead man was Roberts' contact with the cartel, sent there to help transfer the cargo and report everything to his boss in Mexico. But Roberts didn't have time to deal with that now. He had to stop the truck. Zac reached the dock door and Roberts yelled for him to take care of the mess. Zac peered over the edge and looked at the heap, the contents of the man's head oozing into the dirt, and vomited.

Roberts ran down the steps into the turbulent brown chaos, the scorching wind flinging dirt into his face. He lifted his arm to shield his eyes and saw the truck with the over sized hit man hanging off the side heading for the fence.

JONATHAN SAW THE FENCE approaching and wanted to turn the truck, but he was half-way out the window and couldn't get leverage on the steering wheel, so he wrapped his arms around it and braced for the collision. As the truck plowed through the chain-link, a steel fence post struck the killer and peeled him off the truck. He fell with his fists still clinging to long tufts of Jonathan's hair. The sudden release from the killer's grip flung Jonathan back into the cab, and he felt a moment of triumph before a flood of intense pain washed over his scalp. He screamed but was soon overcome by a fit of coughing as the dust storm surrounded the truck, filling the cab with flying dirt, which stuck to the blood trickling down his face. The wind blew harder and threatened to overturn the truck, which was rolling broadside to the storm. Jonathan couldn't see where the exit was, or if there were any cars coming, but he wasn't going to stop. He yanked the wheel towards the right and plodded through another chain link fence, missing the driveway completely. The truck convulsed each time an axle reached the curb and the wheels slammed down onto the roadway. He yanked the wheel towards the right again, turning the truck onto the street.

Facing north now, the interior of the truck cab had more protection from the dust, but the trailer had once again become a sail for the wind to push against, and it tilted, giving Jonathan the feeling it was going to flip and put an end to his freedom flight.

Jonathan knew he had to go faster if he wanted to get away from the killer, so he shoved the gearshift lever forward. The gears ground and the truck shuttered, but he got it into second, and it picked up a little speed. He shifted again, but he wasn't going fast enough for third, and the engine lugged down, straining to pull the truck. Jonathan didn't let up, though, and the truck chugged forward down Sunshine Blvd.

Jonathan gained enough speed to shift into fourth. He repeated the action all the way to seventh, but at that point he became confused. He remembered watching Mark flip a switch and going through the gears a second time. Jonathan looked at the shift knob and spotted a lever on the side. He had found the switch, but he wasn't sure which way to move the gearshift. He was staring at the shift pattern diagram and trying to figure out what to do next when the blast of an air horn broke his concentration. He looked up and saw the railroad crossing. The gates were down and the lights were flashing.

A train was approaching.

He couldn't see it though the dust, or how close it was, or how fast it was going. He didn't know if he could stop in time. What he did know was the people who were chasing him intended to kill him, and they would kill him right here if he stopped for that train.

ROBERTS WATCHED VALDO fall backwards and land on the chain link fence which had been smashed to the ground. The fence caught on the the truck frame and the truck dragged it away from the warehouse. Valdo rolled off the fence and Roberts hurried over to him. He reached out, offering his hand to Valdo, but Valdo stood up without his help.

"Are you okay?"

"I'm fine." Valdo dusted himself off.

"Come on." Roberts ran to his car.

Valdo walked towards his own car but Roberts cut him off with the Charger.

Roberts said, "Get in."

Valdo jumped in Roberts' car and they raced out of the yard. Roberts turned right and burned rubber. Dust shrouded the street, making it impossible to see far enough ahead for the speed they were going, but there was a gouge in the roadway leading away from the warehouse, breadcrumbs for them to follow. A slow moving car emerged from the cloud, and they just missed crashing into it. Roberts slammed on the brakes and swerved left, fishtailing, sliding into the oncoming lanes, and barely avoided colliding with a car on that side. He swerved hard to the right, and the Charger spun around in a circle, coming to a stop in the two-way turn lane in the middle of the street, the car sticking out into lanes on both sides.

Valdo said, "You don't have to get us killed."

"I want my truck back."

"My truck."

"Whatever. We can't have witnesses."

"The truck ain't going that fast. Just follow the marks on the road."

Roberts turned the car around and headed north. They closed in on the truck as it approached the railroad tracks. Valdo and Roberts watched as the railroad crossing gates dropped down in front of the truck, which had nowhere to go.

Roberts said, "Got 'im."

He slowed down and got ready to block the truck in with the car to keep it from turning around, but the truck didn't stop at the crossing. It didn't even slow down. It steered around a car waiting at the crossing and smashed through the gates, launching a burst of boards and splinters into the air. When it hit the slightly raised crossing, the tractor became airborne for a moment before crashing to the ground. A second later, it was the trailer's turn to bounce, but before the rear axles returned to earth, the speeding train arrived. The locomotive barreled through the tail of the trailer, and the truck disappeared behind the train. The train's brakes squealed but it kept rolling.

They sat in silence and watched the freight cars go by. There were a lot of them. The caboose had almost reached the crossing when the train finally came to a stop, blocking Sunshine Blvd.

Roberts turned to Valdo and said, "Too bad about your truck."

EIGHT

JESSE CONRAD WAS STILL IN BED when she got the call. Her mobile phone was her alarm clock, set to go off every morning at 6 AM, play Chopin's Prelude Number 7 and ease her from her sleep. But her ring tone was set to play Heart's "Barracuda", and it woke Jesse with a start. She picked up her phone and saw it was 4 AM and who the call was from.

This was it.

"Eduardo?"

"Yeah. I got the call from Tomás. He tole me to be there at sunrise."

Sunrise was two hours from now, and "there" was on Cowtown Road in Casa Grande, next to the Union Pacific line. That's where the illegals would be waiting, hiding among the rail cars stashed on the side track.

Jesse said, "You got the okay? I can come along?"

"Tomás was not happy, but I tole him you my sister's kid, you want to learn the business. I tole him is better I have a backup, in case I get sick."

"You? I'll bet you've never been sick a day in your life."

"No, I never been real sick. I faked it one time in jail, just to go to the hospital, get away from the putos. Oh, I'm sorry, Jesse."

Jesse laughed. "That's okay, I've heard worse."

Jesse had noticed how older men seemed to act around her. They were protective, chivalrous. At twenty-two years old, she was only five-three and weighed around 100 pounds. To them she looked like a young girl, a daughter, and she was not above exploiting their paternal feelings to get what she wanted. It's a competitive world and a girl needs every advantage. Today she would use the black hair and olive colored skin her Mexican mother had given her to pose as Eduardo's niece, the young girl tagging along with the old man.

Eduardo said, "Where should I pick you up?"

"The Serrano Vista Apartments. Do you know where they are?"

"Those the ones across the street from Sam's Club?"

"Yes. Come in off Elm, you'll see a driveway on the right, just past the park. I'll be downstairs waiting. Oh, what time will you be here?"

"Let me see. Everybody's going the other way, to Phoenix to get to work, so there won't be no traffic. An hour should do it. I'll pick you up at five o'clock."

"I'll be waiting."

"Oh, and Jesse, please don't bring no camera."

"No, you can't bring no camera." That's what Eduardo had told her three weeks ago, when he finally gave in, agreed to take her along on the dangerous run from Casa Grande to Picacho. They had met at Marsala's in Tempe. It was late, nearly closing time. She had the tiramisu with a decaf, he had a beer, Tecate. He tried hard to talk her out of it, told her she was crazy, told her she could be killed. If that happened, who knew what her uncle, Bill Conrad, might do? He might work things out with the court, talk to the judge, get Eduardo sent back to jail or worse.

He told her about his friend, Luis. It was a lie, Luis wasn't his friend, he had hated Luis, but it sounded better that way. "My friend Luis, we go way back, he used to work for Tomás, same as me. Well, he's dead now. He was making the same run I do when he got pulled over by the Border Patrol."

"Eduardo, —"

"They tole him to get out of the van, but he panicked, took off. The cops chased him all the way to Tempe. You heard about that?"

"Yeah, but —"

"It was on the news. He tried to go on the Superstition Freeway but he must of took the corner too fast, cause the tires blew and he rolled the van. That's what the cops said. Somebody said they shot the tires, I don't know. But it flipped off the overpass. Luis died, Jesse. So did the people in the van, and he had that thing stuffed full, like a clown car. Ah, poor Luis."

"That's not going to happen to you, Eduardo. You're too careful. That time last year when you got pulled over, you gave up without a fight."

"That's true. I don't even carry no gun. I ain't gonna give the cops no excuse to shoot me."

"Look, Eduardo, —"

"You know, I'm an old man. If El Señor decides, is my time to die, it don't matter, Jesse. But you, you are just a baby. You have your whole life to live."

"You're a good man, Eduardo. My Uncle Bill certainly thinks so. That's why he took your case."

"God bless Señor Conrad. He saved my life. But that makes it harder. How can I take you with me? I can't. It's too dangerous."

"It'll be okay, I promise."

"I don't think it will be okay with Tomás. He might think you're a cop and kill us both."

"Just tell him the truth."

"I also don't think he's gonna like the truth."

"Why not?"

"You come with me, see how we do it, put it on your website, next time we go, maybe the Border Patrol is there to arrest us."

"I won't publish any specific information, I promise. You trust me, don't you?"

"I do, I trust you, Jesse. I just don't wanna see you get killed. Or me. No, I won't take you."

Jesse waited a long time before saying anything, knowing how uncomfortable people are with silence.

"You know how much this means to me, to my website."

"Yeah, I know, but —"

"Don't you want me to succeed in my profession?"

"Yeah, but —"

"I need cutting edge stories. My readers expect them."

Eduardo didn't say anything, just sat there looking worried. Jesse said, "I feel like a Margarita. Would you like one?"

"No, I still have my beer."

When Jesse flagged down their waitress she ordered a margarita and a Tecate. Eduardo started to object, but the waitress had already gone to fill the order. When the beer arrived, he downed the first bottle and started on the new one. Jesse took a tiny sip of her drink and held it up to get the waitress's attention. She indicated a number two with her other hand.

When another drink arrived, she said, "Oh, she brought it too soon. Can you finish this one for me?"

Eduardo pleaded with his eyes but said he would. He downed the beer and started on the margarita. Jesse took a sip and again signaled she would like another one. This time Eduardo said, "Get me one, too."

Three drinks later Eduardo said, "You can't being no camera."

"I won't."

"He's not gonna want his picture on some website."

"I'm not going to show anybody's face. You have my word."

"I don't know, Jesse."

"You trust me, don't you?"

"Ay yi yi. Señor Conrad tole me you always get your way."

Jesse hugged him and kissed him on the cheek. She said, "Thank you, Eduardo."

Eduardo blushed.

JESSE WAS WAITING IN HER APARTMENT when Eduardo knocked on the door. It was still dark out, and the lights were on over the parking lot where Eduardo led her to an old Chevy C30 pickup truck. It was a dualie—a truck with dual wheels on the rear axle—and it had an over-sized wrought iron utility rack that looked homemade. Bales of hay filled the rack.

Jesse said, "Where are you going to put the people?"

Eduardo smiled and said, "You'll see."

Jesse pulled out her camera and started taking pictures.

Eduardo said, "A camera! Don't get the license plate."

"Trust me."

They climbed into the cab and when Eduardo turned the key, nothing happened. Eduardo said, "Ay, cabron. Not again."

"What?"

"The starter motor gets too hot. Santo says it's because the engine is a 350. He was gonna put a heat shield on it, but he never got around to it."

"Who's Santo?"

"He's my cousin. He knows how to fix cars."

"Can he get it started for us?"

"He lives way out on the other side of Apache Junction. Shit. We're gonna be late. Tomás always wants me there at sunrise."

Jesse said, "Tyler."

Eduardo turned around to see who Tyler was but nobody was there. Jesse punched in a speed dial number on her phone.

"Tyler? Jesse. I need to get a car started … At my apartment … Can you hurry, I'm late for an appointment … Thank you so much."

Jesse put her phone in her fanny pack. "He's on his way."

Fifteen minutes later, a young man in a BMW pulled in the driveway. Eduardo said, "That ain't no mechanic's truck."

The man stepped out of his car and Jesse introduced them.

Eduardo said, "It's the starter. It gets hot."

Tyler said, "350?"

"Yeah, you know about it?"

Tyler walked to the back of his car and pushed a button on his keyless remote. The trunk popped open and revealed a red toolbox with the label Snap-On. He reached over the box and pulled out a creeper dolly, opened the box, and took out a large flathead screwdriver. He walked to the truck and said, "You know the routine?"

Eduardo said, "Yeah."

Tyler said, "Let's do it," lay down on the creeper, and rolled under the engine compartment.

Eduardo climbed into the cab.

Tyler said, "Ready?"

When Eduardo said, "Go ahead," a spark lit up the ground under the engine, which started right up.

Tyler rolled back out and stood up. "I thought you were in a hurry. Go."

Jesse kissed him on the lips and said, "Thank you." She got in the truck and they left.

By the time they got to Casa Grande, the sun was up and the temperature was rising. They met Tomás behind the Union Pacific tracks on Cowtown Road, a little bit south of the Frito Lay plant.

When Jesse and Eduardo arrived, Tomás stepped out from behind a rail car. He was drenched in sweat and looked angry.

"Quien es la chica?" Tomás wanted to know who Jesse was.

"Ella está bien." Eduardo vouched for her.

That seemed to satisfy Tomás until Jesse pulled out her camera. Tomás said, "What the hell is she doing?"

Eduardo said, "It's okay. She's just taking pictures."

Eduardo assured him she wouldn't publish anything that would get him in trouble with La Migra—immigration. She wouldn't show anybody's face, and she wouldn't show anything that would help the cops figure out where they were. They argued for a long time, and eventually they declared an uneasy truce, but Tomás glared at Jesse through soulless eyes every time she snapped a photograph.

Eduardo turned his attention to the job at hand. He untied the ropes holding the bales of hay on his pickup, and pulled two bales out of the stack near the back, revealing his secret. The "bales" on the sides and top were fake. A thin layer of hay was stacked around a wrought iron frame and the interior was hollow.

Tomás whistled towards the freight cars stored along the siding rail. A face appeared for a moment at the edge of a boxcar. There was some chattering and about a dozen men popped out from behind their cover. Jesse was disappointed. She was hoping for a more diverse group—women and children to tug on her readers' heart strings. The men scurried over to the pickup and packed themselves in. Eduardo replaced the hay bales and tied the ropes. It was time to go. Eduardo, Jesse, and a haystack full of secret travelers headed southeast down Cowtown Road. Tomás disappeared among the rail cars.

Jesse said, "How did those people get here?"

Eduardo said, "I never asked. They have to cross the border somewhere. They probably come in down by Calexico. A guy tole me once that's where they jump on the train. When the train slows down in Casa Grande, they jump off and and wait for me. I take them to Picacho. I don't know where they go from there."

They eventually crossed over to the other side of the tracks and continued through town along Main Street. The speed limit dropped until they got back to the road along the tracks. At that point the name of the street changed to Jimmy Kerr Blvd.

Eduardo said, "Oh no," as a Border Patrol truck approached from the other direction. It passed by without even looking at them. Eduardo let out his breath. He said, "Ay yi yi. I can't go to jail again."

Jesse said, "Was it really bad?"

"The guards didn't pay no attention to me, but some of the other prisoners wanted to marry me, you know what I mean?"

Jesse laughed.

"No, really. I don't understand what they saw in me, wrinkled old smuggler from Chihuahua."

Jesse said, "Oh, I understand. You're pretty irresistible."

Eduardo blushed and said, "I know."

Jesse turned to look at the hay. She said, "Are they okay back there?"

"They're fine."

"Are you sure?"

"I'm sure. It's not that far, you know."

"It's awfully hot out. And humid."

"Don't worry, Jesse. I done this lots of times. Nobody ever got sick or nothing."

"But did you ever get this late of a start?"

"No."

"Then they could be dying under that hay."

"They're not dying."

"How do you know?"

"I just know. That hay, it's like insulation."

Jesse spotted a small market. "Pull in there."

Eduardo said, "We're late already."

"Please, Eduardo."

"You're not gonna leave me alone until I stop, are you?"

He pulled into the parking lot and waited with the motor running while Jesse raced into the market. She came out a few minutes later with a case of drinking water and two bags of ice. When she got into the truck, she said, "Find someplace secluded."

Eduardo drove a little farther and made some turns until Jesse said, "There. That access road along the canal." Eduardo started to turn and she said, "Not that one, the one right next to it."

Eduardo pulled off the road and eased the pickup onto a narrow gravel road. On one side was the canal, and on the other was a dirt berm created from the canal's excavation debris. About a half a mile in, Jesse said, "This is good."

Jesse helped Eduardo open the hay bale door. The men shielded their eyes from the daylight and staggered out of their hidey-hole. They were drenched. Some of them were wheezing. Jesse and Eduardo handed each man a bottle as he came out. They guzzled the water and sucked on the ice cubes. Some of them rubbed ice on their skin. Jesse tried to talk to one of them in Spanish, but he didn't seem to know Spanish. She asked him if he spoke English.

He said in broken English, "Are we there?"

Eduardo gestured for him to look around. The nearest buildings were far off in the distance. "We're only stopping to give you some water and let you cool down."

The man said, "Thank you." He had a Middle Eastern accent.

Jesse took out her camera and started taking pictures of the men but turned her attention to a pipe stretched across the canal. It came out of the ground on one side, spanned the canal above the water, and disappeared into the ground on the other side. She wondered what it was carrying. It was large enough to be a sewer pipe.

Eduardo took Jesse by the elbow and walked her along the canal bank out of hearing range of the men. "The coyote won't wait. If we don't get to Picacho soon, these people are going to be stranded."

Before Jesse could respond, a commotion erupted over by the pickup. Jesse and Eduardo turned around to see the men clamoring and pointing to the east. An approaching dust cloud filled the entire horizon. It was as if a massive brown wave had crashed down upon the earth and was about to sweep away everything in its path.

Eduardo said, "Ay yi yi, that's a big one."

Jesse said, "Like 2011."

They sprinted back towards the men, but before they could get there, the raging surge of dirt and debris closed in on them. They fought for breath and covered their eyes as they hustled the men back inside the haystack. They secured their cargo and climbed into the cab. Visibility was down to zero. Eduardo turned the key, but nothing happened. He had forgotten to leave the engine running. Jesse opened the glove compartment but couldn't find a screwdriver, so she grabbed a wrench. She said, "What does the starter look like?"

"A black round thing about this big." He held his hands apart.

Jesse stepped out of the truck and was battered by the dust as she rolled under the truck. The body of the truck funneled the wind passing under it, increasing its speed. Her long black hair was whipping in her face as she searched for the starter. The engine was filthy, covered with decades of grease and dirt. She located a part fitting Eduardo's description bolted onto the right side between the engine and the exhaust pipe. A small cylinder with threaded posts coming out of it was attached to the top of the starter. Bolted to the posts were two electrical cables: a thick red one and a thin purple one. She yelled to Eduardo, "Ready?" but she didn't know if he had heard her. She took the wrench and jammed it between the big post and the engine block. Sparks flew from both ends of the wrench, but the engine didn't budge, so she shoved the bigger end between the big post and the little post. The posts sparked and the engine roared to life. Jesse jumped and her forearm touched the exhaust pipe. She yelled and pulled her arm back, climbed out from under the truck, jumped into the cab, and slammed the door shut.

Eduardo said, "You did it, Jesse. You are really something, you know that?"

Jesse said, "Let's get moving."

Eduardo put the truck in Drive and pressed down lightly on the accelerator.

Jesse looked over her arm. It was a first degree burn, maybe second. She looked up and said, "Go more to the right. I don't want to end up in the canal."

"I can't see nothing over there with the wind blowing on that pile of dirt. But I can see the canal. I'm using it as a guide."

"Just be careful."

"You're the one who wanted to drive to someplace secluded."

"I didn't want those men to die. Hey, Eduardo?"

"Yeah."

"Why didn't you take the freeway? If you had taken the freeway we'd be there already."

"Because a truck full of hay looks less suspicious on a country road." He looked over at her and said, "Hey, do you know what you look like?"

Jesse pulled down the vanity mirror on the visor. She had black streaks on her face from the grease. Her hair was a wild mat with twigs and dried up flower petals in it. She looked at her arms and legs and clothing. There were grease stains everywhere, and her entire body was covered with tan-colored dirt.

Eduardo laughed. "You look like a grease monkey."

The wind was blowing straight towards them and the truck was swaying, but it seemed stable. When they reached the next road crossing, Eduardo stopped and scratched his head. "Do you know how far this canal goes?"

"I have no idea."

"I don't want to turn until the wind dies down. If I turn against the wind, it might catch that hay and blow us over. I think I'll keep driving along the canal. It's going the right way." He crossed the road and continued along the canal for another mile until he came to the next road. He looked for traffic before crossing it, but on the other side, the canal headed north. Eduardo stopped the truck and said, "I guess we gotta turn. He put the truck in reverse and started backing out onto the road.

NINE

JONATHAN HAD ALMOST MADE IT through the railroad crossing when the locomotive plowed into the tail end of the trailer. The trailer stayed attached to the tractor, but the train pushed it across the center divider where it knocked down the street signs and the crossing gate assembly. Three cars and a woman on a bicycle had been waiting in the oncoming lane, and the trailer swept the cars completely off the road into a ditch. One of the cars collided with a saguaro cactus, chopping it in half, the upper half toppling over onto the hood of one of the other cars. The woman on the bicycle fell down and the trailer passed right over without touching her.

Jonathan clenched the steering wheel, fighting to drive in a straight line, keeping his foot on the accelerator, picking up speed, ignoring the stop sign, flying through the intersection. A car driving west swerved to avoid him and crashed into a purple building on the corner.

The trailer swung back and started following the tractor again, but not directly behind it. The force of the impact had damaged the frame, and the axles were tracking a good three feet to the left. When he looked in the mirror, he saw the train had actually twisted the last third of the trailer, mangling the aluminum box.

The tires were now lined up at an angle, chirp-chirping across the asphalt and spitting chunks of black rubber into the air. The wind was still blowing from the east, but instead of swaying and tipping, the trailer was now wagging violently back and forth. A plume of dark gray smoke rose from the tires, mingling with the dust and blowing away.

Jonathan didn't let up.

He wanted to get as far away from the killer as possible, and wanted to shift the transmission into higher gears, but it took every bit of his concentration to keep the truck on the road, so he drove as fast as seventh gear would take him. At one point, a school bus crossed in front of him, and without slowing down he pulled hard on the wheel to go around it on the right. The trailer swung to the left and almost hit the bus.

Through the dust he saw the area around him had changed to residential, small stucco houses in pink and tan. About a mile past the train crash, Jonathan came upon another major cross street. Driving fast and surrounded by blowing dust, he didn't see the stop signs until he was right on top of them and it was too late to brake. Nobody crashed into him this time, but he ran out of road on the other side.

Sunshine Blvd terminated at this intersection.

He jumped the curb and kept driving straight ahead into an open field. The truck caromed across the bumpy terrain, bucking up and down. Everything in the cab that wasn't secured was tossed into the air and onto the floor. His head struck the roof of the cab with every convulsion of the out-of-control machine.

Jonathan was close to panicking.

He yanked the steering wheel hard to the right, side-swiped a palm tree, and with a whump, was back on a road, a gravel road, which was a tremendous improvement over the raw field. He decided he would ditch the truck at the first inhabited building he saw. He wasn't sure what he would do at that point, but he knew he had had his fill of the demolition derby.

In the distance, he saw a large stack of hay bales emerge from the dust cloud. It was moving from right to left across the road, and Jonathan had to think fast. His first instinct was to go around it the way he had done with the school bus, so he yanked the wheel to the left, but changed his mind and decided to stop, jamming his foot down on the brake pedal. Something appeared in the right side mirror. He focused on it and was shocked at what he saw: the side of the trailer. The tail had swung forward, catching up with the tractor.

He had jackknifed it.

The truck smashed into the haystack, which turned out to be a flatbed hay truck, and dragged it forward until they both came to a stop on top of a small bridge. The front corner of the tractor hung over the curb running along the side of the bridge, and the trailer stretched across both the bridge and the remnants of an old obsolete bridge next to it. In the collision, the flatbed had hooked onto the bumper and frame of the tractor, and was dangling over a wide canal filled with rushing water. The water was dark.

Jonathan knew he needed to get out of the truck and run to safety, but he realized if he weren't careful, he could fall into the canal and drown. In spite of the danger, he couldn't help but notice the irony of drowning in the middle of a desert.

A hay bale dropped from the flatbed and plunked down into the water before bobbing up and floating off with the current, and a swarm of men emerged from the hole left by the falling bale. The men scrambled to climb up the hay, over the tractor and onto the bridge. One of them lost his grip and fell into the canal, grabbing another man and dragging him with him. That man grabbed at the men above him, and a half a dozen men ended up in the drink. The men flailed at the water and kicked their legs, and they screamed for help in a foreign language. One of the men slipped below the surface. Jonathan saw the man through the murky water, the pleading in his face, now screaming for help, sinking lower, now gone. The man's fatal struggle against the rushing water brought back agonizing memories for Jonathan. A primal terror emerged from deep inside him, washing over his body, and he began to tremble. In full panic now, he clawed his way to the high side of the truck and jumped onto the concrete bridge. In all the time he had been in Arizona, this was his first venture completely out of the air-conditioned truck, and the oven-blast wind sucked the air out of his lungs. He ran around to the front of the truck and looked for the other men in the water. He saw that a second bale had fallen, and a man was hanging on to it. The man drifted away downstream, while those who had made it to the bridge scurried off in every direction. Before long, they had all disappeared into the haze, down the canal or into the fields.

Jonathan heard a pounding noise below the bridge, so he peered over the edge. People were trapped in the cab of the truck—an old man and a young girl. The man was kicking the door with both feet. It finally popped open and he climbed onto the hood. The girl scooted up behind him, steadying him and pushing him forward. Jonathan felt paralyzed. The girl looked up at Jonathan and said, "Help us."

Struggling to control his fear, Jonathan leaned over the curb as far as he could and stretched out his arm. The man grabbed his hand, and Jonathan pulled him up onto the bridge. The man immediately turned around and grabbed the girl's arm. He lifted her with ease, strong for his age. The three of them half crawled to a spot away from the truck cab where they found better protection from the wind.

The man was Hispanic and looked like a cowboy, weathered and tough in his blue jeans and long sleeve denim shirt. His belt had a big silver buckle with a man riding a bucking bronco engraved on it. His pointed leather boots were old and worn. The only thing missing was the hat. It was probably at the bottom of the canal. The man stood bent over with his hands on his knees, trying to catch his breath. He said, "Thank you, señor."

The girl said, "Why are you thanking him? He just ran us off the road."

Now that he saw her up close, Jonathan realized the girl was actually a young woman. In her early twenties, he figured. She wore khaki shorts and shirt, and an Australian bush hat hung from her neck by the cords. She was covered with dirt and grease, and her long black hair was frightening—a birds' nest. Jonathan wanted to ask her if she were on safari, but decided it was a bad idea.

When the old man caught his breath, he straightened up and looked around, frowning. He said to the girl, "I'll see you later, Jesse," nodded to Jonathan, and walked off into a field.

Jonathan said, "Jesse?"

She didn't look at him, but said, "Yes."

"I'm Jonathan."

Neither one offered to shake hands.

She said, "Why the hell did you run your truck into us?"

Jonathan said, "I couldn't stop. Besides, you came out of nowhere."

"How fast were you going, anyway? Didn't you see the dust storm? You're supposed to slow down or pull off to the side until it passes." She tilted her head, curious now, and examined the twisted wreck.

"I was in a hurry. I was running for my life."

"Yeah, uh huh." Her expression changed and she said, "Oh no." She ran back to the bridge and leaned over the curb, peering at the flatbed.

"What's wrong?"

She squatted down, saying, "I have to get something." She sat down on the curb and slid onto the hood of the flatbed.

"Hey, come back."

She ignored him, grabbing a hand hold on the side mirror,

working her way into the cab.

Jonathan paced the bridge, saying, "That's not a good idea. Come back."

She came out of the cab holding a brown knapsack. It looked expensive, the same as her clothes and hat, but cleaner. She slid her arm through one of the straps, swung it over her shoulder, and climbed out of the cab, working her way to the front of the truck. Jonathan reached down and helped her back up. As she stepped off the flatbed's hood, the semi's bumper wrenched forward and the flatbed slipped off, falling into the canal. Jonathan watched it drop beneath the surface in a torrent of bubbles.

She pulled a camera out of the knapsack and started taking pictures of the tractor and the bridge, saying, "Running for your life, huh? Wow, that's some getaway car."

"That's all I had. Look, I have to leave before he catches up with me."

"Who's 'he'?"

"The guy, the man who killed Mark." He paused before saying, "You should come too."

She walked towards the tail of the trailer, shooting pictures as she went. "Where are we going? And who's Mark?"

Jonathan spotted a rifle on the ground about 100 feet from the wreck. He jogged over to it and said, "Come look at this."

"In a minute." She went to the other side of the bridge and started to shoot the inside of the trailer. She climbed inside the trailer and continued shooting.

He said, "Don't do that. Are you crazy? That thing could fall into the water."

Jesse's voice from inside the trailer said, "It's not going to fall." She jumped out of the trailer and walked over to Jonathan. The wind was starting to die down, but she still had to squint as she stared down at the rifle. She said, "An AK47," and aimed her camera.

Jonathan said, "Were there any more in the trailer?"

"No, just some boards." She took about 20 pictures of the rifle. She looked up and turned her camera towards him, saying, "What's your last name, Jonathan?"

"Starker. Look, we have to get out of here."

"And how long have you been driving trucks?"

"About ten minutes. Come on, let's go."

She looked up and said, "So you've never driven a truck before?"

"No, this is my first time."

She looked back at the wreck and said, "Well, they say the first time can be painful."

Jonathan was confused for a moment. He smiled and shook his head. "You have no idea."

VALDO SAID, "GO AROUND IT," and Roberts jammed the car in reverse. Tires squealing, he backed up and spun the car 180 degrees in one fluid motion, changed gears and shot back down Sunshine Blvd.

Roberts turned his head and said with a cocky grin, "Bondurant School. Took a driving course when I first got to Phoenix." He passed a car on the right and turned into the warehouse driveway, slamming on the brakes and spinning the car around again.

Valdo said, "What the hell are you stopping here for?"

"I need the van."

"I don't see no van."

"It'll be here shortly."

"What do you need a van for?"

"That truck still had a crate in it. With this dust storm and the confusion from the crash, we might get lucky and retrieve the crate before law enforcement stumbles upon it."

"Forget that one. Just take the crates you got and get them the hell out of here. We really gotta get rid of the guy who can tie us to the truck."

"You go ahead and track him down, then call me and tell me what's going on."

"How do I get around the train?"

"Go down to the freeway and head south. That's left on I-10 east."

"Left on the freeway."

"Correct. Stay on the freeway for two miles, then get off and turn left on 87, cross the tracks and turn left again. Follow the road along the tracks back to the scene of the accident."

"87, left, left."

"You got it."

Valdo jumped in his car and raced to the freeway. He got off on 87 and doubled back up along the tracks. By the time he got to Sunshine Blvd, officers from the Eloy Police Department were directing traffic away from the scene. Valdo had no choice but to turn right and follow the other cars. It didn't matter, though. He spotted the divots the damaged trailer had made in the roadbed. The police had directed him down the course taken by the truck. He still had a chance to retrieve the few rifles still in the trailer when the truck was stolen, but what he wanted was to find the guy who stole it.

The truck had left a trail of debris in its wake, chunks of tire, scraps of wood and—guns. Apparently no one had noticed the pile of guns lying on the side of the road. The police hadn't gotten around to following the truck yet and the other drivers were too busy trying to navigate through the dust. Valdo pulled over by the rifles. The line of cars behind him did the same, playing follow the leader. A police officer started walking towards the parked cars, but Valdo waved the cars on and when they were moving again, he flashed the officer an okay sign with his fingers. The officer glared at him, but got a call on his radio and rushed back to the accident scene. Valdo waited until there was a lull in the traffic and the police officers were preoccupied before opening the trunk and throwing the guns in. There were five of them. He closed the trunk and left, leaving the pieces of crate behind.

A mile up from the accident, the road ended in a T. The other cars were turning left, but the trail of debris headed straight into a field. Valdo saw that Sunshine Blvd started up again just to the right of the intersection, so he made a right turn, a quick left turn, and parked the car. He got out and walked into the field. There were rifles scattered along a fifty-yard path from the intersection to the road he was parked on. He pulled out his phone and called Roberts.

Roberts said, "Valdo, what's your 20?"

"My what?"

"Your location."

Valdo said, "I'm on Sunshine Blvd., farther down. The guy dumped the guns in a field."

"How do you know about the guns? Who told you?"

"I'm looking at them. You better come get them. I'm going after the truck."

"Zac is following me in a cargo van. Hey, the cops are diverting traffic onto Sunshine Blvd."

"Yeah, just keep going. When you get to the end, turn right and left. The field is right there."

"What?"

"The field with the guns. You can't miss it."

"On the right?"

"On the left."

"You said … never mind."

Valdo followed the breadcrumbs, stopping three more times and getting out to retrieve guns off the gravel roadbed. By the third time, the wind wasn't as bad and visibility was improving. Finally, he was able to make out a large red object in the distance—his truck. Maybe it wasn't so bad. Maybe he could still take the tractor down to Manny.

JONATHAN SPOTTED A LARGE WHITE CAR approaching from the south. At a distance it looked like a police car, but then he saw how old it was. When it got close, he realized Mark's killer was driving. He turned to see Jesse snapping pictures of the car. Jonathan said, "He's here, we have to go."

She said, "Is that the man who killed Mark?"

Jonathan started to tremble again. He wanted to run but he couldn't leave this fool here to be slaughtered. He grabbed Jesse's camera and said to her, "This is not a joke. That man has a gun."

Jesse yanked the camera back and took pictures of the killer stepping out of his car. When she saw his full size, she said, "Whoa." The killer held a large pistol, but he wasn't aiming it or anything, just keeping his arms at his sides as he walked slowly towards them.

Jonathan said, "He has a gun."

"I see it." She started backing up as she resumed snapping pictures.

Jonathan started backing up, too. They ran out of room when they reached the canal. To his horror, Jonathan was faced with getting shot or jumping into the water.

But the killer stopped.

Jonathan looked over and saw Jesse aiming a small, shiny handgun at the killer.

A red Dodge Charger came racing up to the white car. It skidded to a halt, and a middle-aged man dressed like Jimmy Buffet stepped out. He looked at Jesse's pistol and said to her, "Don't shoot, I'm a federal agent." He looked at the killer. Jonathan thought he saw the man wink. The man said, "Everything's under control. Put the gun down."

Jonathan said, "He's lying."

Jesse said, "Let's see some ID."

The agent said, "Okay. Just stay calm. I'm reaching into my back pocket."

The killer shook his head in disgust.

The agent reached into his back pocket and pulled out a wallet. He opened the wallet and said, "See? Now put the gun down."

Jesse turned to Jonathan.

Jonathan said, "Don't listen to him. That's the same thing he said to Mark."

The agent looked shocked. The killer was trying not to.

Without being asked, the agent tossed his wallet over by Jesse's feet and said, "Have a look."

It startled Jonathan; he flinched and his foot slipped. He fell over onto Jesse, knocking her off balance. She started to fall and grabbed hold of Jonathan's shirt. The gravel gave way beneath their feet and they tumbled down the concrete bank with their limbs entwined, rolling over each other until they hit the water with a plunk.

TEN

THE WATER WAS COLD, colder still because Jonathan had just been roasting in the desert heat.

He felt as if he were reliving a memory. He was 11, back in Newport Beach, struggling against a wave that had just crashed in front of him, icy water slamming him down, holding him under, the salt stinging his sinuses. What had his father told him? Push off the bottom and grab a lungful of air before it pulls you back down. Push off the bottom.

He couldn't feel the bottom.

He tried to kick, but his legs were tied together. He sank deeper. His lungs burned. He couldn't hold his breath any longer. The air burst out of his mouth in a torrent of bubbles and rushed to the surface. He ached to follow those bubbles. The urge was overwhelming: to breathe in, to fill his empty lungs back up, even if it meant filling them with the dirty water surrounding him. It would be the last breath he ever took. He knew from his experience in the surf he could fight the urge, but for how long? He realized his eyes were closed. He always closed his eyes to keep the sand out when a wave crashed down on him. There was no sand here. He opened his eyes and looked up, straining to see through the yellowish water that glowed from the sunlight above, struggling in vain to find the surface. He looked down at his legs. A tarp covered them, tangled them, held them together. He reached down and yanked hard on the canvas, kicking and twisting until finally he was free. Now he could swim to the surface, but ...

It was too late.

His vision narrowed and he saw gray clouds closing in. He was passing out. He felt a warm body next to his. Somebody was hugging him. Was he hallucinating? He felt himself floating upwards, and he kicked his legs to speed up the motion.

After an eternity his head broke the surface and he gasped for breath, exploding into a fit of coughing. He felt an arm around his neck—a bony little arm. He had been rescued by Jesse who was now dragging him along the surface. He turned over and said, "I can swim."

Jesse let go of him and said, "Then hurry."

The water next to him splashed and he realized the splashes were bullets striking the surface, bullets meant for him.

Jesse said, "Come on," and Jonathan swam hard in her direction. She ducked behind a hay bale bobbing along the canal and he followed right behind her. He looked up to see the killer walking along the bank, aiming towards them. Bullets thumped into the bale and into the water around them splashing and hissing. The smell of scorched hay filled his nostrils. He dropped as low in the water as he could.

When Jonathan had viewed the water from above, it seemed to be moving slowly, but now—here in the middle of it—he realized the current was swift, swift enough to carry them out of range when the killer stopped to reload.

VALDO SHOVED A FULL MAGAZINE into the pistol, but didn't fire any more rounds. The hay bale had floated too far away. He would have to run to catch up with it, and his bruised ribs wouldn't allow running.

Roberts said, "Go after them you idiot. They're getting away."

Valdo said, "Calm down. They're not going nowhere. I'll get them at the next bridge."

"Just drive along the canal. You'll catch up with them."

"We don't know where this dirt road ends. I could end up having to back up for miles."

"It runs along the entire canal."

"Bullshit. You don't know."

"Go, dammit. You're wasting time."

Valdo turned and said, "I'll get them at the bridge." He jumped in his car, sped back to the paved road and turned right without stopping, slowing down just enough to keep from crashing. The car fishtailed as he stomped on the accelerator. The road was crowded with cars and trucks which had been diverted from the train wreck, and Valdo weaved through the congestion at high speed. He drove a mile to the next paved road and turned right. There weren't any cars now and he really opened it up until he came upon the canal. He pulled over and looked around; there was nobody in sight. He walked onto a footbridge just upstream of the road and set up his ambush.

SAFE NOW, Jesse pulled herself up onto the bale. Jonathan stayed in the water. She glared at him and said, "What the hell have you gotten me into?"

He said, "I told you to run, but you had to take your pictures."

"My camera!" She reached over her shoulder and felt around. Nothing.

"It's at the bottom of the canal. You owe me a camera."

"How do you figure that?"

"It was in my knapsack when you threw me into the canal." She reached down into the water in front of her, smiled and said, "Ah, here it is."

"Your camera?"

"No, my phone." She held it up.

"It's soaked."

"It's supposed to be water proof. Let's see … yep, it still works."

"Good. Call the police. I've had enough of this."

She said, "In a minute," held her phone up and started snapping pictures of Jonathan on the hay bale.

She wasn't about to call the police. What would she tell them? That she helped smuggle undocumented immigrants into the country? They might not understand that she did it for a story, a story that was gone, sunk to the bottom of the canal. Besides, she was in the middle of a better news story. She knew that the moment the big guy aimed a pistol at them.

Jonathan said, "Are you crazy?"

"Just a few more. About calling the police …"

"Well, never mind the police for now. The first thing we have to do is get out of the water. You know they'll be coming after us."

Jesse said, "You're right." She slid off the bale and swam to the side of the canal. She tried to get a grip on the concrete to climb out, but it was too steep. She swam farther downstream and tried again.

JONATHAN KEPT WATCH, looking behind them and along the banks, expecting to see the gunmen at any moment. He had lost his glasses when he fell into the canal, and had to strain to see anything far away. Up ahead he saw the image of a bridge fade into view through the dust. There was something on the bridge.

The silhouette of a man. A big man.

Jonathan said, "Get back here."

"Why?"

He pointed in the direction of the bridge. She looked to see what he was talking about.

He said, "Come on."

She swam towards the bale as they drifted closer to the bridge, but the current was fighting her. Now Jonathan could clearly see the killer in the dark suit. Jonathan edged along the side of the bale and reached out for Jesse. When she stretched her hand out, she drifted away and had to swim hard to catch back up. She stretched her hand out again and this time he was able to grab it and pull her in. Without a word, they took a deep breath and ducked under the bale.

VALDO SAW SOMETHING approaching the bridge. It was a bale of hay and some debris from the wreck. Was this the bale he was looking for? He scanned the murky water, murkier still because of the dark pall cast over it by the dust storm. There was no sign of his prey, so he decided this one must be from earlier and he would have to wait. It was also possible they had drowned.

His cell phone rang. It was Roberts.

"Yeah?"

"Have you located our hijacker and his little sidekick?"

"I'm at the bridge. They'll be here if they don't find a way out. I can't talk right now, they could come floating by any minute."

"Do I need to emphasize the importance of your keeping me up to date on any develo—"

Valdo hung up. He thought he heard something.

It was a gasp, and it came from the other side of the bridge. He ran over and watched a bale disappear into the dust cloud. He jumped back into his car, drove north to Houser Road, turned left, drove a mile and turned left on Tumbleweed Road. The canal was a half mile down Tumbleweed.

He parked the car in the dirt and started to step out, but a delivery truck was coming towards the bridge, so he waited for the truck to pass. This time he had to set up on the actual road, since there was no footbridge. He set up on the downstream side of the bridge. He had seen how the couple had hidden underwater as they approached the last bridge. He counted on them doing the same thing here, and when they came up for air on the other side he would be waiting for them.

PAST THE BRIDGE NOW, Jonathan was surprised to see Jesse pull her phone out and start taking pictures again. He said, "That was close. We won't be that lucky again." He scanned the bank and said, "How do we get out?"

Jesse stopped taking pictures and squinted a little, saying, "The sewer line."

"What sewer line?"

"At least I think it's a sewer line."

"What are you talking about?"

"We parked right by a sewer line. Some kind of pipe, anyway. It crosses over the canal before the bridge."

"How does that help us?"

"Eduardo's truck had a tarp on it, and a rope. That's what you were tangled in. We could toss that rope over the pipe and climb out."

They searched around the bale. When they couldn't find the tarp, Jesse took a breath and disappeared into the murky water. She was gone a long time, but finally emerged with a rope in her hand. She pulled on the rope until the tarp became visible. Jesse untied the rope from the tarp and coiled it up. She tied a knot near the end and said, "You're going to have to swim ahead of me and catch the rope."

Jonathan said, "I'll throw the rope. You catch it."

"No, I'll throw the rope. I have more experience."

"How much experience does it take to throw a rope?"

"None, if you're playing around. Plenty if your life depends on it."

"And you have this experience?"

"Yes."

"Where'd you get it?"

"Rodeo. I started when I was six, roping sheep, and moved up to calves. Look, there's the pipe. Swim to the other side of it."

Jonathan froze.

"What are you waiting for?"

"Come on, I need you to … hey, look at that." Before Jonathan could respond, she shoved one end of the rope in his hand and swam towards the right bank with the other.

The concrete on the bank had a crack that went all the way through. Part of the wall was broken and jutting out into the canal, and there was a man stuck in the gap. She swam up to the man and said, "Hey, give me a hand," just as she realized he was dead. She yanked the body out, wound the rope around the protruding concrete and tied it off. The bale drifted past and the rope tightened up. Jonathan hung on to the rope, let go of the bale and swam with Jesse pulling the rope hand-over-hand. He collided with the dead body, shoved it aside, and continued swimming. The body drifted away.

When he reached her, Jesse said, "Climb out."

Jonathan said, "You first."

"Damn you're stubborn."

Gripping the concrete, Jonathan pushed her upward. She climbed out of the water and immediately turned around to help pull him out. They rolled away from the bank and sprawled shivering in the dirt, exhausted.

Jonathan said, "Was that one of the guys in the hay truck?"

"Yeah."

"A friend?"

"A passenger."

Jonathan couldn't rest. After a minute he stood up and said, "Now what?"

Jesse said, "We can't stay here."

"No we can't. When we don't show up at the next bridge he'll start looking for us here along the canal."

Jonathan scanned the horizon as best he could. The wind had died down to a breeze, improving visibility. He said, "Which way do we go?"

Jesse said, "Follow me," stood up, and said, "Ow." She grabbed her leg.

"You're bleeding."

"That son-of-a-bitch shot me. Dammit." She looked at the blood on her hand and wiped it on her pants. "I didn't even feel it. I guess I was numb from the cold."

Jonathan knelt down and examined her wound. Up close now, Jonathan got a good look at Jesse. Their adventure had transformed her appearance. She was quite short, especially without her hat, which was lost in the action. She seemed younger, too. She had a slight build, and with her hair and clothes soaked and clinging to her body, she looked small and vulnerable. "It's not too bad, but we'll need to sanitize it and get a dressing on it."

"Later, not here."

"Then let me help you." He reached his arm around her.

She pushed him away. "Get off me."

"I was just trying to help."

"I can walk." She pointed and said, "That way."

VALDO'S PHONE RANG as he waited at the bridge, but he ignored it. A bale of hay appeared upstream, floating towards the bridge, and he followed it until it was well downstream. This time, nobody popped up and gasped. He watched it drift away before calling

Roberts.

Roberts said, "Did you get them?"

"They never showed. They must have found a way out."

"We're not finished over here yet. You find them. We'll catch up with you as soon as we can." Roberts hung up without waiting for a reply.

Valdo got in his car and cruised along the canal bank until he came to a large pipe spanning the canal. He got out and walked around. He didn't see any signs there of his prey, but he was convinced the big pipe had to be the key. He backed up to the road, drove north across the bridge, and started down the other side of the canal. He stopped at the pipe and got out.

There it was.

The ground just east of the pipe was moist, and wet footprints trailed away from the canal, fading out before reaching the brush.

They were heading north.

Valdo first searched along the roads north of the canal. They probably weren't stupid enough to walk along the road, but he had to check. They could have gotten a ride out of the area. If they did, he would have to find them some other way. There was one place they would go if they knew the area. Valdo had seen a sign for an airport. That's where he would look next.

JONATHAN AND JESSE came upon a road. They held back until they were sure no cars were coming before scooting across as quickly as they could. There was a fence on the other side, but they found an opening and wandered into a field of cotton. Dust drifted gently across the field, covering them, choking them. They walked until they couldn't see the road and sat down.

Jonathan said, "Let's see that leg."

There was a bloody groove along the outside of her left calf, but the bleeding was slow.

Jesse said, "Turn around."

Jonathan turned around. He heard Jesse fiddling with her clothes. When she said it was okay to turn around, he saw that she had removed her undershirt. Jesse tore the tank top into a long strip. She wrapped the strip around the wound, tied it off, stood up, and said, "Come on."

As they continued their journey. Jonathan said, "Where are we going?"

"To the airport."

"Airport?" The word alone made him anxious. "There's an airport out here?"

"Yes, there is."

"How do you know how to get there?"

"It's north."

"Which way is north? I can't see the sun."

"North is the direction these rows of cotton are running."

"Oh yeah. Too bad the battery's dead on my phone. It would be a lot easier if we could use the GPS. Oh no." He stopped and searched his pockets.

"What is it?"

"My phone. It's gone. I must have lost it in the canal."

"Well, it could have been worse. You could have lost an expensive camera. At least I still have my ... " She stuck her hand into her fanny pack and said, "Dammit. You owe me a camera and a phone." Her eyes widened and a pained expression washed over her face. "Dammit." She held up her open fanny pack. "My snubby."

"Your what?"

"My revolver. I dropped it when you pushed me into the canal."

"Well, what do you need a gun for?"

She gave him a look that made him feel stupid. "Wouldn't you like to have one right about now?"

"I see your point. I'll tell you what. I'll replace your camera and your phone and your gun."

She sighed. "That one was special."

"How can a gun be special?"

"It was a graduation present."

"A graduation present? What kind of psychopath gives a girl a gun for graduation? A car I could see, but a gun?"

"You're calling my dad a psychopath? You? The guy who just crashed a truck into a bridge?"

Silence hung over them for a while before Jonathan said, "I'm thirsty."

"Me, too. We'd better go."

A minute into their hike, Jesse said, "So who's Mark?"

"The guy who owned the truck."

"You stole the truck?"

"Yeah. No. I didn't steal it, they did, after they killed Mark."

"Why did they kill him?"

"I don't know. To get the truck, I suppose."

"How do you fit into all of this?"

"I needed to get to Phoenix. To Mesa. Mark was going to Arizona and offered to give me a ride."

"You're not from here?"

"No, I'm from California."

"I love California. I love the beach."

"Me, too. I used to go surfing with my dad."

"You don't go anymore?"

Jonathan didn't answer.

Jesse said, "So you came here in Mark's truck."

"Yeah. We were parked somewhere in the boonies when those guys showed up."

"Do you remember where you were?"

"Near a casino. I do remember hearing gun fire."

"Maricopa?"

"Yeah, that's it."

"So if they shot Mark, why didn't they shoot you?"

"I was hiding in the sleeper cab. I tried to sneak out but they saw me so I took the truck."

"You drove the truck from Maricopa?"

"No, they did. It's complicated."

"Tell me about about it."

"Maybe later."

"Okay."

They walked quietly for a while. When they crossed a stretch of field which had been recently irrigated, Jonathan's running shoes kept getting sucked down in the mud. Every so often he had to stop and pull on them until they popped out of the glop. He noticed Jesse didn't have that problem. Her hiking boots must have been designed for primitive terrain.

Jonathan said, "You were transporting undocumented immigrants, weren't you?"

"Yeah."

"Is that what you do? Are you a coyote?"

Jesse laughed. It was the first time he had seen her smile. Jesse said, "No, I'm not a coyote."

"Then what were you doing with them?"

"I'm a journalist."

"That explains a lot."

"I'm working on a—hey, what did you mean by that?"

"I mean we have people shooting at us and all you want to do is take pictures and ask questions."

"Oh. Anyway, I'm working on a story about illegal immigration. I tagged along on one of the runs. It was a good story, until some idiot ran into us."

"Do you work for a newspaper?"

"No way. There's no future in dead tree media."

"So who do you work for?"

"Myself."

"I don't get it."

"I worked for a local television station for a year. Now I run my own blog."

"Is there any money in that?"

"There can be, if you get enough followers. So what do you do?"

"I create graphic novels."

"Oh, comic books."

"No, not comic books. Graphic novels. There's a difference."

"Relax. I know what a graphic novel is. I'm just messing with you. So, have you sold any?"

"A few."

"You know, there's a big comic book convention going on in Mesa this weekend."

"I know. That's what I came out here for."

"Really? You came all the way from California for the convention?"

"Yeah."

Jesse said, "Heads up," and stopped.

They had come upon another road. Stooping down behind a low stand of mesquite and desert broom plants, they watched the killer's big white car cruise up and come to a stop directly across from them. Sweat dripped down Jonathan's forehead, mixing with the dust, turning into mud and stinging his eyes, but he didn't dare move to wipe his face. The car drove away slowly and when it was out of view they crossed the road and headed into the next field, which was bare dirt.

Jonathan said, "Keep going north?"

Jesse said, "We should head more to the west. We're going to have cross Tumbleweed Road at some point, and we're not that far from the airport."

"Does this airport have a name?"

"The Eloy Municipal Airport."

Jonathan laughed.

"What's so funny?"

"Is that anything like the Hooterville Municipal Airport?"

"For your information, Mister Big City, the Eloy Airport is the world's largest skydiving center. Other countries send their Special Forces there to train."

"All right, I apologize for insulting your airport. What are we going to do when we get there?"

"A friend of mine works there. He can help us."

"Is your friend a special forces skydiver?"

"He's an aircraft mechanic."

JONATHAN FOLLOWED JESSE northwest until they could see Tumbleweed Road in the distance. They turned north again, following the course of the road. When at one point a car approached, they had to throw themselves down and lie flat in the mud until it passed. It wasn't the white car, but they didn't want to take a chance. Close to the airport now, they scurried across the road and Jesse led them to a hangar. Opening a side door, Jesse peeked inside.

"Tyler?" she said. Nobody answered. "He's not here."

They walked in, and Jonathan told Jesse to sit down on a crate next to the door.

She said, "Tyler," again and kept walking.

Jonathan grabbed her by the arms and sat her down. She glared at him but stayed seated. He walked over by the office and tried to get inside but the door was locked. Next to the office he found a refrigerator with cans of Pepsi in it. He grabbed two cans and handed one to Jesse.

"Thank you. Why don't you sit down, too?"

"No thanks." He popped open the other soda and took a swig. "I need to find something." He walked back by the office and found a first aid kit hanging on the wall. "Here we go." He brought an armful of first aid supplies over to the crate. "Let's have a look." He untied the bloody t-shirt and removed it from her leg.

"Ouch."

"Sorry."

"That's okay."

The wound was fairly clean; the makeshift bandage had done its job. He poured hydrogen peroxide over the cut, wrapped it in a clean bandage and said, "There."

They sat for a while in silence and drank their sodas. Finally, Jonathan said, "We should call the police."

"I'm not sure that's such a good idea."

"I think it's a very good idea. I just witnessed a murder and an attempted murder."

"By a man with a badge."

"So?"

"So, how do we know he doesn't have connections with the local police?"

"Aren't you being a little paranoid?"

"How can you not be paranoid after what we just went through?"

"Then what do you think we should do?"

"We should call my Uncle Bill. He's a lawyer."

"What, so we can sue those guys?"

"No, smart ass. Bill has a lot of connections. He used to work for the U.S. Attorney's office."

"Well, let's call him, then."

"We need to find Tyler, have him let us in the office. He might be in the saloon."

"The saloon? Off Tumbleweed Road? What is this, Ovest?"

"What?"

"Never mind."

"It's a bar and grill. With everybody grounded, he could be over there."

"Tell me what he looks like and I'll go check around."

"No, you won't. I'm going with you."

"You need to stay off that leg."

"I'm fine."

"You've been shot."

"It's not that bad."

"You're staying here."

"Look, your big brother routine is kind of cute, but you're operating on my territory. I know my way around, and I know some of the people who work here. If we're going to survive this, you're going to have to follow my lead. Okay?"

"Okay."

THE ENTRANCE TO THE AIRPORT was lined with concrete barriers. Valdo pulled in, creeping along between them with his foot on the brake pedal, scanning the buildings on either side. They could be hiding in any of them. He rounded the corner and stopped in front of the Bent Prop Saloon and Eatery. That's where Valdo would go if he had just hiked two miles in this weather. The parking lot was full so he left his car double-parked and went to hunt on foot. Heads turned when Valdo opened the door and stared inside. The weather must have shut down operations at the airport, because the saloon was filled with customers. Music blared from a juke box, competing with laughter and conversation and a dozen television sets perched high on the walls.

The bartender said, "Come in or get out, but shut the door."

Valdo didn't acknowledge him. His eyes panned slowly from one side of the room to the other. He turned around and left.

ROBERTS CALLED VALDO to get a progress report. Valdo told him he was still searching the buildings around the airport. If Valdo failed to locate them, Roberts would have to move the hunt to a higher level, be forced to rely on his connections at the bureau for information. At first, he didn't know how he would keep track of the investigation without raising suspicions. On the surface, there was no reason for the ATF to be involved in this. Of course, since their shipment of guns had failed to arrive in Nogales, they would eventually track down the truck and put two and two together. But Roberts couldn't wait that long. He needed to find those two and eliminate them before they went to the police. He came up with a way to involve the ATF early on. When he had secured the last weapon from the roadway, an AK47, he tossed it into the trailer. The ATF would be called in, and would know immediately their illegal shipment was missing. Roberts would be able to waltz right through the middle of the panic and confusion. No one would ever notice him in the chaos.

Jesse peeked out the hangar door, looking left and right.

No sign of the killer.

Stepping outside, she signaled for Jonathan to follow as she scurried to the next building. Working her way along the length of the building, she waited for two cars and a pickup truck to pass before leading Jonathan across Tumbleweed Road, slipping from building to building until she reached the parking lot across from the Bent Prop Saloon. She motioned for him to squat-walk as they moved among the cars towards the saloon. She peeked around a car and got a look at the saloon door.

There was the killer.

She froze for a moment before ducking down low. Jonathan, confused, followed her lead. The killer turned around, walked to his double-parked car, and drove away.

Jonathan said, "He's not giving up."

Jesse said, "Nope," stood up, and walked over to the saloon.

When they stepped inside, the bartender looked up and laughed. Jesse said, "What's so funny?"

Jonathan nudged her and nodded towards the mirror behind

the bar.

She was covered in mud that had stuck to her skin and clothes and had dried and cracked. Her hair was filthy and matted. She frowned and said to Jonathan, "Jeez, I knew you were grungy. I didn't realize I was too."

The bartender, a middle-aged man with a black beard and a pot belly said, "Hey, Jess. How was the mud bath?"

"Wonderful. Hey, have you seen Tyler?"

"What do you want with that jerk?"

"Have you seen him or not?"

"He was just here. Why don't you hang around, have something to eat? He'll be back."

Food.

"Oh, yeah. Uh, I don't have my purse with me. Can I open a tab?"

"Anything for you, Sweetheart."

"Better yet, charge it to Tyler."

The bartender laughed. "You got it."

She turned to Jonathan. "Cheeseburgers sound good?"

"Cheeseburgers sound very good."

She said to the bartender, "Two double cheeseburgers and two Dogfish Head ales."

Jonathan said, "No ale for me, please."

The bartender said, "What'll ya have?"

"Do you have Beaver Buzz?"

"No."

"Kore?"

"No."

"All right, then, you must have Monster."

"I'm afraid not."

Jesse said, "He'll have a Mountain Dew."

The bartender turned to Jonathan, who said, "Yeah, that'll work."

The bartender said, "You got it," and handed the order to a waitress.

Jesse shook her head.

Jonathan said, "What?"

"You don't go into a bar and order a power drink."

"Well, excuse me."

The place was packed and they had to stand by the bar and wait for a table to open. Jesse noticed a group of men on the other side of the saloon looking their way. One of the men was agitated, pointing at them and saying something to the others. She moved in close to Jonathan and whispered, "Those men over there are staring at us."

Jonathan started to turn and Jesse said, "Don't … don't be conspicuous. Use the mirror."

Jonathan tilted his head toward the mirror and said, "Do you know them?"

"I've never seen them before."

The man who was pointing stood up. His eyes bored in on them as he walked quickly in their direction. He was almost up to the bar when Jesse said, "Get ready to leave."

ELEVEN

JESSE WATCHED THE MAN march right up to Jonathan and say, "Are you Jonathan Starker?" He had a thick German accent.

Jonathan said, "Why?"

"So you are he?"

"Yes I am. What do you want?"

"I am so glad to meet you." He extended his hand. "I love your novels. I have the entire West Wave Trilogy."

Jonathan shook his hand and said, "Thank you."

The man turned to Jesse, offered his hand, and said, "You are his girlfriend?"

Jesse said, "Uh—"

"You must be very proud."

Jesse shook his hand and said, "Delirious."

The man said, "Please, you will sit with us?"

Jonathan and Jesse said in unison, "Sure."

"Wonderful. I am called Albrecht."

They followed Albrecht to his table, where the men stood up, introducing themselves one-by-one with a handshake, a handshake and a bow for Jesse. Their names sounded strange to her, difficult in English, though she payed close attention. She would jot them down later while she still remembered them. Two of the men excused themselves, leaving places for Jonathan and Jesse to sit. When they all sat down, one of the men said, "How did you hurt your leg?"

Jesse said, "I got shot."

They all thought her joke was funny.

The burgers arrived, and they devoured them as Albrecht rambled on about the glories of Jonathan's work. None of the others were familiar with it, although they had all seen his picture on the billboards. Jesse studied Jonathan's face and nodded, wondering why she hadn't made the connection. She was a reporter. It was her job to observe people.

Albrecht said, "The convention, I have tickets, but I can't attend because we have extra training this weekend."

Jonathan said, "I'm sorry to hear that."

"No, no. Look how it turned out. Jonathan Starker is sitting at my table eating a cheeseburger."

A news bulletin on one of the televisions caught Jesse's attention. It was live coverage at a taped-off railroad crossing in Eloy. The camera zoomed in on a splintered crossing gate. A moment later it cut away to the mangled semi. She couldn't hear the news reader, but there was clearly a connection between the truck and the train crash. She nudged Jonathan's elbow and nodded towards it. She looked at Jonathan, her eyes demanding an explanation. He looked the other way.

Tyler walked up to the table and Jesse stood up, throwing her arms around him. She introduced Jonathan to Tyler and they shook hands. Tyler eyed them and seemed confused by their filthy condition.

Jesse introduced each man at the table, apparently pronouncing their names correctly. After all the hands were shaken, Jonathan and Jesse thanked the men for their hospitality, and started to leave, but Albrecht stopped them to beg for Jonathan's autograph.

Jonathan sketched out a comic book character onto Albrecht's note pad, and scrawled his signature under it. Albrecht was embarrassingly thankful. He also wouldn't allow Tyler to pay for the meals.

When they started to walk away, Jesse limped and said, "Ow."

Tyler said, "What happened?"

One of the Germans said "She got shot," and they all laughed.

Jesse said, "Let's talk outside."

Jonathan followed Jesse and Tyler towards the door.

Jesse tiptoed out of the saloon, looking left and right, scanning the surroundings.

Tyler said, "What are you looking for?"

Jesse said, "The guy who shot me. Come on, let's go to the hangar."

They started across the road when the white car darted in front of them, skidding to a stop. The killer stepped out of the car and reached into his coat.

VALDO HAD THEM: the truck thief, the girl, and some guy wearing a baseball cap. He aimed his .45 at the girl, calculating she might still have her revolver. "That way," he said, "behind the building. Come on, move." They hesitated and he shoved the truck thief. They turned and walked around the corner where they came upon two men standing by a dumpster smoking cigarettes.

Two more witnesses. This was going to be a bloodbath.

Before Valdo could squeeze the trigger, one of the smokers grabbed his gun from him. Valdo couldn't believe it, it happened so quickly. The man who took his gun turned to the guy who stole the truck and said in a thick German accent, "You better call the police, Mr. Starker."

The girl said, "We can't."

The guy with the ball cap seemed upset. "Why not?"

"I don't have time to explain. You'll have to trust me."

The German said, "Well what do you want us to do with him?"

She said, "Could you hold him long enough for us to get out of here?"

"Why don't we just dispose of him for you?"

"No, don't kill him."

The German seemed to think it was funny. Valdo didn't like the way he laughed about it.

The German said, "You go then, we'll take care of your giant."

The girl, the truck thief, and the ball cap guy took off. The German with the gun smiled at Valdo and said, "Look at me, giant."

When he turned to look at him, the other German circled around Valdo. The man—now behind him—whispered in his ear, "Good night, giant," and everything went black.

BACK INSIDE THE HANGAR, Jesse said to Jonathan, "Wait here a minute," and walked into the office with Tyler.

Once inside, she grabbed a rubber band off his desk and tied her hair in a pony tail as she told him about the truck crash and their escape from the two men. When she was finished, Tyler said, "Why haven't you called the police?"

"Tyler, this guy was the police. He was a federal agent. At least he said he was."

"I don't like this at all. Some guy feeds you a story about a murder and you believe him?"

"I was there. They were shooting at us."

"The cop was shooting at you?"

She squinted her eyes. She hadn't actually seen him shooting, just the big guy. "Well, he was there. He tried to distract me so the other guy could shoot us."

"And how did he do that?"

"He showed me his badge." Once she said it, it sounded lame to her, too. "I mean he threw it at my feet so I would take my eyes off of them. I had them covered and he tried to distract me."

"You had them covered?"

"Yes."

"You drew—on a cop?"

"Well, yes."

"And you wonder why he shot at you?"

Jesse ran the scene through her mind. Could she have been mistaken? Was she helping a fugitive escape the law? She looked at Jonathan through the window in the door. Of course. What was she thinking? This guy's no criminal, he's a writer. His picture is plastered all over the valley.

"Look, Tyler, I don't want to do anything until I talk to Uncle Bill. I just need your help getting the heck out of Dodge."

"I know what you're doing. This is another one of your stories, isn't it? Only this time, you're not just risking your own life, you're going to get that poor schmuck out there killed, too."

"We're not going to get killed. We just need to get away from here, then Uncle Bill will know what to do."

Tyler looked at the door. "Call your friend in here. He can decide for himself."

"No."

Tyler opened the door and said, said, "Come on in, uh …"

"I told you, his name is Jonathan."

"Come on in, Jonathan."

Jonathan said, "Are you done telling your secrets?"

Jesse said, "We don't have any secrets. Look, we have a decision to make. Do we contact the police, or do we run? It's your call."

Jonathan said, "I don't want to stay here. I want to get as far away from here as possible. Then we can talk to the police."

"Okay. Tyler, I need to use your phone."

Tyler, who was sitting on the edge of a desk, stepped aside.

She punched in a number. It was on speaker and everybody heard the ringing. A man answered. "Hello, who's calling?"

"Uncle Bill? It's Jesse."

"Oh hi, Princess. What can I do for you?"

Jonathan raised his eyebrows and Jesse felt embarrassed. She took it off speaker. "Uncle Bill, could I stay at your place for a few days?"

"Sure, Princess. What for?"

"My apartment is being fumigated."

"No problem. Mi casa yada yada."

"Thank you so much. What's the alarm code?"

"450366."

She wrote it down on one of Tyler's note pads. "Uncle Bill, are you having a good time on your honeymoon?"

"It's been … unbelievable."

"That's great. Say hi to Kotryna for me."

"I will."

"Love you, Uncle Bill. Bye."

Jesse said, "They're on a honeymoon cruise in Lithuania."

Tyler said, "Kotryna? That's what, number four?"

"Shut up."

Tyler smiled and said, "You're staying at your uncle's place at Stellar?"

"Yes."

"I can fly you there. No chance of running into the police."

"I thought the planes were grounded?"

"It's clear enough. I might have to change the air filters when I get back."

"Okay. Let's go."

Jonathan said, "We can't."

Jesse said, "Why not?"

"I don't fly"

"It's only a fifteen minute flight."

"I don't fly. I can't fly."

* * *

Jonathan said, "Could you drive us?" He didn't care that he looked like a coward. He was not getting on that plane.

Tyler pointed to his motorcycle. "It'll be cozy with the three of us."

Jesse said, "Where's your Beemer?"

"It's up at Falcon Field. I had to shuttle a plane over here."

Jesse said, "We'll take the Ninja. You can hitch a ride home with one of your buddies."

Jonathan thought, Now she's bossing Tyler around.

Tyler threw up his hands. "Fine. Take it."

Jesse said, "One more thing."

"What?"

"I need to borrow your XD."

"What happened to your Smith?"

"I lost it."

"The one Papa Joe gave you?"

"Yeah." She made pouty lips.

He walked over to a tool box and took a black and silver pistol out of the top drawer. "Here. There's one in the chamber."

Jonathan said, "Do you think that's a good idea?"

Jesse said, "I thought we covered that already." She took the gun and zipped it into her fanny pack. "I'll be careful."

Tyler said, "You'd better go."

Jesse grabbed the handlebars, threw her leg over the motorcycle, and pushed the starter button. The engine purred. "Hop on," she said.

Jonathan climbed onto the seat behind Jesse. There was no separate passenger seat and no passenger foot pegs. Jesse pulled in the clutch and popped it into gear.

"Ow, she said," reaching for her leg.

Jonathan said, "Does it hurt?"

"Yeah." She popped the transmission back into neutral. "Ow. I don't know. It's gonna be a bitch to shift. It would be so much easier to fly."

Jonathan decided to take a chance. He had clocked countless hours on his motorcycle simulator. He knew how to shift, how to accelerate, how to brake. There was no reason he couldn't transfer his virtual reality experience to the real world. Of course, he was risking embarrassment if he screwed up and dumped the bike. Maybe even risking injury. But if the choice was between being totally humiliated and getting on that plane, it was no choice at all.

"I'll drive," he said.

Tyler said, "You ride motorcycles?"

"Not this model, but yeah."

Jonathan and Jesse traded places.

Tyler said, "Now be very gentle with the accelerator. A little bit goes a long way. This bike has an ungodly amount of horsepower and you have to respect it."

"Okay."

"I'm serious. Nice and easy."

"Got it. Hey, what's the shift pattern?"

"One down and five up."

Jonathan squeezed the clutch and pressed the gearshift lever with his toe. It was just like his simulator. He revved the engine and released the clutch. The front wheel leapt into the air, the bike rotating on the back wheel, almost flipping back on them, but Jonathan pulled the clutch in and it settled down.

Tyler said, "I told you, nice and easy."

"Sorry."

Jesse said, "Please don't kill us."

Jonathan revved the engine lower this time, eased the clutch out, and the bike rolled smoothly out of the hangar.

WHEN VALDO WOKE UP, it was pitch black. He felt around, trying to figure out where he was, finding cartons and hand tools. He was inside some kind of storage shed. There was a thin crack of light—the door. He slammed his body against it, but it was thick steel and wouldn't budge. He felt inside his coat and found his .45, aimed it at the door latch, squeezed the trigger, and click. Those pendejos had emptied it. He pounded on the door, kept pounding until his fists were raw, and pounded some more. Finally someone yelled, "Hey, is there somebody in there?"

Valdo said, "Yeah, stupid. Let me out."

"Well, hold on. I'll get the key."

A minute later he heard a key working a lock.

"Hang on. Almost done."

The door opened and Valdo shielded his eyes from the sunlight. "Are you okay?"

Valdo didn't answer, didn't even look at the man, just pushed past him and worked his way back to his car, reloading his pistol as he went. He looked up when he heard the motorcycle. The truck thief was driving a rice burner with the girl wrapped behind him. They flew right past him to the edge of the lot, where they slowed to a crawl and picked their way through some brush to a dirt road on the other side. They accelerated and were gone.

Valdo started his car and followed their trail. He almost got stuck in the brush, but finally made it through. The dust stirred up by the bike lingered in the air, so he was able to track them. He should probably have called Roberts to fill him in on this development, but hey, screw Roberts.

Valdo followed the dust trail several miles until it ended at the intersection of a paved two-lane highway. Which way? Across the highway, the road faded out into the desert. What good would that do them? If they turned right, they would end up back in Eloy. They won't want to go back there. Valdo turned left onto the highway and pressed the accelerator.

He slowed down when he reached the Coolidge city limits. The road widened and was apparently the main drag. Unless they knew somebody here, the bikers would be passing straight through. He drove slowly and cruised through town, catching up with them just past the Walmart. They were turning left at the light. Valdo kept his distance. Patience.

JONATHAN COULDN'T HEAR JESSE over the road noise. He said, "You what?"

"I have to pee."

"Where?"

He looked for some place that might have a rest room, but couldn't find any. They had left Coolidge far behind them and were speeding through open desert.

Jesse said, "There's a trading post up ahead."

A short while later, he saw the sign for the Blackwater Trading Post. He pulled off into the gravel parking lot.

Jesse said, "Drop me off at the door, then get out of view from the road. When you see me come back out, drive over and get me."

He dropped her off and pulled the motorcycle around the back of the building.

Several Native American men were sitting on a fallen tree trunk at edge of the lot, passing around a bottle in a paper bag. He nodded to them and they nodded back. He kept the bike running and watched. When Jesse reappeared at the door the white car bolted across the driveway towards the trading post, slamming its brakes and almost running her over. The killer jumped out and grabbed her by the arm.

Jonathan revved the engine and dropped the clutch. The rear wheel spun out and slid sideways.

He had dumped the bike.

TWELVE

Jesse told herself to keep cool. She twisted and tugged her arm but it felt as if a bear had clamped onto it.

She needed a distraction.

She pulled her other arm forward, wound up, and hammered him in the jaw with her elbow, immediately yanking her arm free. She darted away, but not before he grabbed her ponytail. Her feet flew out from under her and she slammed to the ground on her back. She rolled over and kicked him with both feet as he reached for her. He didn't move, but the kick pushed her backwards across the ground and out of his grip. She pulled Tyler's pistol from her fanny pack and fired two quick rounds into the man's chest. He fell down, but stood back up and reached into his coat. Jonathan, who had managed to set the bike upright and restart the engine, rammed the motorcycle into him, and he fell down again. Jesse jumped on behind Jonathan and they sped away. When they reached the pavement, Jonathan twisted the accelerator back. The engine roared and the front tire climbed high into the air. It lowered when he shifted into second and raised up again until third. The scenery became a blur as the motorcycle whisked them away from the trading post. Finally she said, "Too fast, slow down." He let up on the accelerator and brought it back down to the speed limit.

VALDO DUSTED HIMSELF OFF and hobbled over to his car, where he wrote down the motorcycle's license plate number in a spiral notebook. He pulled out onto the highway and tried to follow them, but after an hour of searching, he gave up and headed back to Eloy.

Back at the warehouse, he opened the trunk on his car and took out a clean coat in a bag, bringing it inside the building where he hung it up on a run of electrical conduit. He took off the coat he was wearing, set it down on the back of a chair, unbuttoned his dress shirt, and placed it on top of the coat. When he removed his undershirt, his bare chest showed three large bruises. The largest of the three had what looked like a bullet hole in the center, only it wasn't bleeding.

Roberts said, "I see the dent from the magnum, but where did those other two come from?

"That bitch shot me with a 9."

"Huh. Somebody taught her to double tap."

Valdo felt his rib below the hole. He was sure it was cracked.

Roberts said, "You're lucky she didn't go Mozambique on you, shoot you in the face."

"Yeah. Crazy bitch."

Both men laughed, but Valdo was thinking what a good little fighter she was. Not many men could have gotten away from him, yet she did. He said, "Do we know who they are?"

"The man who stole the truck is one Jonathan Starker. I found his personal belongings in the truck."

"His belongings?" Valdo had caught him entering the truck. Or maybe he was exiting and changed his mind. "What did he have in there?"

"Well, that's where the problem comes in. He had a travel bag. That tells me he was in the truck already. Did you check inside the sleeper cab when you drove over here?"

"No."

Valdo had screwed up. He had never bungled an assignment before, but everything about this one seemed to be jinxed.

Roberts said, "This raises an important question. Just how much did he see?"

"The way he was talking at the canal? Sounds like he saw too much."

"I believe you are correct, big guy. But a more important question is what if he goes to the police?"

"He hasn't so far."

"Indeed. Don't you find that interesting?"

"He saw your badge. He's scared if he goes to the cops, you're gonna get him. Or the ATF will."

"Exactly. Of course, at some point he may decide to take his chances and turn himself in."

"He needs to be stopped before he does."

"So we turn up the heat. This guy is running like a rabbit. If he becomes a suspect in the hijacking—if the police are after him—he'll keep running. Until we catch up with him."

"Why would he be a suspect?"

"I left his bag in the truck, so the police already know who he is. Witnesses have ID'd him driving the truck through the railroad crossing. And that pickup he pushed off the bridge was transporting illegals."

Valdo said, "Really?"

Roberts shook his head. "You'll like this. Border Patrol just happened to be crossing the canal about five miles downstream when a bunch of them came floating by on bales of hay. They scooped up the whole lot of them. They'll confirm Starker was the driver. Hell, they might even try to pin the warehouse manager on him."

"How do you figure?"

"If he was in the truck all along, he would have been at the warehouse around the time of the murder."

"Oh, you're right."

Roberts was turning out to be smarter than Valdo had thought. Roberts said, "That just leaves one loose end."

"The girl."

"The girl."

Valdo, ready to tell him about the license plate number, said, "I think I can help with that."

Roberts said, "They went to the airport, so they know their way around. But Starker is from out of state, so the girl must be local."

"Look, I—"

"Did anybody at the airport know her?"

"I—"

"Did you even ask about her?"

Roberts wouldn't shut up, so Valdo blurted out, "I have a license number."

"A licence number. To what?"

"They got a motorcycle from somewhere. I followed them to a trading post down the highway. That's where the girlfriend shot me. I saw their license plate." He tore a page out of a notebook and held it out to Roberts. Roberts was furious.

"Dammit. Why didn't you call me?"

"I was chasing them. I didn't have time to stop and make a phone call."

Roberts snatched the paper and punched a number on his phone. "Stupid. I could have called this in already."

Roberts told the person on the phone he needed the call to be confidential, to keep it between the two of them. He gave the license plate number and told him to expedite it.

Roberts turned to Valdo and said, "It'll take a little longer because we're keeping this off the radar. And next time you call me."

* * *

JESSE GUIDED JONATHAN down to Chandler, being careful to keep him off the main roads. Finally she pointed to a circular cobblestone driveway next to a two story home. "Turn in here."

He pulled up to a garage door. "This is your Uncle Bill's house?"

"One of them."

"Is Uncle Bill rich?"

"He does all right."

She punched the alarm code into the key pad, and the door rolled up. Inside the garage sat a late model Audi. He pushed the motorcycle into the garage, and she pushed a button on the wall to roll the garage door back down.

"Come on. Oh, take your shoes off first." She led him through a door into the house. Once inside, she reactivated the alarm. "Follow me." She led him into a hallway and stopped to open a closet. She pulled out a set of towels and continued down the hall to an open door. "Here. You can sleep in this room."

He looked into the room. She handed him the towels and said, "You're about my uncle's size. I'll bring you some of his clothes."

"He won't mind?"

"No."

"Oh, that's right, Princess."

"Shut up and take a shower. You stink."

He walked into the room and closed the door.

JONATHAN WALKED OVER to a roll top desk in the corner of the room. He opened the desk and located a pen and a pad of paper. He wrote down the security codes he had watched Jesse use to get them into the house, and tearing off the sheet, folded it and slid it into his wallet before walking into the attached bathroom. On the vanity counter was a new toothbrush still in its wrapper, a new stick of deodorant, and a new disposable razor. When he looked into the mirror, all the energy that had pushed him forward through the day drained from his body. Nothing would feel better than to fall onto the bed and go to sleep. But she was right: he stank.

After his shower, Jonathan found the clothes laid out for him. He got dressed, sprawled out on the bed, closed his eyes—for just a minute or two, and fell asleep.

JESSE WENT THROUGH her uncle's closet and drawers and put together some casual clothes for Jonathan to wear. She knocked on his door, and when nobody answered, she cracked the door enough to hear the shower running. She went inside to lay the clothes out on the bed, telling herself out loud, "Now it's my turn."

She walked down the hall to 'her' room. It had been her room when she was going to college. Uncle Bill let her stay there because it was close to ASU and her parents lived 100 miles away. Now her uncle reserved it for his nieces and nephews when they came over to swim. Several of them kept changes of clothes there, Jesse included.

She took her clothes off and let them drop to the floor, stepped into the shower, and turned the knobs. Lukewarm water flowed from the over-sized shower head, becoming hotter as it traveled the long run from the water heater. She propped her leg up on the built-in shower seat and peeled off the bandaging. It bled a little. She washed the grease off her arm and examined her burn, which she had forgotten about in the excitement. Luckily it was only red, not blistered.

She had never enjoyed a shower as much as this one. After she scrubbed herself, she sat down and let the steaming water flow over her body. The shower was her refuge, the place where she could decompress, review her day, make her plans.

The story was turning out to be even bigger than she had hoped. Jonathan didn't just witness a murder, steal a truck, and crash into a bunch of illegal immigrants. He was a celebrity. And he took out a train!

Why hadn't he mentioned the train?

WHEN JONATHAN WOKE UP, the smell of grilled steak filled the house. He followed his nose to the kitchen and found Jesse standing over a Wolf range. He said, "Wow."

Jesse said, "I'm hungry. Are you hungry?"

"Oh, yeah." He noticed it was getting dark outside. "Man, how long was I sleeping?"

The door bell rang. She said, "Get that, will you?"

"What's the alarm code?"

"You won't need it."

He walked to the front door and when he opened it the alarm didn't go off. At the door stood a tall black woman with long, straight black hair, wearing a black pant suit with black shoes. She was exceptionally well built and there was something familiar about her.

She looked exactly like Mara.

It was as if someone had used his character from the Trilogy series to design a real woman. Without thinking he said, "Mara."

"Neela," she said. "May I come in?"

Jesse called from the kitchen, "Let her in."

Neela walked in without Jonathan's permission. "And you are?"

Jonathan hesitated.

"Oh, you're the boy on the billboard."

Jonathan reached out his hand. "Jonathan Starker."

"I'm pleased to meet you, Jonathan Starker. Are you a friend of Jesse's?"

"Uh, yes."

"Well I'm Jesse's cousin."

Jesse appeared from around the corner. "Food's on."

Jonathan and Neela sat down around the oak and steel kitchen table. Jesse served Jonathan and herself rib eye steaks, fried potatoes, and salad. She served Neela the same, except instead of steak, she had grilled salmon. Jesse poured wine into Neela's glass and asked Jonathan if he wanted some.

"No, thank you."

She poured some into her own glass, bowed her head, and crossed herself. Catholic. She remained silent for a moment, crossed again, and said, "Enjoy."

Neela said, "Well, this is a pleasant surprise. Salmon and sirah. My favorites. It's almost as if you knew I was coming over."

Jesse smiled.

Neela said, "Bill called and told me you'd be staying here for a while. But then you knew he would. Didn't want me to worry when the alarm system was switched off and on. Of course, when it was switched off and stayed off, I thought I should check it out. But you knew that, too, didn't you? That's how you summoned me here."

Jesse said, "I don't know what you're talking about," and raised her glass. "To Neela."

Neela raised her glass. "To conniving little brats."

They made small talk as they ate. When they finished, Jesse said, "Neela, I need to find some papers upstairs in Uncle Bill's office. Can you give me a hand?"

Neela said, "Sure."

Jonathan said, "If you two are going to talk about me, you can do it here."

Neela looked at Jesse. Jeese said, "Okay."

Jesse said, "Jonathan, why don't you tell Neela what happened to you. Start at the beginning."

Jonathan told Neela how he had hitched a ride with Mark, and how he witnessed the murder in the desert, recorded it on his iPhone, and lost the phone in the canal. When he described the killer getting shot but getting back up, Neela said, "He must have been wearing a vest."

Jonathan told her how he saw them drag Mark and another man out into the desert, and how he hid in the sleeper cab while the killer drove the truck to Eloy.

Jesse looked as if she were listening more intently than Neela was. Neela was cool and showed no emotion until he got to the part where he stole the truck from the hijackers.

She said, "You know how to drive a truck?"

"Apparently not."

He told her how he drove through the crossing gate and how the train clipped the trailer.

She said, "That was you?"

"I guess so."

"That was all over the news. My God. You sure stirred things up out in Eloy."

Jonathan continued but Jesse interrupted.

"Why didn't you tell me about the train?"

"It didn't seem pertinent at the time."

Jesse shot him a dirty look.

Neela said to Jonathan, "Go on."

Jonathan brought the story up to where he crashed into Jesse, then Jesse took over. She told Neela about the truck ramming the pickup.

Neela said, "That was Eduardo's flat bed?"

"Yeah."

"Bill told me you we on some kind of fool's errand with Eduardo. You know, your father is right. Bill indulges you entirely too much."

Jesse went through the rest of the story, how they went into the canal, and walked to the airport where they borrowed Tyler's bike. Jonathan was glad she left out the part where he refused to fly.

Neela retrieved a pen and a pad from her coat and said, "Jonathan, what was the name of the truck driver?"

"His name is, was Mark. Mark Talmeier."

A sick look came over Neela's face, and she dropped the pen and pad on the table.

"Mark Talmeier? They killed Mark?"

"Yes. Do you know him?"

"I used to work with him. He trained me." Her eyes welled up.

Jesse became upset, too. She said, "Everybody knows Mark. Mark was a retired police officer—a hero."

Neela sat quietly for a long time. She took her phone out, opened an app, and pressed some icons on the screen. "There," she said, "Your alarm is back on. Make sure it stays on."

Jesse said, "I'll make sure and turn it back on if I go out."

"You're not going anywhere, especially not in public. You need to stay right where you are."

"But—"

"Jesse? "

"Yes, mother."

"Good girl. Now, those doors stay closed. Nobody comes in this house, unless you are absolutely sure that it's the police, and if the police come to the door, do exactly what they say. Don't resist, don't show any weapons. If they take you into custody, say nothing. Give no explanation. Don't try to tell them what happened. Say nothing. Nothing. Ask for your attorney, and that's all."

"So what, I sit in jail and wait for Uncle Bill to get back from Europe?"

"Bill won't be coming home for a while. Oh, you didn't hear?"

"Hear what?"

"Bill had a heart attack. They had to airlift him off the cruise ship."

"But I just talked to him."

"And he didn't say anything? That's Bill for you."

"Poor Uncle Bill."

"Bill will be fine. But you listen to me, Jesse. This isn't like the time you caught Councilman Vargas with his pants down. This is your life. I'm going to find out everything I can about the men who are after you, and I'm going to do everything I can to protect you. But Bill is the one with the connections. He can help you in ways I can't."

"You're not going to tell him, are you, not in his condition?"

"Absolutely not. You know, up until now, I have never withheld information from him, especially when it came to his little Princess."

Jesse smiled and said, "Screw you."

Neela said, "Now let's have a look at that leg wound."

Once Neela was satisfied Jesse's wound wasn't serious, she turned to Jonathan.

"You haven't shaved lately."

"No, but there's a new razor in the guest bathroom. I was going to shave in the morning."

"Don't. Not until I come back here tomorrow."

"You don't want me to shave?"

"No. There's something else … you were wearing glasses in your billboard photo."

"Yes, I wear glasses. I lost them in the canal."

"What is your prescription?"

"What?"

"What is your vision?"

"20-150 in both eyes."

"Okay. I'll be right back." She left the room and walked upstairs.

JESSE LOOKED AT THE CLOCK. She said, "Let's see what the news has to say about you," and moved into the living room. She picked up a remote control and turned on the television, an enormous plasma screen with Dolby stereo.

The Channel 4 News was just coming on. The big story was the haboob and the 20 car pile-up it caused on I-10 outside of Casa Grande. Immediately following that was the story of the train crash.

The news reader was a young blonde. She was standing in front of the accident scene at the railroad crossing, smiling, showing a large set of teeth so white they glowed. She said:

"THERE WAS CHAOS IN ELOY TODAY AS A RUNAWAY BIG RIG COLLIDED WITH A UNION PACIFIC FREIGHT TRAIN AND A PICKUP TRUCK FULL OF UNDOCUMENTED IMMIGRANTS."

Jesse said, "Enjoy your story, Charlene. I've got the inside scoop."

Jonathan turned his head and stared at Jesse.

Jesse said, "I used to work with her."

The news program showed footage of the train crossing with the crime scene tape, and the car that Jonathan had swept off the road. The driver of the car was not injured, and gave Charlene a live interview. After the interview, they showed footage of the truck at the bridge.

"WHEN THE POLICE ARRIVED AT THE SCENE, THE DRIVER OF THE TRUCK HAD ALREADY FLED THE SCENE. TRAFFIC IN THE AREA WAS TIED UP FOR HOURS AS POLICE WORKED TO SORT EVERYTHING OUT."

Jesse turned the television off. She said, "They didn't say anything about Eduardo's truck."

Jonathan said, "Probably didn't see it. I can't believe you climbed back into it."

"I had to get my camera. You still owe me a camera."

"I said I'd replace it."

"Dammit. I wish I had the photos I took of the wreck."

Neela walked into the living room. "I made some calls."

Jesse said, "To whom?"

"You don't want to know. Now, you are not to contact anyone, not even family."

Jonathan stood up and said, "My mother. I promised to call her when I got to Phoenix. She'll be worried sick when she hears about Mark."

Neela said, "Jonathan, you just told me you witnessed a murder and left the scene of an accident. You have a thug and a supposed federal agent looking for you, intent on killing you. If you contact your mother, she'll …"

"What?"

"Jonathan, is there any way that those men could find out who you are, what your identity is? Did you leave anything behind in that truck?"

"My suitcase. It has all my information."

Neela sighed. "All right. I need to do some digging. You need to stay put and keep your head down. No phone calls, no emails, no blog postings." She glared at Jesse. "I'm serious. No contact with anybody. I'll be back in the morning."

THIRTEEN

MONDAY MORNING Valdo looked over the printout Roberts had given him. On the page was a photo of a young man with close cropped blond hair. It was the man outside the saloon, the one with the baseball cap. Beneath the photo was a name and address:

TYLER ANDERSON
2515 E. SESAME ST
TEMPE, ARIZONA 85218

The printout indicated that he was full owner of Anderson Aircraft Maintenance in Eloy, Arizona.

Valdo decided he would check out Anderson's home address first. He searched on his Thomas Brothers atlas and mapped out the location. When he arrived there, he pulled the Pelican case from the back seat and took out the MK II and the suppressor. He got out of the car, walked up to the house, and rang the bell. Nobody answered, so he rang again. There were no sounds coming from the house and no car in the driveway. Maybe the guy was working. He decided to drive to Eloy. When he got there he found Anderson Aircraft Maintenance in a hangar at the Eloy Airport.

* * *

TYLER WAS WORKING on an airplane engine, but he was thinking about Jesse. It had been six months since he had broken off their relationship, and he still couldn't get her off his mind. He had been in love with her, but after four years he was tired of her obsessions—her obsession with college, her obsession with her Channel 4 job, and now her obsession with her news blog. She put so much time and passion into her career there wasn't much left over for him. Finally he had enough.

He had almost succeeded in forgetting her. He had met other girls, usually in night clubs up in Scottsdale. These girls gave him plenty of attention. The first one took him to bed the night they met. The sex was incredible, maybe because it had been over four years for him. He soon found out she wasn't very interesting outside of the bedroom, which made it awkward when she expected a relationship with him. She had a hard time taking no for an answer and pestered him with texts and phone calls to the point he had to change his phone number. After that he was reluctant to give out his number to the girls he went home with.

Now Jesse calls him up and asks for his help, stirring up old feelings. The business with that Starker guy, though, was classic Jesse: intense, in trouble, on the edge of danger. Thrilling, and maddening at the same time. He pitied Starker. All she wanted from him was a great story. At least that was how it seemed. The whole thing made it hard to focus, but he had no choice. The plane had to be ready by Monday evening.

Tyler had drained the oil and removed the oil filter—the instruments were showing some unusual oil pressure readings on Saturday. Now he was performing a post-mortem examination of the oil filter. He was about to cut it open when he noticed the man slipping into the hangar. He hadn't rung the buzzer or announced his presence, but once Tyler got a glimpse of him, he knew it was more than just rude behavior. It was the man outside the saloon, the one who drew on him and Jesse and Starker. Tyler edged over to his tool chest, reached into the top drawer, and remembered.

He had loaned his gun to Jesse.

Tyler grabbed a breaker bar and backed away towards the big roll-up hangar door.

The man raised a suppressed pistol and aimed it at Tyler, asking, "Is there anybody else here?"

"No."

"Are you expecting anybody soon?"

Tyler hesitated.

"If you have to think about it, then nobody is coming."

"What do you want?"

"I need some information. Put that down and get in there." He waved the gun at the office.

Tyler lead the man past the plane though the office door. The man put his foot onto the desk and shoved it out of the way. He pointed the gun at the chair and said, "Sit down."

Tyler sat down.

"Put your hands behind your back, behind the chair." He pulled some zip ties out of his pocket, secured Tyler's hands to each other and to the chair, and secured his legs to the chair legs. "I need to know who was riding your motorcycle yesterday."

"I wish I knew. Someone stole it."

The man showed a sarcastic smile. "Now, how did I know you were going to say that?" He held the gun to Tyler's temple and said, "I'll ask you again. Who did you give your motorcycle to?"

"I'm telling you the truth. The dust storm shut everything down, so I went to the saloon to grab lunch. When I came back, someone had broken into the hangar. I didn't realize my bike was missing until it was time to drive home."

The man walked over to the desk and turned everything over

before rummaging through the drawers. He turned to Tyler and said, "This was a lot easier when people used a Rolodex." He walked back to Tyler and popped open the cell phone holster on Tyler's hip, pulling out the phone, trying to unlock the screen. "How do you do this?"

"You'll have to figure that out by yourself."

"Roberts will know."

"Who's Roberts?"

The man put the gun back up to Tyler's head.

JESSE HAD ALMOST FINISHED frying the bacon when Jonathan walked into the kitchen.

Jonathan said, "How long have you been up?"

"A couple hours. I had some writing to do."

Jesse handed him a plate of scrambled eggs. "You want some coffee?"

"Yes, thank you."

Jesse turned on a small television set next to the kitchen table. Charlene was on again:

"A MAN AND HIS YOUNG SON WERE HIKING IN THE DESERT THIS MORNING WEST OF THE AK CHIN CASINO WHEN THEY MADE A GRISLY DISCOVERY: THE BODIES OF TWO MEN, APPARENTLY THE VICTIMS OF FOUL PLAY. ACCORDING TO THE PINAL COUNTY SHERIFF'S DEPARTMENT, THE MEN HAD BEEN SHOT TO DEATH. THE SHERIFF'S SPOKESPERSON TOLD REPORTERS THE MEN MAY HAVE BEEN CONNECTED WITH YESTERDAY'S TRAIN WRECK IN ELOY. THEY ARE LOOKING FOR A MAN THEY SAY IS A PERSON OF INTEREST IN THAT INCIDENT."

Jonathan said, "That's them. That's Mark and the guy they dragged out of the trailer."

Jesse said, "Well, that confirms your story."

"What? You didn't believe me?"

Charlene continued:

"THE MAN THEY ARE LOOKING FOR IS 28-YEAR-OLD JONATHAN STARKER OF LA MIRADA, CALIFORNIA. STARKER WAS SAID TO HAVE BEEN TRAVELING WITH THE OWNER OF THE TRUCK, AND MAY HAVE ACTUALLY BEEN THE DRIVER OF THE TRUCK WHEN IT STRUCK THE TRAIN."

They heard a noise at the front door. Jesse reached into the cupboard and grabbed her pistol just as Neela entered the kitchen. She was carrying a gym bag.

Neela looked at the gun and said, "Is that for me?"

Jesse said, "It might be if you sneak in like that."

"Who's sneaking? Hey, look at you." She nodded towards the television. A photograph of Jonathan was on the screen with his name captioned beneath it.

Jonathan said, "Oh, crap."

Neela said, "Crap indeed." Reaching into the gym bag, she pulled out a cell phone and handed it to Jesse. "Hang on to this. It's a burner. This is so I can call you. Do not call out. Now, let's have a look at that leg."

Jesse said, "That's not necessary. It's a lot better already."

"You don't have a choice. Come with me."

Jesse followed her to the bathroom. Neela closed the door and said, "Take your pants off."

"I was shot in the leg, not in the butt."

Neela reached in the gym bag and took out a syringe and a small vial of medicine. "You're getting an antibiotic. Drop your pants and touch your toes."

Jesse complied and Neela administered the shot.

"Okay, now let's see the leg."

Neela removed the bandage and flushed the wound with hydrogen peroxide, then dried it with a sterile gauze pad. She said, "It's superficial. It doesn't seem to be bleeding, so I'm not going to stitch it up. Just let me know if it does start to bleed, or if it becomes inflamed." She handed Jesse a bottle of pills. "Take one of these four times a day until they're gone."

"Okay. Thanks. While we're in here, what did you find out about Jonathan?"

"What do you mean?"

"I know you, Neela. You ran all kinds of background checks on him the moment you left here. So what do we know about him?"

"He checks out. 28-years-old, hugely successful graphic novelist."

"I already knew that. What else did you find out?"

"He's kind of a recluse, lives with his mother. His father died in a drowning accident on the Kern River when he was twelve. Since then he developed a fear of water."

"Fear of water?"

"Yep. Won't go near the water."

"He swam in the canal."

"Did he do so willingly?"

"Not really. They were shooting at us. Come to think of it, I'm not even sure he meant for us to go into the water. He might have been just ducking the bullets. What else?"

"The boy's a mess. In the past few years he's added to his aquaphobia. Now he's afraid of crowds."

"Crowds? He said he was going to that convention in Mesa. Conventions are by definition crowds."

"Yeah, well he was supposed to be there Saturday, but he never showed up, pissed off a lot of people. Oh, and he's also afraid of flying."

"Yeah, I saw that. It freaked him out when Tyler wanted to fly us out of Eloy."

"Well, it explains why he tagged along with Mark."

"Yeah."

"Look, Jesse, you're digging yourself a pit, shielding this guy from the law. At some point you're going to have to turn him in. My first thought is to wait until Bill gets back, but with Mark getting shot, you could end up in so deep, even Bill might not be able to keep his Princess out of trouble."

"I'm not worried."

"You should be. Jesse, no news story is worth your life."

"What are you talking about?"

"I'm talking about the reason you're hanging on to this guy. A story like this is too juicy for you to let go of, but you're gambling with your life, Honey."

"Well, we're going to wait for Bill. Look, we'd better get back out there before Jonathan gets annoyed."

"He knows we're talking about him. He's a sharp guy. Cute, too."

They walked back into the kitchen, where Jonathan had just finished his breakfast.

Neela said, "Your turn, Blondie."

"My turn for what?"

"You'll see. Come on."

Jonathan followed Neela back to the bathroom. When they were out of sight, Jesse opened a laptop on the counter and logged into her WordPress blog. She typed the headline:

MYSTERY KILLINGS IN MARICOPA TIED TO COMIC BOOK WRITER

She paused for a moment. What could she write without giving away her involvement? And what information did she have, really? She didn't know the names of her attackers, she didn't have any photographs. She opened a text file and wrote down some notes about the previous day's adventure, then logged out of her blog and navigated to Google. There she typed in the key phrase Jonathan Starker and hit enter. Google returned 1.5 million results. Impressive. She clicked on the Wikipedia link. She found out where Jonathan was born, who his parents were, and the history of his writing career. Jonathan had sold his first graphic novel at the age of 15, and had consistently published successful works culminating in his West Wave Trilogy. He had recently signed a contract for the movie production of all three installments.

Jesse searched the key phrase West Wave. She scanned the search results and clicked on westwavetrilogy.com. The web page was graphically rich, a showcase of Jonathan's creations, dramatic and colorful. The characters where highly stylized, the men ripped and powerful like the heroes in Greek mythology. The women were as tall as the men and powerfully built, ridiculous in their war-tattered clothing.

Wow. Look at the way this guy draws women. He needs to find a girlfriend.

She clicked the page-turn link and there, on the next page, was a character named Mara who bore an uncanny resemblance to Neela. She was going to have fun teasing her about that.

Jesse heard a key opening the locks on the front door and worked the remote control on the television until she could see the camera feed from the porch. It was her sister, Maria, with her six children. Jesse called back to Neela, "We have company."

Neela said, "Damn, they weren't supposed to be here today."

The kids burst into the house and swarmed their Aunt Jesse—except for the oldest, Chelsea, who had just turned 13 and was trying hard to act bored.

Maria, who was six months pregnant, stood in the hallway and said, "Well, this is a surprise."

Jesse said, "It certainly is."

"Uncle Bill said we could use his pool. It's so hot and the kids are driving me crazy. What are you doing here?"

"My apartment is being fumigated. Uncle Bill said I could stay here a couple days."

"In your room, I suppose."

"Yeah."

"I saw Neela's car out front. Where is she?"

"I think she's upstairs. She had some phone calls to make."

"Oh, okay. Could you hold onto Justin for me? I need to go change into my bathing suit. Kids, don't go outside until I get back. And do what your Aunt Jesse says."

Without waiting for an answer, she handed her the baby she was holding and walked down the hallway. Justin grabbed Jesse's hair and tugged hard. She pulled his hand away and poked him in the belly. He laughed and so did she. A few moments later Maria came back, dressed in a one-piece bathing suit.

"The guest room bed looked like somebody slept in it. Is someone else staying here?"

How could she explain Jonathan?

"Yeah, a friend of mine was passing though, so I asked Uncle Bill if he could stay here, too."

"He? You have a new boyfriend?"

"No, he's just a guy I met at work."

"Oh. Are you and Tyler getting back together?"

"No, we're not. What makes you think we would?"

"No reason. I just think he's the one."

Neela walked into the kitchen and hugged Maria, then said, "I thought you weren't coming over until Wednesday."

"I couldn't wait that long. The air conditioner is acting up and I'm dying, stuck inside with the kids."

"Well, you've got to tell me when there's a change of plans. If the security system notifies me that someone's at the house when they're not supposed to be, I've got to check it out."

"And come in with guns blazing, right?"

Neela laughed. "It wouldn't be the first time."

Maria herded the kids out to the swimming pool, except for Chelsea, who plopped down on the living room sofa in front of the television. She navigated the remote control to a reality show. Neela went back to see about Jonathan.

Jesse carried the laptop into the living room and sat down on a reclining chair. She needed to catch up with news events, especially anything concerning Jonathan. There were plenty of articles about the crash and the killings. A few more law enforcement agencies had become involved since the last time she checked. So far it was the Pinal County Sheriff (PCSO), the Eloy Police Department (EPD), the Department of Public Safety (DPS), the National Transportation and Safety Administration (NTSA), Immigrations and Customs Enforcement (ICE), and the Bureau of Alcohol, Tobacco, Firearms, and Explosives (ATF).

NEELA SAID, "You're a beautiful man, Jonathan. You know that, don't you?"

Jonathan blushed.

"It's a shame I had to cut off all that gorgeous blond hair."

She had clipped the hair on his head and his beard down to the same length as his five o'clock shadow, then dyed it all black. He refused at first, but she convinced him his life depended on it. She said the billboards all around town were like wanted posters, and now that his face was on the news, he had no choice but to disguise himself if he wanted to stay alive. Her phone timer rang and she said, "Okay, that's long enough."

She held his head over the sink and rinsed out the dye, massaging his scalp with her long fingernails, then dried his head with a towel. She stepped back and looked him over and shook her head in approval. "Nice. I like it. Let's see what you think. Oh wait." She reached into her bag and pulled out a box of contact lenses. "Here. Have you ever worn contacts?"

"Yes. I don't care for them."

"Well, let's hope it's only for a few days. In the meantime, I think you look great."

He inserted the contact lenses and turned towards the mirror. "Wow," he said. "I wouldn't even recognize myself."

"You're very handsome with short hair. Manly. Come on, it's time to strut the cat walk."

They went into the living room. Jesse and Chelsea didn't look up until Neela said, "Chelsea, have you met Jesse's friend, Jack?"

Jesse did a double-take, then smiled. Chelsea's mouth dropped open and her eyes got wide.

Jesse said, "Say hello, Chelsea, and stop drooling."

Chelsea's cheeks turned bright red. She said, "I'm not drooling, you jerk," and she stormed out of the room.

Jonathan blushed again. Jesse and Neela laughed.

ROBERTS ASKED VALDO what he found out from Anderson.

"He wouldn't tell me nothing."

"What? Why didn't you try to persuade him?"

"I don't do that."

"Oh, you can kill but you can't torture?" Valdo scowled at him and Roberts said, "What, it upsets your delicate sensibilities?"

Valdo said, "Here, see what you can find on this," and tossed him a cell phone.

Roberts unlocked the screen and opened the Contacts app, flipping through the names. When he got to Conrad he recognized the thumbnail photo. It was the girl. He opened her contact page. Her name was Jesse Conrad and it had a phone number but no address. Roberts told Valdo to go to his hotel room and stay put while he did some research on her.

When he got the information, he decided to go by himself to see her. She might not have gotten a good look at him, but she would certainly remember Valdo. Who could forget that big moose? The problem he faced was he had never before engaged in physical violence. He had never even drawn his weapon in the field. But this was a good initiation for him, dealing with this little girl. How much trouble could she be? He set out for the most recent address listed on the printout:

JESSENIA CONRAD
1215 E. ELLIOT ROAD APT 143
GILBERT, ARIZONA 85212

He exited the Superstition Freeway at Gilbert Road and headed south. He was almost to Elliot Road when he saw the flashing blue and red lights in his rear view mirror. He turned onto a side street and parked. A uniformed Gilbert Police officer approached the Charger. Roberts was ready for him. He had his wallet open with his badge showing.

"Hello officer, what seems to be the problem?"

"You were speeding in a twenty five mile-per-hour zone."

Roberts squinted at the officer's name tag. "Twenty five? I must have missed the sign, Officer Kohler. I'm in a bit of a hurry. Official business." He held up the badge for the officer to see. Kohler kept writing.

Roberts said, "Uh, hey buddy, How about a little professional courtesy?"

"Professional courtesy? What's that?"

When Officer Kohler handed him the citation, Roberts snatched it and tossed it into the back seat. Nothing like getting pulled over by Barney Fife.

Roberts drove to the apartment and pulled into a visitor's parking spot. He found apartment 143 and knocked on the door, ready to force his way in and silence the girl, but nobody answered. He knocked again, and the door on the apartment next to it opened. A middle-aged women stepped out and said, "Can I help you?"

Roberts showed her his badge and said, "I'm looking for a Jessenia Conrad. Do you know when she'll be home?"

"Jessenia? Oh, you mean Jesse. She's a lovely girl. A little intense."

"Well?"

"No, I haven't seen her all day. But then, sometimes she's gone for days at a time, on assignments. She's a journalist."

A journalist. He had seen that on the report. Not a good sign.

"Listen, ma'am, if you see Ms. Conrad, I'd appreciate it if you didn't mention I was here looking for her."

"Why, is she in some kind of trouble?"

"I can't divulge that information, ma'am, but it's very important that you don't say anything to anybody about my presence here today. I wouldn't want to have to arrest you for impeding a federal investigation."

She said, "No, I won't say anything," and hurried back into her apartment.

Back at the car, Roberts decided to try Ms. Conrad's previous address:

15029 W. Piper Cub Lane
Chandler, Arizona 85226

He set his GPS and headed west on Elliot.

The house was in a nice upper-middle class neighborhood on the west side of Chandler. He parked the car, walked up to the house, and pushed the button on the intercom. A woman's voice answered.

"Yes?"

"Federal agent, may I come in?"

"What's this about?"

"I would really like to come inside and talk, ma'am."

"Let me see your badge. Hold it up to the camera."

Camera. Damn.

He looked up to see a closed circuit camera in the corner above the door. "You need to let me inside the house, ma'am. I'm investigating a murder."

"Let me see your badge."

"Ma'am, you're obstructing a federal investigation."

"Do you have a warrant?"

"No, but if I have to get one, we're going to tear this place apart. It'll go a lot easier on you if you just cooperate with me now."

"I'm afraid I can't let you in without a warrant."

Roberts drew his service pistol and held it up to the camera. "I've about had it with your attitude. If you don't open the door, I'm going to break it open."

"If I'm in fear of my life I'll be forced to defend myself."

"What the hell is that supposed to mean?"

"I can't let some stranger come barging into the house."

"I know Jessenia Conrad is in there."

"I don't know what you're talking about."

"You are harboring a fugitive and impeding a federal investigation."

"Show me your badge, Mr. Federal Agent."

Again with the badge.

He reached up and smashed the video camera with his pistol.

"There's my badge."

The sound of a gun slide being racked came from the other side of the door.

"I know she's in there. I know she is because you haven't called the police."

"I thought you were the police. And by the way, you haven't called for backup, either. So I really have nothing more to say. Have a nice day."

He stormed off to his car and parked farther down the street.

FOURTEEN

JONATHAN TURNED TO NEELA, who was de-cocking her pistol. "This has gone far enough. I'm going to turn myself in to the police before somebody else gets hurt."

Jesse said, "You can't. We don't know who this clown is connected with. If he is a federal agent, there might be others who are corrupt. He could get to you."

Jonathan motioned towards the back door. "What about those kids? I can't put them in danger."

Neela said, "Jesse and I will keep the house secure until the pool party is over. The safest thing is for everyone to stay put."

Jesse said, "Neela, we should bring Maria in on this, for her own safety."

Neela said, "No. The less she knows, the better. You need to keep an eye on the other cameras while I run the video past a friend of mine. We need to find out more about that idiot."

A voice came from the kitchen. "He's not going to hurt us, is he?" Chelsea was standing in the doorway. She looked terrified. Neela walked over and put her arms around her.

"No, Honey. He's just full of bluster."

"Why does he want Jesse?" She looked at Jesse and said, "What did you do? Are you in trouble?"

Jonathan said, "Jesse didn't do anything. I witnessed a crime, and he wants to ask her about me."

Chelsea said, "If he's a federal agent, why don't you talk to him?"

Jesse said, "It's complicated, but there's really nothing to worry about."

Chelsea said, "Okay."

Neela said, "Chelsea Honey, I need to ask you a favor."

"What's that?"

"You know I would never ask you to keep a secret from your mother, but I think it would be better if you waited until you got home to tell her about this."

"Why?"

"I don't want to upset her while she's here. She has all those kids to take care of, to drive home."

"I understand. I won't say anything."

"And I don't want that man finding out where you live. There's some masking tape in the den. I want you to sneak out to your car and tape over your license plate. That man can't see the back of the car from where he's parked. Just stay low and move in from the side door."

She looked at Jonathan with big doe eyes and said, "I'll do it. I'm not afraid."

Jonathan said, "Won't they get pulled over by the police if it's taped over?"

Neela said, "That doesn't matter. Bill will take care of it. Maria will just think somebody played a prank on them."

Chelsea found the tape and slid out the back door, while Neela watched her on the security camera, ready to intervene if something went wrong. Chelsea stooped down, scooted over behind the car, and pulled a strip of tape off the roll, sticking it onto the license plate. She pulled off another strip and stuck it on, repeating the action until it was covered. When she came back in the house, Neela said, "Good job, Sweetheart. Why don't you go outside now and enjoy the pool?"

"All right." She hugged Neela and went outside, glancing back at Jonathan.

Jonathan said, "She's pretty upset. Won't Maria pick up on that?"

Jesse said, "She's thirteen. She's always upset. She won't seem any different."

VALDO PULLED IN BEHIND ROBERTS. Valdo had been catching up on his sleep when Roberts called him and told him to come over so he could take a shift watching the house.

When he got there, Roberts said, "My gut tells me Conrad is in there."

Valdo said, "Is she the one you talked to?"

"I don't think so. Conrad's only 22. The bitch on the intercom sounded older."

"We could take her by force."

"This isn't southeast L.A. Around here people notice when they hear gunfire. Let's wait them out. Besides, we want the girl and the guy who hijacked the truck, both of them. That's going to be a lot harder to do if you kill the girl."

"Well, he's probably in the house with her."

"He very well ... the point is ... Dammit, we're going to wait."

Was Roberts losing it?

"If we wait too long, the cops will be all over this."

"I know, I know. Let's ... let's wait it out for now. If it goes on for too long, we can always sneak in. You get the overnight shift. I'll be back in the morning. Did you bring the cell phone charger I gave you? I want you to call me if anything happens—anything."

The damn cell phone.

"Yeah, I brought it."

"Good."

Roberts drove away and Valdo settled in.

* * *

JONATHAN WATCHED AS MARIA packed up her kids and headed for the SUV. He caught Chelsea sneaking a glance at him while she was carrying her baby brother out the door. Jesse rushed into a back room the moment they left and came out with a digital SLR camera and a tripod. She attached an enormous zoom lens to the camera and carried it out the back door. Jonathan looked to Neela, who was watching the security monitors on the laptop.

Neela motioned towards the door with a tilt of her head. "Go on, go with her. Just stay down."

Jonathan stuck his head out the door and saw Jesse hiding behind a bush. She was positioning the lens through an opening in the branches. Jonathan stooped down and crab-walked over to Jesse.

"Stay down," she said.

Maria backed out of the driveway and a car down the street started its engine. It wasn't the Charger, it was the killer's big white Ford. The camera started clicking its faux shutter sound. The clicks came rapidly, one after another, and Jesse slowly swiveled the camera around, panning to track the man as he approached the house and caught up with Maria and the kids.

Jesse said, "I got you, you ugly son-of-a-bitch."

"Aren't you worried about Maria?"

"No. He's just trying to get the license plate number. He won't go far unless he sees you or me leave. He had a clear view of the car doors, so he knows we didn't sneak into it. Look."

The man had turned around and was heading back down the street, where he made another u-turn, parking at his original location.

Jesse said, "Okay, we got what we need," and sneaked back into the house with Jonathan close behind.

Inside the house, Neela said, "Let's have a look."

They went into the living room, where Jesse turned on the television and navigated to Source:Media. She synchronized the camera and television with a bluetooth connection, and the camera's display appeared on the big screen. She set the camera to DCIM and selected the first image: a close-up of the man driving the car.

Jonathan said, "That's him."

Neela said, "That's the man who shot at you?"

"Yes."

"The man who shot Mark?"

"Yes."

"Well, now we have photographs of two of the men involved in this. I'll work my sources and we'll find out what is going on."

Jesse said, "That other man keeps saying he's a federal agent. Do you think he might actually be a federal agent?"

Neela said, "He … feels like a federal agent. The clothes look like undercover DEA. Jonathan, is there anything you can remember, anything at all, that can help us?"

Jonathan said, "I told you everything I know."

Neela said, "Sometimes there can be some small detail that doesn't seem important, doesn't stand out at the time. It can be the key to an investigation."

Jonathan said, "Yes, I know. I've seen cop shows."

"Don't be that way. I'm trying to save your life. Now I want you to think back to the desert, to where they shot Mark. Run it through in your mind, step by step, as if you were watching a movie of the event. Start with the first time you saw the men."

"It was in the morning. We were waiting for somebody to come so we could deliver the freight."

"Go on."

"The red car came flying down the road. I mean, it was really moving, bouncing up and down. Dirt and rocks were flying. Mark knew something wasn't right, so he checked his gun and took it with him."

"What can you remember about the gun?"

"He had a name for it. He called it his—"

"His Python?"

"Yes, that was it."

"He shot that man with his Python and the guy stood back up?"

"Yes. Didn't you say the guy was probably wearing a vest?"

"Yes, but I didn't know what he was shot with. I assumed it was with a 9 or something."

"What difference does it make?"

"Mark's Python is a .357 Magnum. He loved that gun. He kept using it even after everyone else switched to 9mm autos."

"So a .357 Magnum should have penetrated the vest?"

"Penetrated it or caused enough trauma to his torso that he shouldn't be standing back up and chasing you all over the place. But go on. What happened next."

"It was weird. Mark pointed his gun at the guy and told him to leave, but the guy just kept talking."

"What did he talk about?"

"Guns. He was talking about guns. The way you people do."

"You people?" She tilted her head and raised an eyebrow.

"No, I don't mean it like that. I mean your family. You, Jesse, the guy at the airport."

Jesse said, "Tyler. He let me borrow his XD."

"What happened to your Smith?"

"I lost it in the canal."

"The snubby? The one Papa Joe gave you for your graduation?"

"Uh-huh."

"Oh, Honey, I'm so sorry."

"That's okay."

Jonathan said, "See? That's what I'm talking about. You and your guns."

Neela said to Jesse, "So anyway, you shot him with Tyler's nine?"

"Yeah. I need to get it back to him. That, and his motorcycle."

"Don't worry about that right now. I'll get in touch with Tyler. Jonathan, when the other guy stepped out of the car, do you remember what he said? Did he say he was a federal agent?"

"Yes. He held up his badge. Mark told him to throw it to him, but when he tossed it at his feet, the big guy tried to shoot him."

"The same as he did at the canal?"

"No, at the canal he didn't wait, he just threw the wallet right away."

"Did he say the same thing both times?"

Then it came to Jonathan. Of course. Why hadn't he remembered this before?

"No. In the desert he said he was with the ATF."

Jesse said, "The ATF is one of the agencies investigating the crash."

Neela said, "Why would the ATF be investigating a train wreck? Do you know what was on that truck?"

Jonathan said, "Mark said they were machine parts. But after the truck crashed, there were guns on the ground."

Jesse said, "AK47s. I photographed them."

"Show me the photos."

"I can't. I lost my camera when I lost my snubby."

Neela said, "Okay then. It was a shipment of guns."

Jonathan said, "I guess."

"And a man claiming to be with the ATF is after you guys. Hmm. I'm going to have to think about this."

Neela downloaded the photos from the DSLR and the security cameras to a thumb drive and left, driving right by the big guy's car, slowing down and giving him the evil eye. The guy didn't bother to follow her.

* * *

Jesse cooked a frozen pizza. They each took a slice and sat down in front of the television to watch the evening news. There was Charlene, standing in front of the FBI building in Phoenix:

"The investigation into the shocking hijack/murder of retired Phoenix Police Detective Mark Talmeier is being headed up by the Federal Bureau of Investigation here in Phoenix. The focus of the investigation is centered around comic book writer Jonathan Starker."

The screen showed a photo of Jonathan.

"According to Detective Talmeier's mother, Rita Talmeier, Jonathan Starker had ridden along with her son in his big rig. That's the same truck that is responsible for the collision with the Union Pacific freight train in Eloy yesterday."

The screen showed the scene from the crash.

"In addition, witnesses have identified the driver of the truck at the time of the accident as Starker. Los Angeles County Sheriff's deputies took Starker's mother in for questioning late this afternoon."

The screen switched to a scene of a SWAT team breaking down the front door at Jonathan's mother's house with a battering ram.
Jonathan shot up in his chair. He said, "That's my house!"
The camera came back to Charlene:

"Elma Starker, 64, claims she hasn't heard from her son since he left with Detective Talmeier on Saturday."

The station went to a commercial break.

The commercial break ended and Charlene came back on the screen with a special segment on Officer Mark Talmeier. They showcased his career with the police force, from the time he was a recruit, through his years on the beat, his undercover work in narcotics, his promotion to detective. They interviewed the officers who worked with him. There was universal praise for Mark as a tough, smart, compassionate police officer who devoted himself to his job and to the community. They talked about the bullet he took for his fellow officer—the bullet that ended the career he so loved.

Jonathan was impressed. He hadn't known what a great man Mark was. The horror of witnessing his murder was now compounded with a greater sense of loss.

The segment ended with a police department spokesperson vowing to find the killer and bring him to justice.

Jesse said, "Did Neela tell you about Mark?"

"Only that he trained her."

"Mark was Neela's boss when she joined the force. This was back when Uncle Bill was with the Attorney General's office. He knew Mark, by reputation and through working with him, so he pulled a few strings to get Neela stationed under his command. Mark mentored Neela, taught her how to be a cop. She told me how he never reprimanded her or the other cops in public. Whenever she screwed up, he pulled her aside before he gave her hell. Professional all the way. Mark is an icon in the Phoenix PD."

Jonathan said, "I can see that about him, the way he was with me on the way over."

"Neela doesn't show it, but she's very upset over Mark's murder. She wants to shoot that guy down the street. I told her not to, that she should wait until Uncle Bill gets well enough to help, but if this thing gets out of hand, I don't know if I can hold her back."

Jesse looked at the television. The news had moved on to a story on how to wash your hands properly. She turned it off.

"The point is, every cop in Phoenix feels the same way she does, only they feel that way about you."

Jonathan shuddered.

Jesse said, "Listen, I don't want you to worry. I'm only telling you this so you understand the gravity of the situation."

"I've known that since I watched Mark get murdered."

"I'm sure you have. I just don't want you to start thinking you're a hero, turning yourself in."

Jonathan didn't reply.

"Well, anyway, I need to take care of a few things. Do you mind keeping an eye on the security cameras?"

"I can do that."

Jesse said, "Thanks," and walked back to her room.

SOON JONATHAN NOTICED a young girl on the screen. She was walking up to the house.

It was Chelsea.

He yelled towards the hallway to the back rooms, "Jesse?"

There was no reply.

Chelsea knocked on the door. Jonathan took out his wallet and fumbled to find the paper with the code, punched it in the keypad, and let her in.

He said, "What are you doing back here?"

Chelsea walked over close to him and said, "I wanted to help." Her eyes had a glassy appearance that made him feel nervous.

Jesse came out of her room and said, "What's going on here?" She seemed worried.

Jesse looked at Chelsea, then at Jonathan, then at Chelsea. She shook her head in disgust and said, "Does your mother know you're here?"

"I told her I was going over to Sandra's house. Sandra dropped me off here."

"You know I have to call her and rat on you."

"Please, Aunt Jesse, don't call her yet. I just got here."

Jonathan made up his mind he was going to turn himself in first thing in the morning. For the time being, he wanted to get away from Chelsea. He said he had to go to the bathroom, but when he came out, she was waiting in the hallway.

Chelsea said, "Are you and Jesse going together?"

"No."

"Oh. Do you have a girlfriend?"

"Um, I need to check something." He went back into his room, but Chelsea followed him.

She said, "Do you ever date younger women?"

Jonathan just stared at her, then walked out of the room. He settled down in the living room on the sofa.

Chelsea planted herself on the sofa next to him and said, "What's it like living in California?"

"How did you know I lived in California?"

"I'm not stupid. It's all over the news. They say you killed a cop."

"I didn't kill anybody."

"I knew you wouldn't do anything like that. So what's it like, living in California? Do you live at the beach?"

"No, I don't."

"Do you know any movie stars?"

Jesse called out from the kitchen, "Chelsea, come give me a hand."

Thank you, Jesse.

Chelsea came back to the living room with a bowl of antipasto and sat back down next to Jonathan. Jesse came out with salad bowls.

Jesse said to Chelsea, "Have some pizza."

Chelsea said, "No, thank you," and poked at a small pile of antipasto. She made it a point to let Jonathan know that she doesn't eat much. She asked for some wine. When she was told she could have milk or soda, she announced that she'd had wine before.

Jesse said, "I'm sure you have, but we're not going to be the ones who give it to you."

Chelsea's face turned red and she left the table. Jonathan and Jesse tried not to laugh.

After dinner, Neela came by to take Chelsea home.

JONATHAN ASKED JESSE if he could use the laptop.

Jesse said, "As long as you don't make contact with anyone."

"I know, I know."

Jonathan navigated to the West Wave Twitter feed. There was a running verbal war going on among his fans. Some of them were certain Jonathan was innocent of the crime, while others were convinced he had snapped. He was tempted to email his agent, Deb, and find out what was going to happen with his movie. Three times he accessed his email account, and three times he chickened out.

The news articles about the murders were all bad. Some of them didn't even bother to use the word alleged in front of the words killer or murderer. Public officials and political pundits were starting to weigh in on the subject. Some of them were condemning the violence in his movie. Others were calling for stricter gun control laws. Law enforcement agencies in California and Arizona were announcing their determination to find him and bring him to justice.

He watched a video on CNN's home page. They had brought a psychiatrist into the studio to speculate on Jonathan's mental condition. He pointed out "Starker" had grown up isolated, and thought perhaps the loss of his father had fueled feelings of abandonment. Images from his graphic novels where offered as proof of his violent fantasies as well as possible anger towards women. The shrink implied these facts, taken together, indicated Jonathan fit the profile of a serial killer, and asserted that in his demented mind there must be something common among the men he shot which made them Jonathan's 'perfect' victims. The icing on the cake was the interview with his next-door neighbor who said Jonathan was a quiet man who kept to himself.

Neela returned and told them they could relax now, she was keeping watch over the house.

Jesse said, "Then I'm going for a swim. The sun is down and the water looks great." She said to Jonathan, "You want to join me?"

"Are you sure it's safe?"

Neela called out from down the hall, "Don't worry, I have things under control." She walked back to the living room and said, "Go ahead. You two enjoy the pool." She said to Jonathan, "There's a bathing suit you can use in your dresser."

He squirmed. "I, uh, I don't feel like swimming right now."

Neela and Jesse exchanged knowing glances.

Jesse said, "Well come on out, anyway. No point in being stuck inside," and walked back to her room.

He went to the back patio and sat down at a wrought iron table. Neela soon followed. She put the laptop on the table and set a pistol down next to it.

Jonathan said, "Why are you doing all this?"

"All what?"

"Helping me. Protecting me."

"You're a friend of Jesse's. We take care of our friends."

Jonathan shook his head. "Look at the trouble you're getting yourselves into. And you don't even know me. Have you read what they're saying about me? They think I'm a psycho."

"Jesse trusts you, and I trust Jesse. Well, let me rephrase that. Jesse is a good judge of character."

"I want you to know how much I appreciate you—your whole family."

"Yeah, well don't get mushy about it. Look, Jonathan, I wanted to talk to you about Jesse."

"What about her."

"I'm very fond of her."

"I can see that."

"She probably seems like a pretty tough chick to you."

"She can handle herself."

"She's very young." He could tell she was reaching for the right words. "I don't want to see anything happen to her."

"Neither do I."

"She thinks she's worldly, but she's still quite innocent."

"Innocent?"

"Here's the deal. You are to keep your hands off of her."

"What? She doesn't even like me."

"I'm just saying, I'm looking over your shoulder. If you take advantage of her, you're going to be in a world of hurt."

Before he could reply, Jesse walked out to the patio. Jonathan tried hard to keep his eyes off her, but he was compelled to look. She wore a skimpy yellow bikini that showed off her smooth, olive-color skin, and her body was so firm, almost athletic, shapelier than it had seemed when she had climbed out of the canal. He realized he was staring and fumbled for something to say, but his mouth was dry. Finally he said, "What about your gunshot wound?"

"The chlorine water will be good for it. It's not that bad, anyway." She dived into the deep end of the pool.

Neela said, "I like that, your concern about the wound. Just remember what I told you." She scooped up the gun and the computer and walked back into the house.

Jonathan watched Jesse as she swam back and forth across the pool several times, then climbed out and walked to the table. She dried herself off and sat down next to him.

"So, did Neela give you the 'keep your hands off my baby cousin' speech?"

"Yes, she did."

"What did you say?"

"I told her it wouldn't be a problem since you don't even like me."

Jesse laughed. "You're okay. I was the baby of the family—the youngest sibling. Until the grandchildren arrived. Everybody thinks they have to protect me."

"I saw how you dealt with that guy at the trading post. I told Neela you can handle yourself."

"Thank you."

"Can I ask you something?"

"Maybe."

"About Neela."

"Neela is my Uncle Bill's private investigator."

"She seems awfully close to your uncle. Is she related to him?"

Jesse laughed.

"Can't you see the resemblance? Actually, Bill sort of adopted Neela. Her parents were killed when she was little. She went through a series of foster homes, got herself in trouble with the law—big trouble. She was only ten. Uncle Bill intervened for her. He was working for the Assistant Attorney General at the time. He took her home. She and my aunt raised her, sent her to college and everything. Uncle Bill never had any children of his own. That's probably why he's always so kind to all his nieces and nephews."

"What kind of trouble did Neela get into?"

"Oh, so you're the journalist now?"

"I just wondered."

"You don't need to know that. Neela's a member of the family. You're not."

"Point taken."

"So, it looks as if you have an admirer."

"What, who?"

"Chelsea."

Jonathan felt himself blush and said, "Oh, man. As if I don't have enough problems."

"She is cute, don't you think?"

"Well sure, but—"

"I'm just messing with you. When it comes to romance, the women in my family are kind of aggressive. Except for me. I guess I'm the exception."

"I didn't want to hurt her feelings."

"You handled it just fine."

Neela came out and sat down at the table. She handed them printouts, and held up a photo of Agent Roberts, saying, "Here's what we have so far. James T. Roberts. He is indeed an agent with the Bureau of Alcohol, Tobacco, Firearms, and Explosives. He was formerly an agent with the FBI. He was disciplined two years ago for failing to follow protocol, effectively ending any hope for advancement. At that time he applied for a job with the ATF, and was stationed in Phoenix."

Jesse said, "Did you get any information on any operations he might be a part of?"

"Nothing definite. They're on lockdown at the agency as far as information is concerned, but it's buzzing. Whatever it is, it's big. I'm keeping my ears open. The most important thing right now is to find out Roberts' status in this mess."

Jesse said, "What else do you have?"

"I was right to suspect a California connection. The big boy is one Valdo Esposito." She pointed to the printout of Valdo's photograph, and everyone picked up their copies. "Mr. Esposito works for a Jimmy 'Shades' Deguardia. Jimmy is a mid-level player on the West Coast. Old school mafia. It seems Mr. Esposito started out in collections and moved up to security chief in one of Jimmy's nightclubs. He is not known as a hit man."

Jesse said, "So what's he doing in Arizona?"

"I haven't figured that out yet. There's a lot of heat among the Mexican gangs lately. And nobody here knows anything about Esposito. Roberts could have thought there was an advantage to bringing in a fresh face for whatever he's doing. That makes more sense than Jimmy expanding his reach eastward."

Jesse said, "Getting back to the ATF, how are they involved in this?"

"Well, here's the kicker: you know that truck pretty boy here ran into that train? And the AK47 on the road?"

Jonathan said, "We figured that must have been what they were hauling."

Jesse said, "But they would have had time to remove a single gun. That means they left it there on purpose."

Neela said, "And why would they do that?"

Jesse said, "So they could keep the ATF, that is Roberts, involved in the investigation without raising suspicion."

Neela said, "Smart girl. Maybe you should go into the PI business."

Jonathan said, "So what does that tell us about Roberts and the ATF?"

Jesse said, "Nothing, unfortunately. Except that they're not telling local law enforcement what's really going on."

Neela said, "Or the FBI. I'm not sensing the same kind of buzz at the bureau. I mean, they are certainly into this, but I'm convinced they're out of the loop. As for the locals, they're not only out of the loop, they're out for blood. And frankly, I can't blame them."

Jonathan said, "Yeah, my blood. What are we going to do?"

Neela said, "We're going to stash you guys away from here for a couple days until we can bring you in safely. Jesse, I'm trying to get ahold of Papa Joe, send you up to the Conrad compound until this blows over."

Jonathan said, "Papa Joe?"

Jesse said, "My dad. My parents are retired. They live up north, in Young." She said to Neela, "Won't they just follow us up there?"

Neela said, "We're going to fly you out of here. If we do it right, it will be days before they realize you're gone. That'll give us enough time to straighten this mess out."

Jonathan said, "Fly? I don't fly."

Neela said, "Don't worry about it. I've got it covered."

Jonathan said, "I'm not worried about it, because I'm not flying. Take Jesse up there. Turn me in. I'm not flying."

Neela said, "Okay, okay, we'll work this out tomorrow. Is there anything else you want to know?"

Jonathan said, "Can you find out how my mother's doing?"

Neela hesitated for a moment, then said, "I'll work something out to get a message to her."

Jonathan said, "Don't take any chances."

Neela said, "Do you trust me or don't you?"

Jonathan held his hands up in a defensive posture.

Neela said, "That's more like it."

FIFTEEN

IT WAS ALMOST SUNRISE when Roberts pulled up behind Valdo. He opened his phone and punched in Valdo's speed dial number. It rang a dozen times before Roberts closed his phone and got out of his car. He walked up to Valdo's car and knocked on the driver side window. Valdo rolled the window down.

"Why won't you answer your phone?"

"Because I'm right here."

"I told you it's … ah, never mind. Anything happen overnight?"

"The black chick came back, then left again. Look, there she is again."

They watched the woman park in the driveway and enter the house.

Roberts said, "You're right. Big girl, but hot. I ran the plates on the Porsche. It belongs to William Conrad, the owner of the house. He's the little girl's uncle, some hot shot attorney. The woman is a P.I., works for him. Name's Neela Conrad, but they don't look related."

Valdo nodded.

Roberts said, "I'll take over now. You go get some sleep."

Valdo said, "So it's just you and me watching the house?"

Roberts said, "I don't want to bring the others into this unless it gets out of hand. I'd rather clean it up myself."

"Whatever. But I ain't gonna wait forever."

"We won't."

"You know, while I was sitting here, I saw an airplane fly over really low. If I didn't know better, I'd swear that it landed in the back yard."

"Stellar Airpark."

"Stellar Airpark?"

"Yeah, it's a private airport. A lot of these houses have hangars built onto them."

"So they could just fly away and nobody would know?"

"You're smarter than you look."

Valdo said, "Screw you," rolled the window up and drove away.

Roberts went back to his car.

JONATHAN WOKE UP and got dressed. He walked out to the living room to find Jesse and Neela drinking coffee and watching the news on television. The President of the United States was weighing in on the shootings. He said they were an example of runaway gun violence, and called for Congress to enact "common sense" gun control legislation.

Jonathan said, "How did it ever get this far?"

Everybody turned around.

Jesse said, "Good morning. How 'bout some coffee?"

Jonathan said, "Yes, that would be excellent."

Neela said, "I'll get it for you. How do you like it?"

"Cream and sugar. Lots of sugar."

Jonathan sat down on the couch and Neela went out to the kitchen.

Jesse said, "We're getting out of here this morning."

Jonathan said, "As long as it's not on a plane."

There was a long pause.

Finally Jesse said, "Neela and I have a plan. But enjoy your coffee, then we'll talk."

Neela walked into the room and set a cup of coffee down on an end table next to Jonathan. Jonathan picked it up and took a sip. He said, "So, are we driving up to …"

Jesse said, "Young."

Neela said, "Law enforcement doesn't know about Jesse. Even if the ATF were running a secret operation, our sources would tell us if they were looking for her. That means Roberts is a rogue, as far as his interest in her is concerned."

Jonathan said, "Anybody can find out about Jesse's parents. Like I said, what's to keep them from following us to their house?"

Neela said, "They won't know she's left, not for a while, anyway. We're going to create a diversion when we leave. That will give you at least a couple days. But don't worry, we won't leave you hanging any longer than we have to."

Jonathan yawned and rubbed his eyes, trying to shake the residual sleep from his head.

Jesse said, "Finish your coffee. You seem to need it."

Jonathan tilted the cup back, draining it. He started feeling even sleepier and was having trouble keeping his eyes open.

Neela said, "He's ready. I'll make the call."

She set a briefcase down on the coffee table and opened it. Inside were several rows of cell phones, lined up in pairs. She grabbed one of the phones and popped the back plate off, took a battery out of the briefcase and inserted it into the phone. She put the phone back together and pressed the power button. When the phone powered up, she punched in some numbers and held it to her ear. She said, "Hello? I'd like to report a drunk driver. Okay, I'll wait, but hurry. He's parked now but he might start driving again." She put the phone on hold and said to Jonathan, "Chandler Police." Jonathan yawned. She took the call off hold and a few moments later said,

"Yes. No, I wish to remain anonymous. For my own safety. Yes, he's right outside in his car. A red Dodge Charger. He was weaving all over the road. Yes, I saw him drinking. He sideswiped a tree, then he stopped, but he looks as if he's getting ready to drive away. He's on South Stellar Parkway just north of Kitty Hawk. Thank you. I'll keep an eye on him. Please hurry." She pulled the battery out and returned it with the phone to the briefcase.

Jesse said, "Very good. Do we have everything?"

Jonathan said, "I think I need to lie down for a few minutes."

Neela said, "Go ahead. Just lie down on the couch. We'll wake you."

Jonathan slumped over and fell asleep.

ROBERTS WATCHED the patrol car drive past, the police officer giving him the eye. The car turned around at the corner and came back, stopping at an angle partially in front of his car, blocking him in. Roberts sighed as the patrolman exited his car, hands covering his sidearm, and walked up to the driver side window.

"What can I do for you, officer?"

"Have you been drinking, sir?"

"No, I have not. Look, I'm law enforcement. I'm going to reach into my coat pocket to retrieve my badge."

"Keep your hands where I can see them."

"Look, I—"

"Shut up and step out of the car."

Roberts shook his head as he slowly opened the door and stepped out of the car.

The patrolman said, "Put your hands on your head."

As Roberts did so, the patrolman shoved him, turning him around until he was facing the car. Another patrol car turned onto the street. The second patrolman walked up with his hand covering his pistol. The first patrolman reached under Roberts' coat and took possession of his pistol, handing it to the other officer, then reached into Robert's coat pocket and pulled out his wallet. He opened it and examined his ID and badge.

"So, you're ATF? What are you doing here?"

"I'm on a stake-out. Confidential. Somebody call on me?"

"We got a report of a drunk driver at this location in a car that fits this description."

"Shit!" He looked at the house. So far none of the cars had moved. "I told you this is confidential. You're better off forgetting about it."

The patrolman leaned into the car and rummaged around, looking under the seat. He pulled out the bottle of vodka. "What is this?"

"I have no idea how that got there."

"Don't move." He walked over to his patrol car. After about five minutes, he came back to the Charger with a Breathalyzer kit.

Roberts said, "I'm not taking any tests."

The patrolman said, "Fine," pulled Roberts' hand back, snapping a handcuff on his wrist, pulled the other hand back and cuffed it. He patted Roberts down before walking him over to his patrol car. He shoved him into the back seat and slammed the door shut.

JONATHAN HEARD HIS MOTHER tell him to get up, that it was time to go. She was calling him from inside their home. He stepped through the shattered front door and almost fell into a swirling pool of water. He saw his father slip beneath the surface of the water and disappear.

He felt someone grab his arm and realized he had been dreaming. He turned his head, and there was Mara from West Wave, only she wasn't in costume. Was he still dreaming? Jonathan looked down to see he was lying on a couch in a puddle of drool. He sat up and looked around the room.

Mara slid her arms under his and pulled upward, saying, "We have to go now."

He said, "Okay," and stood up. He started to walk, but his legs seemed far away. "Where are we going?"

"We're getting you away from here, remember?"

"Where's here?"

He turned and stared into her eyes, saying, "Mara, you've come to save me." He heard laughter from across the room. He looked over and saw it was coming from a beautiful young woman who was carrying a backpack. "Oh, I know you," he said. "But I didn't create you, did I?"

The woman said, "No, I'm real, not like Mara."

Mara said, "Who's Mara?" which didn't make sense to him. The woman who was real laughed even harder. Mara said, "Come on, quit clowning around. He's talking to the cop."

Jonathan said, "Who's talking to the cop?"

Mara said, "Never mind," and pulled Jonathan along as he plopped his feet down one after the other. "That's right. Left foot, right foot. Keep going."

He said, "Where are we going? You never said where we're going."

Mara said, "You'll see."

He stumbled along next to Mara down a hallway until they reached a door. The other woman opened the door and stepped out. They followed her into a large white room with a high ceiling and an airplane in the middle of a white painted floor. It was a funny looking plane. He said, "Did you know you have an airplane in your garage?"

Mara said, "This is a hangar."

"Oh. Well it doesn't matter because I don't fly."

"You don't have to, Honey. I just wanted to show you something."

"Okay, but you should know that I don't fly."

Mara said to the real woman, "Go get a pillow and a couple blankets." The woman hurried back into the house.

He said to Mara, "I know her."

"Yes you do."

"I like her, she's real."

"You poor boy."

The woman returned with her arms full of blankets, which she put into the plane. Mara walked him over to the plane and showed him inside. There was a space on the floor in the back of the plane covered with blankets, with a pillow on one side. It looked inviting—he was having trouble staying awake.

Mara said, "We've fixed you a bed. You'll be safe here. You can get some sleep now."

He climbed into the plane, said, "They'll never think to look for me here," and lay down on the makeshift bed.

Mara climbed into the front of the cockpit, and the young woman climbed in next to Jonathan. She curled up, keeping her head low.

He said, "Are you sleeping with me?"

The woman said, "Shhhh."

He closed his eyes, but opened them when the engine started. "What's going on?"

Mara said, "Nothing. I'm just doing some maintenance on the plane. Go back to sleep."

The plane started to move.

He said, "Where are we going?"

Mara said, "I'm just testing the wheels."

"Oh, okay." He closed his eyes again. The humming of the engine and the rolling of the wheels made him even sleepier. He was dozing off when the engine started revving. He sat up and said, "What are you doing?"

Mara said, "It's okay. This will only take a minute."

The plane started rolling faster. He said, "I don't fly," just as the plane left the runway and became airborne. "Oh, crap. I'm flying. Is this real?"

Mara said, "Yes, this is very real."

He said, "I told you I don't fly. Why am I flying?"

"You had to, Jonathan. It was the only way."

"I'm dizzy."

The other woman said, "It's the drugs."

He said, "I'm going to throw up."

Mara said, "You throw up in my plane and I'll toss you out."

He gagged, vomited his coffee onto the young woman, and passed out.

SIXTEEN

Jesse gagged at the mess Jonathan had made on her pants and the floor of the plane but composed herself.

Jonathan opened his eyes and sat up, his head swaying. He looked at the puke and said, "I'm sorry."

Jesse didn't reply. She scraped her pants off with one of the blankets. She folded the blanket and handed it to him. "Here, wipe your mouth."

After Jonathan cleaned himself up, Jesse handed him a bottle of water. He took a long swig.

He said, "Jesse?"

"That's my name."

He looked at Neela and squinted. He turned and peered out the window.

"Did you have to drug me? There wasn't any other way?"

Jesse said, "Why don't you lie down? I'll wake you up after we land."

"No. I didn't choose to fly, but as long as I'm here, I might as well experience it."

Neela said, "Taking it like a man." When Jesse started taking pictures, Neela said, "Did you ask Bill if you could take his camera?

Oh, what am I saying?"

The darkness below gave way to the sunrise, revealing the vast desert floor, and Jesse started snapping photos of Jonathan, who by now had his face pressed against the window.

The plane started gaining altitude.

Jonathan said, "What is that mountain?"

Neela said, "Those are the Superstitions. Over there is the Salt River." She pointed to the left. "We'll be following that for a while." She was enjoying playing tour guide.

Jonathan said, "Lakes."

"Yes. That one is Canyon Lake. The one back there is Saguaro. We'll pass over Apache on our way to Roosevelt. When we reach Roosevelt, we turn north."

"To Young."

"Yes."

"You know, I never heard of Young before."

"It's in the center of Pleasant Valley."

"Sounds nice."

"Yeah, tell that to the Grahams and the Tewksburys."

"Who?"

"The people who wiped each other out in the Pleasant Valley War."

"You're kidding."

"Nope. Both families were killed off in the feud."

"What were they feuding over?"

"Cattle and sheep. You know, the usual."

"You're not going to start singing, are you?"

"Hey, he's funny." She smiled and pointed out the window. "Roosevelt Lake."

"It's a lot bigger than the others."

The plane banked and turned north, leveling off. The ground was flat and dry and rocky, but soon they approached another range of mountains and began to climb again. The farther they flew, the higher the mountains rose, and the greener the landscape below became. Creosote and mesquite gave way to saguaro and palo verde, then to thick stands of cedar and pine until the land was blanketed in green in all directions.

Jonathan said, "I didn't know there were forests like this in Arizona."

Jesse kept taking photos over his shoulder.

Finally the plane leveled off. Neela turned around and said, "Jesse, grab that briefcase."

Jesse put her camera down, placed the briefcase on her lap, and opened it. It was the briefcase with the cell phones.

"Take three of them."

Jesse pulled three phones out and started to put them into her backpack.

Neela said, "Don't forget the batteries."

She pulled out three batteries and put them with the phones.

"Okay. If you need to call me, put the battery in, make the call, then take it back out. Use one phone for one call, then the next phone for the next, etc. Cycle through them."

Jonathan said, "Aren't you being a little over-cautious?"

Neela said, "A little caution could save your life. Don't use the phones unless you have to. If we need to contact you, we'll call Joe on the shortwave."

Jonathan said, "Shortwave?"

Jesse said, "My father doesn't own a telephone."

"Why not?"

"He's a little—"

"Paranoid," Neela said.

Jonathan said, "More than you?"

"Oh yeah."

Jesse said, "That's enough. Remember to get Tyler his motorcycle."

Neela said, "I will. Look up ahead, everyone."

The plane flew over the top of the mountain, and below them was a vast, green valley covered with farms and ranches. The plane started to bank to the left and lose altitude.

Neela said, "I want everyone strapped in and all cargo tied down."

Jonathan looked terrified. "Oh, no."

"Don't worry. Neela knows what she's doing,"

Neela said, "Thank you, Sweetheart. I wouldn't let anything happen to Bill's little Princess. Now buckle up, it's time to land."

Jonathan looked around. "Where's the airport?"

Neela said, "We're not using the airport."

"Then how can we land?"

"We'll be fine, Honey," Neela said, shooting a glance towards Jesse.

Jesse reached over and strapped Jonathan in.

Jonathan said, "I'm serious. Where are we supposed to land?"

Neela said, "Jonathan, this is a STOL aircraft—Short Take Off and Landing. It's designed to use a small landing strip."

"What landing strip? There is no landing strip. You just said so."

"There," Neela said, pointing towards the ground.

"Where? I don't see anything."

"There. Right down there."

"There? That's a dirt road." Jonathan started rocking back and forth.

Jesse reached over and rubbed Jonathan's shoulders. "It's okay. Neela knows what she's doing."

Jonathan calmed down.

Neela reached back and patted Jonathan's leg. "Trust me Jonathan. I'll take good care of you." She turned back and pushed forward on the yoke. The plane banked and dropped quickly.

Jonathan said, "Oh, crap."

Neela dropped the engine speed to an idle and the plane glided in around a mountain peak. When they had made a complete circle around the peak, they were only 20 feet above the tree tops and flying slowly. The dirt road came back into view. When they reached the road, Neela straightened out their direction and set the plane down, coming to a stop about a hundred feet down the road.

Jonathan sighed.

Neela said, "Hurry up."

Jesse said, "Oh, here. Almost forgot," and handed her Tyler's pistol.

Neela said, "I'll get it to him. You be careful now."

"Thanks."

Jonathan said, "Wait. Are you sure you don't want to hang on to the gun?"

Jesse said, "Don't worry, we won't need it. Now say thank you to Neela and let her get out of here."

Jonathan turned to Neela and said, "Thank you. For everything."

"My pleasure. I'd give you a kiss goodbye but you're kind of disgusting right now." She smiled and gave Jonathan a wink.

Jonathan and Jesse climbed out of the plane and watched as it took off and banked up and around the mountain.

"Why did you give her the gun?"

"I've got more. I keep my guns at my folks' house."

"Yeah, but what if something happens before we get there? We might need it."

"Wow, now who's the gun nut?"

"It's just that we seem like sitting ducks out here." He gestured in a circle at the wilderness around them.

"It's not that far." Jesse slung the backpack over her shoulder and started down the road. Jonathan followed close behind.

JONATHAN FOLLOWED JESSE down the dirt road for a quarter mile until she stopped in front of a gravel driveway.

"Your parents' house?"

"Shh."

Three large dogs came running down the driveway. Jesse said, "Don't move."

Jonathan said, "Is it okay?"

"It's fine. Just don't move."

The dogs closed in cautiously, eying the strangers, sniffing the air, analyzing their scent. The largest dog, a male, was growling, the fur on its back bristling.

Jesse said, "Diablo."

At this, the dogs ran up to her, excited, circling her and shoving their heads under her hand, begging to be petted. The male jumped up, putting his huge front paws on Jesse's shoulders and licking her face. On its hind legs Diablo stood taller than she was. The other two dogs rubbed up against Jonathan, almost knocking him over.

She said, "They won't hurt you. You're with me." She nuzzled Diablo and said in baby talk, "You're just a great big puppy, aren't you?"

"What kind of dogs are these?"

"Guess."

"I was going to say Labrador Retriever, but they're too big. I'm thinking they're some kind of Great Dane-Lab mix, except they have those black markings. And those paws, they're huge. Are they still growing?"

No, they're fully grown."

"I give up. What are they?"

"These sweet puppies are Anatolian Shepherd dogs."

"Really? I've never heard of them."

"They're from Turkey. The shepherds there use them to guard the flocks. They say that two or three of these can actually take on a pack of wolves."

"You believe that?"

"Well, that could be bragging on the part of the shepherds, but it could be true."

"I imagine they're here for security."

"Papa bought and trained them for security, but they're really Mama's babies."

Jesse started down the driveway. Diablo walked next to her, on her left, and the other dogs followed them. Jonathan brought up the rear. He noticed the dogs had shed a layer of fur on his pants.

The driveway wound around a hill and through some brush and pine trees, ending in front of a two-story ranch house with a large covered porch.

Jesse said, "The truck's not here. They must have gone into town," and stepped up onto the porch. There was a combination security lock on the front door. She punched in some numbers, opened the door, and stepped inside. Diablo started towards the door, but she said, "Not you. Back!" and the dogs stood back, allowing Jonathan and Jesse to enter the house. She said, "Close the door," and worked the keypad on the alarm system control panel. "I'm going to take a shower, help yourself to the fridge," She walked down a hallway, pointing to a door as she passed it. "This is the guest bathroom."

Jonathan went to the kitchen and found a glass in the cupboard, filled it at the sink and sat down at the kitchen table. It was quiet in the house, and he let himself relax. He was sipping on his water and listening to the songbirds chatter outside when he heard a car pulling up to the house. He hurried to the living room and peeked out the window in time to see a big four-wheel-drive pickup truck come to a stop in front of the house. A man was driving, and a woman was his passenger. When they stepped out, Jonathan saw they were older, probably in their mid sixties. The man had a medium build and a full gray beard. He was wearing a cowboy hat and boots. The woman was short and a little heavy, and when she got closer to the house Jonathan could tell she was Jesse's mother. She looked like an exact, older copy of Jesse: the same black hair, the same dark eyes, the same beautiful skin, only brown instead of olive. The man worked the security lock and opened the door, letting the woman in first. They had barely cleared the doorway when the man said, "Who the hell are you?" He was aiming a large handgun at Jonathan and staring at him with bright blue eyes.

SEVENTEEN

"I'M JONATHAN STARKER."

"What are you doing in my home?"

"Jesse brought me here."

He looked Jonathan up and down. "How do you know my Jesse?"

"I ran into her in Eloy."

The woman said, "Joe, put that gun away." She had a thick Mexican accent. "You're scaring Jesse's boyfriend."

Jonathan said, "Uh, I'm not actually her ..." He decided not to finish the sentence, under the circumstances.

Joe said, "Where's Jesse?"

"She's taking a shower."

Joe put the gun back into his belt holster. The woman grabbed Jonathan in a bear hug and kissed his cheek. "You are welcome here, Jonathan." She let go and stepped back, smiling, looking him over. "I am Maria, Jesse's mama. Can I get you something to eat?"

"No, that's okay. Thank you."

"No no, you need to eat. Look at you. You're so skinny."

"No, really, I'm fine."

"Come on." She took Jonathan by the hand and led him into the kitchen. "Sit. I'll see what we have." She opened the refrigerator and grabbed a package of ham and a package of Swiss cheese. "Do you like mustard or mayonnaise on your sandwich?"

"Mayo."

She spread mayonnaise on both slices of twelve-grain bread, slapped several slices of ham and cheese on them, put the sandwich together, sliced it diagonally and put it on a plate. She lay the plate down in front of him and said, "You want some milk?"

"No, thank you."

"Oh, it's still early. Let me make you some coffee."

The thought of coffee made him nauseous. He vaguely remembered vomiting the last cup he had drank, but for some reason said, "Yes, coffee would be good."

As she was putting the coffee grounds into the drip basket, Joe walked into the kitchen with both arms full of groceries. He set them down on the table and left, coming back a minute later with more. Marie said, "Thank you, Joseph." She turned to Jonathan and said, "We just got back from Payson."

Joe said, "I don't know why you like shopping at Walmart. I hate that place."

"Because everything is cheaper there."

"Yeah, but it's a mob. I'd rather shop at Safeway. Safeway is cleaner, too."

"When you are in charge of the groceries, you can shop where you want."

"Yeah, yeah."

"Joe, you never said hello to Jonathan." She turned to Jonathan and said, "Please excuse my husband. He is very old and forgets his manners."

Joe sighed heavily and offered his hand. "Joseph Conrad."

When Jonathan reached out, Joe gripped his hand so tight it hurt. His words said welcome but his eyes said watch your ass.

Maria said, "Don't let him scare you. He is really a big softy." She put her arm around Joe's waist.

Joe said, "You see what I have to put up with around here?"

Jonathan ate his breakfast while Maria put the groceries away. When he had finished, Maria said, "Come out here with us, Jonathan," and guided him to the living room. A few minutes later, Jesse joined them, her hair wrapped in a towel. They sat in silence for a long time before Maria said to Jesse, "So what's going on, Jess?" Jesse told their story.

Joe sat forward in his leather chair. "You shot him with a 9 and he kept coming? How close were you when you shot him?"

Jesse said, "I don't know, it just happened so fast. I wasn't right next to him but I wasn't very far away, either. I was on the ground and he was coming after me. I used a two-handed grip and aimed at center mass like you taught me. It stunned him but he got back up."

"Body armor. He was wearing a Kevlar vest."

"That's what Neela said. I'm glad he was wearing it. I don't want to kill anybody."

Joe stroked his chin. "The man is a professional. I've been watching the news reports—"

"Yeah, I saw the television. When did you get that?"

Maria said, "I made him buy me a TV. I got tired of living like a hermit."

Joe said, "I've been following the news reports." He turned to Jonathan. "They say you shot a man in Riverside." He squinted. "You know, you look different than your photo."

Jesse said, "Neela gave him a make-over."

"Smart girl. As I was saying, they aren't sure if you shot him in California or kidnapped him and shot him in Arizona when you killed the driver and hijacked the truck."

Jonathan said, "I didn't shoot anybody."

"So the driver makes two murders. They also found a guy in the the trailer you were pulling. His head was smashed."

"Crap. I have no idea where he came from."

"That makes three murders."

"I didn't kill him either. I swear I don't know anything about him or the guy from Riverside. The only murder I saw was Mark Talmeier."

"Well, this is some mess you dragged us into. How do we know you're telling the truth?"

Jesse said, "Papa, when I saw the inside of the trailer there wasn't a body in it."

Jonathan said, "If I only had my phone. I recorded the whole thing on my phone."

Joe said, "Okay, then let's see your phone."

"I lost it. I think I dropped it in the canal."

"That's very convenient. How do we even know you're who you say you are?"

Jesse said, "I looked him up."

Jonathan said, "You looked me up?"

"Of course I did. I'm a journalist. It's my job."

"So you didn't believe me?"

"I believed you. I just had to make sure."

Joe said, "Okay. Okay." He turned to Jonathan. "What exactly were you hauling in that truck?"

"Mark said it was machinery, but when it crashed, guns fell out of it."

Jesse said, "I saw one of the guns. It was an AK47."

Joe said, "Really?"

"Yeah."

"And the guy said he was with the ATF?"

Jonathan said, "Yes."

"Sounds like Fast and Furious."

"The movie?"

"The scandal."

Jonathan shook his head. "I've never heard of it."

"I'm not surprised. Fast and Furious was a gunwalking opera- tion run by the ATF back in 2010."

"Gunwalking?"

"Yeah. What it boils down to is the ATF let a couple thousand high powered rifles walk into Mexico, supposedly as a way to catch people buying illegal weapons. Those weapons showed up in the hands of the drug cartels. Over a hundred Mexican citizens have been murdered with those weapons, as well as one of our Border Patrol agents."

"Wow. And you think this could be related to that?"

"Or some other operation. What I can't figure out is why they killed Mark. That part doesn't make sense."

Jesse said, "Maybe Mark was doing some undercover work."

"Maybe."

Jonathan said, "Do you really think the ATF would murder people?"

"I don't know. I'm sure Neela's looking into it. Maybe she'll come up with something to help connect the dots. In the meantime, we need to be ready for anything. I wonder how long it will take them to figure out you're here."

Jesse said, "It could take a while. On paper, it looks as if Neela took off from Stellar and landed the plane ten minutes later at the Chandler airport."

"I'm sure she was careful about covering things up, but they'll come knocking eventually. I've got a couple bug-out bags for you in case you need to leave in a hurry."

Jonathan said, "Leave? Leave where?"

Joe said, "Don't worry about that just yet. That would be a last resort. Anything short of a full out assault and we can protect you here. You ever used a firearm?"

"I have a .22 rifle. I used to go target shooting with my father."

"Well that's a start. Jesse, why don't you take him out to the hill and show him how to use a handgun."

Jonathan said, "Do you really think it will come to that?"

Joe said, "I hope not. Jesse, make sure he practices with one of my CZ52s."

Jonathan followed Jesse to a door at the back of the kitchen. Jesse opened the padlock on the door and swung the bolt back out of the way. She flipped a light switch and led Jonathan down into the basement.

Jonathan said, "Holy crap. Are you guys getting ready to start a war?"

"My family has been collecting guns for over a hundred fifty years." She walked over to an antique rifle sitting on a display and picked it up. "This was used by my sixth great-grandfather at Gettysburg." She handed it to Jonathan.

"It's beautiful. What kind is it?"

"It's a Spencer Repeating Rifle."

"He was able to keep it after the war?"

"The Union Army let him buy it. He paid ten dollars for it. He took it home and was able to feed his family with it." She took the rifle back and set it on the display.

My great-great-grandfather fought in the first World War. He brought home quite a few war souvenirs, including this one." She held up a pistol.

Jonathan said, ".45."

"That's right."

"That's what Esposito used to shoot Mark."

She put it down and said, "By the time grandpa died he had assembled a collection of every kind of rifle and handgun used by either side in the war. Papa's father fought in Korea. When he got back he continued the hobby, then passed it on to Papa, who fought in Vietnam. Papa has a copy of almost every type of small arms used in World War Two, Korea, Vietnam, and both Iraq wars. He's thinking about opening a museum."

"Every gun from World War Two?"

"Almost."

"Does he have a Tommy gun?"

"Right over here. He has two different magazines, the military stick, and a 50 round drum, like the old gangsters."

"He's allowed to own a machine gun?"

"Submachine gun. He had to pay $200 for a tax stamp."

"That's all he had to do?"

"Other than pay twenty grand for the gun."

"Wow. Could I see it?"

"Sure." She picked up the Tommy gun and inspected the chamber. "Here, it's not loaded."

Jonathan took the gun and looked it over. He lined the sights up at an air vent and pulled the trigger. He said, "Nice," and hung the Thompson back on the wall.

Jesse walked over to a stack of military ammo cases, took a box out of it, put the box in a gym bag, and repeated the action on two more cases. She grabbed three handguns off the wall: a large barreled revolver in a Western holster, a small black pistol in a black nylon holster, and a medium-sized pistol in a weatherworn military holster. She put the revolver and the military handguns in the gym bag and clipped the small gun onto her belt. She handed the bag to Jonathan and said, "You can carry this," slung a different bag over her shoulder and said, "Come on."

JESSE AND JONATHAN got into the pickup truck, Jesse driving with Jonathan riding shotgun. It was hot out so they kept the windows closed and the air conditioner on. They drove down the driveway and turned left, following the dirt road as it wound around hills and over streams, and the trees grew thicker and greener as they went, cedars and junipers, pinyon trees and tall ponderosa pine. They were deep in the woods when Jesse pulled onto a trail, the truck's tires gripping the quartzite beneath the pine needles, pulling them forward until they came to a stop behind a stand of pine trees. She turned the steering wheel and backed the truck around until the bed was facing a barren hill about 50 yards away. They stepped out of the truck and were immersed in the smell of the forest.

She set up the weapons and ammo and drinking water bottles on the tailgate, handed Jonathan the heavy gym bag, and marched towards the hill, saying, "Come on." When they got to the base of the hill, Jesse reached into it and pulled out a steel gong on a two-legged stand. She walked half-way back, Jonathan in tow, set up six small targets shaped like squirrels, and walked back to the truck where an actual squirrel was examining a water bottle. The squirrel leapt onto a tree branch and up the pine tree. Jesse slid the gun out of the cowboy holster and inserted a large brass-jacketed cartridge into each of the six chambers.

Jonathan watched Jesse hold the revolver in both hands and squeeze the trigger. A flame shot out of the long silver muzzle and the gong far off in the distance made a clank.

She said, "Now look at my feet. See? This is a Weaver stance." She held the gun out to Jonathan. "Your turn. Have you ever shot a handgun?"

Jonathan didn't answer.

"I'll take that as a no."

"I have."

"Okay, what did you shoot?"

"A Desert Eagle."

"Are you kidding me? You have experience with a .50 caliber auto?"

He had talked himself into a corner.

She said, "Where did you shoot a Desert Eagle?"

"Deadly Combat II."

"Deadly what?"

"Deadly Combat II. It's VR—Virtual Reality."

She laughed. "So you've shot a Desert Eagle in a video game?"

"Virtual Reality. It's three dimensional. You have to wear special head gear an—"

She laughed even harder.

He said, "Actually, virtual reality shooting is an efficient way to develop hand-eye coordination."

"Did you read that on the box?"

He didn't answer.

"Okay, prove it." She held the revolver in front of him.

Jonathan took it and turned towards the target.

"Don't forget the Weaver stance."

Jonathan adjusted his feet, took aim and fired, missing the target by several feet. "It feels awkward."

"Wait, wait a minute. The Weaver stance isn't the only stance. Try standing the way you do when you shoot in your video games. Just relax and do what you know."

Jonathan closed his eyes, thinking about Deadly Combat, let out a sigh, opened his eyes, raised the revolver and fired.

The target clanked.

She said, "Yes! Okay, try double-tapping."

"Try what?"

"Fire two rounds in rapid succession."

Clank clank.

"Again."

Clank clank.

"You're really good at this."

"Thanks. That's six bullets. It's empty."

"Six rounds. They're called rounds. The bullet is just the projectile."

"So, let's put some more rounds in."

"Later. I brought the Redhawk for fun." She took the revolver from Jonathan, set it down on the tailgate, and picked up a slender black pistol. "Papa wants you to learn how to use this."

"Why that one?"

"His reasoning is if we run across Esposito, he's going to be wearing his body armor, so if we can't get away from him, we're going to have to shoot him in the head. Papa doesn't have confidence in your ability to do that. Although after watching what you just did ..."

"I hope is doesn't come to that."

"Me, too. Anyway, Papa has opted for having you carry a penetrating round, something that has a chance to defeat his armor. This is a CZ52. It shoots Russian Tokarev rounds. Penetrating rounds."

Jesse showed Jonathan how to load the ammo into the magazines, how to insert the magazines into the grip, how to rack the slide, how to work the safety/decocker, and how to release the magazine. He had no trouble dealing with the rudimentary iron sites and was able to hit the targets repeatedly. All the while she kept taking pictures of him.

After going through the 50 round box of Tokarev ammo, she gave him the Redhawk to shoot while she practiced with her Glock 26. Eventually they both ran out of ammo and had to head back home.

After dinner, Joe nodded towards Jonathan and said, "How'd he do out there?"

Jesse said, "Surprisingly well. He's a deadeye with the Blackhawk."

"And the CZ?"

"Pretty good, once he got used to the sights. By the time the ammo ran out, he was hitting the gong almost every time."

"What about the tactical target? Did you do any close-in work?"

"No."

"Don't you think it's kind of important?"

"Yeah, but I like to shoot for distance."

"That's fine for elk, but close up is where he'll need to defend himself."

"You're right. Well, we're going back out tomorrow."

EIGHTEEN

TUESDAY MORNING, Valdo was sitting across the table from Roberts at Lo-Lo's Restaurant in South Phoenix. Roberts had called and told him to meet him there. Valdo was working on a plate of chicken and waffles; Roberts was leafing through some papers.

Valdo said, "You didn't call to have me take over last night. We're not watching the house, or what?"

"Don't need to."

"Why not?"

"Nobody's there."

"How do you know that?"

"The P.I. She goes into the house, then three hours later another car shows up. She gets out of that car, gets in her BMW, and drives off. So I thought about what you said, about them flying out. I did some checking and came up with this interesting document." He handed a paper to Valdo.

"What is this?"

"The flight plans submitted for Stellar Airpark yesterday. It seems the P.I. took the lawyer's plane out for a ten mile jaunt."

"Ten miles?" said Roberts.

"Yeah, from Stellar Airpark in West Chandler to the Chandler

Airport in East Chandler."

Valdo put his fork down. "Dammit. They could've driven off from the airport, gone anywhere. Hell, they could've taken a plane from there back to Cali."

"Yeah, they could, except that every cop in California and Arizona is looking for him. His face is on every newspaper, every television screen. So the question is: where would you go if you wanted to disappear?"

"I'd go to Mexico."

"Exactly, because you've got family there. The Conrad girl brought Starker with her to her uncle's house. My gut tells me her family is still protecting them."

"So where else does she have family?"

"Everywhere. Her sister is a surgeon. She lives in Tucson. Her other sister is an accountant. She lives in Glendale."

"In L.A.?"

"Glendale Arizona."

"Oh. Is that a place to hide out?"

"Not really."

"So where did they go?"

"Oh, I'm not finished. She has a brother who is a network administrator for the Phoenix Police department. He lives in Queen Creek."

"Queen Creek is secluded?"

"Not secluded enough."

Valdo took a swig of coffee. "Any more relatives?"

"Oh yeah. Twins."

"Twins?"

"Twin brothers."

Valdo took a bite of chicken and said with his mouth full, "Jeez, what are these people, Mormons?"

"Catholic. Like you."

"Used to be. So where are these twins?"

"In the Navy. They're SEALs. I couldn't find out where they are. Classified bullshit."

"Any more relatives?"

"Indeed there are. She has another sister. This sister is a sister."

"What are you talking about?"

"She's a nun."

"A nun? Where does she live?"

"Tonapah."

"Where's that?"

"West of Phoenix. But I doubt she's hiding among the good sisters."

Valdo put down the drumstick he was working on and said, "Listen, culero. I'm tired of hearing where she isn't."

Heads turned in the restaurant.

Roberts motioned to keep it down.

Valdo said, "Just tell me. Where do you think she went?"

"Young."

"That don't mean nothing to me. Where the hell is Young?"

"Up north."

"North what?"

"Arizona."

"What makes you think they went to Young?"

"Young is in the boonies. This place is so secluded there isn't even a paved road going all the way up there. It's the perfect place to hide."

"So what? A lot of places are in the boonies. Why would she pick Young?"

"Because she grew up there. She knows the area."

"So she knows people there."

"She sure does. Her parents still live there."

"Huh. So why did you go though all that other shit? Why didn't you just say you think she went to hide out with her parents?"

"I wanted to give you enough time to finish your waffles."

"Yeah, well I'm finished. Let's go take care of those two. We taking my car or yours?"

"We'll have to take yours. They took mine away from me."

"How'd you get here?"

"I used Uber."

"What's that, a taxi?"

"Yeah, kind of."

Roberts paid the check and they left the restaurant. They drove up towards Globe, then down the hill to HWY 288. The two-lane road dropped down and they crossed the Salt River on a one-lane bridge, gaining altitude again as the highway rose up into the Sierra Anchas.

Eventually the pavement ended and they were driving on gravel.

"YOU SAID IT WAS COOLER up the mountains." Valdo wiped the sweat off his face with a hankerchief. "Why is it so hot?"

"It's this damn humidity. We should've had rain by now. You know, it wouldn't be that bad if your air conditioner worked. When was the last time you had it charged?"

"I never use it. In L.A. you just open the window."

"That isn't going to help here." He took a swig of vodka from the bottle he had brought along.

Valdo pressed the button and the driver side window slid down. "Jeez, it's like a blast furnace." He brought it back up quickly. "And this gravel road is tearing up my finish."

Roberts said, "Just like a Mexican, worried about your car. Besides, what difference does it make? This thing's ready for the scrap heap."

"Bullshit."

Roberts leaned over and looked at the guages. "57,000. What is that, 157,000?"

"Two hundred."

"257,00 miles?"

"This car is like new. The engine's smooth, the interior's cherry, the finish was pretty decent."

"The A/C is shit."

When they reached the highest point of the road, Roberts had Valdo pull over so he could take a leak. He walked over to a sign that said Honey Creek Divide and peed on it. He got back in the car and pointed off into the distance. There was a wide, green valley on a plateau surrounded by forest.

Roberts said, "Young." He pulled out his cell phone and spoke into it, "Joseph Conrad, Young Arizona," but nothing happened. He looked at the screen and said, "Dead zone."

They drove down the mountain and into the town of Young, where Roberts was able to get enough bars on his phone to get directions to the Conrad home.

Valdo drove to the edge of the gravel drive. The temperature in Young was bearable and they had rolled down their windows twenty miles back, but when they stopped, the dust they had stirred up from the road caught up with them, wafting into the car.

Valdo said, "Dammit. It's gonna take me a week to get this car clean."

Roberts was looking at his phone.

Valdo said, "So is this the place?"

"I think so. Let's find out—"

Three huge dogs appeared from nowhere and leapt towards the windows. Valdo was barely able to roll them up without getting bitten. The dogs snarled and barked at them, slobbering up the glass. Valdo put it in gear and turned onto the drive, the agitated canines following along. They came to a stop in front of a ranch house. An older man in a cowboy hat stood on the porch, a pistol dangling from his hand. The man said, "Diablo, leave it," and the dogs sat down quietly. The man said, "Whatever you're selling, we're not buying."

Valdo heard a woman's voice coming from the house. "Joe?"

The man said, "Stay in the house, Maria."

Roberts held his badge up to the window and said, "ATF."

The man said, "Do you have a warrant?"

"No, but I can get one."

"Then go get one."

"Look, it'll go a lot easier on you if you cooperate."

"It'll go a lot easier on you if you turn around and leave. Now."

Valdo said, "You're going to answer some questions, old man." He opened the door and started to step out of the car.

"I beg to differ, and so do my dogs. Diablo, watchum."

Diablo growled.

Valdo froze.

Valdo said, "You better call off your dogs or I'm gonna shoot 'em."

The voice from inside the house said, "Go ahead and shoot 'em."

The old man looked down and rubbed his forehead with his fingertips. He looked up and said, "You've done it now, mister."

An older Hispanic woman stepped out of the house carrying a lever action rifle. She said, "But if you shoot my dogs, then I'm gonna have to shoot you." She kept moving forward. "But I'm an old woman. My eyes don't work so good no more. I'll have to shoot a lot of bullets to make sure you don't shoot back." She reached the end of the porch and stepped onto the driveway. "I guess I'll just have to keep shooting until you start to change shape. You know, just to be sure."

The man said, "She isn't kidding."

A drop of muddy sweat ran down the side of Valdo's face.

The woman moved forward again, stopping about 20 feet from the car. "That's what going to happen to you if you shoot my dogs," she said. "Come to think of it, I might just shoot you anyway."

She brought the gun stock up to her shoulder and lined the sites up on Valdo. Everybody froze. Nobody said a word. In the silence they heard a squirrel chatting in a nearby tree. A bluejay called out in the distance. The wind blew and rustled the leaves in the aspen trees.

The woman pulled the lever down and back up, cocking the gun.

Valdo jumped back into the car and jammed it into gear. Without closing the door, he hit the accelerator and spun his tires. He tried to turn the car around in the driveway but drove off the edge and ran over a sapling. The door struck a branch of the sapling, banging shut and bouncing back open. Valdo kept on accelerating out of the driveway and onto the road, the door flapping back and forth. A quarter mile away, he stopped to shut the door. It had been twisted a little by the impact with the tree, and he had to slam it shut three times before it would close.

JONATHAN HAD FUN at his tactical shooting lesson. The more time he spent with Jesse, the more he liked being with her. On the way back, he was enjoying watching her wrestle with the steering wheel, making the four-wheel drive truck work hard, climbing up the narrow path. She stopped before pulling onto the main dirt road and narrowly missed colliding with the big white car careening away.

Jonathan said, "That's them! They've found us."

"They found Mama is more like it."

"What do you mean?"

"I mean they looked scared, judging by their speed and direction of travel."

"Aren't you worried about your parents?"

"You don't know my parents."

When they got back, Jonathan grabbed the tote bags while Jesse ran into the house. When he got to the kitchen, everybody was seated around the table.

Maria stood up and said, "Sit down, Jonathan. Let me make you something to eat."

Jonathan said, "No thank you, Maria."

"Well have some coffee, then."

"Sure."

Maria dumped the coffee pot and began to make a fresh batch.

Joe said, "That was half a pot."

Maria said, "I don't want to serve our guest stale coffee."

"But I just made it ten minutes ago."

"When you make it, it tastes stale."

Jesse said, "It seems we missed some excitement."

Jonathan said, "What happened? We saw the car."

Joe said, "Those two clowns picked on the wrong dogs."

Jonathan said, "I don't understand."

Joe told him how Maria had chased off the two men instead of letting him handle it calmly. He admonished her, saying, "Maria, I told you when I bought you that gun, if you shoot something, you have to skin it yourself." He winked at Jonathan. "Son, This is a good time to think bout what you're getting yourself into. You see what this crazy old lady is like. I feel it's only fair to warn you that Jesse takes after her."

Jesse said, "He's not getting himself into anything."

Joe said, "Calm down, Princess. Hey, didn't you say Neela gave you a phone to use?"

Jesse took one of the phones out of the case and inserted the battery. She punched in the speed dial number and handed it to Joe. Joe talked to Neela for a minute. After he hung up the phone Jesse took the battery out.

Joe said, "Neela didn't have much good news. Bill is still delayed and in bad shape. She said that you two are to stay put. The police are still looking for Jonathan. Now that the reward is up to a quarter million they're receiving hundreds of tips."

Jesse said, "That's it?"

"She said to call back at six."

NINETEEN

VALDO AND ROBERTS DROVE NORTH out of Young to State Route 260, then west until they reached Star Valley. They stopped in a place called Rustlers' Hole. It was a strip club but it was too early for a show.

Roberts downed a shot of Wild Turkey chased with beer and said, "What the hell happened back there? You were acting like a scared little bitch."

Valdo said, "That woman's crazy."

"She wasn't going to shoot us."

"Oh, yes she was. You can be sure of it."

"Some hit man you are. You go around killing people you shouldn't be killing, the people you're supposed to kill you let get away, and then you piss your pants over a little Mexican grandma with a pop gun." Roberts took a bite of his hamburger.

"You don't know Mexican women. It don't matter if they're just out of diapers or back in them again, they're all crazy."

Roberts just shook his head.

"She reminds me of my Nana from Oaxaca. That woman was really crazy. When I talked back to her she used to hit me with her mano."

"Her what?"

"Mano stone. It's like a rolling pin only it's made out of stone."

"Oh. Right. Listen, we need to find a way to get past those dogs. As long as they're guarding the place, we'll never be able to sneak up on those assholes."

"She used it to make tortillas. Like she couldn't just buy tortillas at the mercado."

"Yeah, well, some folks are used to the old ways."

"What kind of Nana hits her grandson with a stone?"

"I never thought about it."

"A crazy Mexican Nana."

"Maybe your Nana wasn't typical," Roberts said, munching on a French fry. "Maybe she's an exception. What about your other grandmother?"

"I wouldn't know. Besides, she's not Mexican."

"Oh, that's right. I forgot you're a mutt."

"Samoan."

"Samoan? That makes sense." Roberts washed the fries down with his beer. He put the bottle down and looked at the label. "Four Peaks. Pretty good."

"Half Samoan, on my father's side."

"How did that happen?"

"The longshoreman's strike."

"The what?"

"The longshoreman's strike of '71. All the west coast ports were closed, so the ships had to unload in Mexico. The Mexicans drove the cargo up to the states."

"Yeah?"

"My father was a merchant marine."

"Yeah?"

"His ship was docked in Ensenada. The way my uncle tells it, that's how he met my mother."

"Oh yeah, that's right." He started to laugh. "I forgot, your mother was a stripper."

"Exotic dancer."

Roberts kept laughing. "Oh jeez, what was the name of that place where she worked?"

"Leave it alone."

"Wait, it's right on the tip of my tongue."

"I said shut up."

"Harem. Yeah, that's it. The Harem Club. Hey, you must feel pretty comfortable in this place. Does it feel like home?" The laughing turned into a fit of choking.

Valdo stood up and went to the rest room. When he came back, Roberts had stopped choking. Valdo said, "Let's go back and finish this."

Roberts chugged down his beer and said, "I have an idea." He motioned the waitress to come over and said to her, "Three twelve ounce sirloins."

The waitress said, "How would you like them?"

"Raw, in a doggie bag."

They left the bar and drove to Payson, stopping in the Home Depot where they picked up a package of D-Con rat poison. They headed back to Young, returning to the ranch and parking at the edge of the property. Roberts poured the rat bait pellets into a plastic grocery bag and set it on the floor board. He stomped on it, grinding his heel into it, put the steaks into the bag and shook the bag around, saying, "It's Shake and Bake for dinner." He stepped out of the car and walked towards the house, and found himself surrounded by the dogs. He held the bag open and let the steaks drop out. The dogs responded by sniffing the steaks, which allowed him to back away and return to the car. They watched the dogs sniff the steaks. Roberts said, "Eat it, stupid," but the dogs wouldn't.

Valdo said, "They must've trained them."

"Ya think? Gimme your phone." Roberts took Valdo's cell phone and punched in some numbers. He put the phone up to his ear and waited before saying, "Hi, I'm calling about the guy who killed the cop? You had his picture on TV … Yeah, that's him. Well I just saw him up here in Young. He was at the restaurant … Yeah, I'm sure … Yeah, anonymous … Case number 4588? … Thanks."

Valdo said, "Now how are we gonna get this guy before the cops do?"

"Relax, I'm flushing them out. They're not going to search the house. They're going to go there like every other house and knock on the door. The old couple will act dumb around law enforcement and our two rabbits will run scared as soon as they think nobody's looking. All we have to do is watch and wait."

"Yeah, and what happens if they question me?"

"You're just a guy I hired to drive me up here."

"You think they're not going to connect me to Cornwall?"

"Dammit. I forgot about that. You know, that was a stupid move on your part. I guess we're going to have to put you up in Star Vally for a day or two."

JESSE KEPT LOOKOUT, scanning the area through her camera's telephoto lens. Later that afternoon she saw the white car return, this time stopping at the intersection of the main road. Snapping the shutter, she called her father out to the porch. Jonathan followed.

"Look. They're back."

Joe said, "I knew they would be."

Jonathan said, "What do we do?"

Joe said, "Nothing for now. Those two won't come onto the property without the dogs telling us about it. I do think it's time to prepare for the real cops. If those two clowns figured out where you are, the Feds can't be far behind."

Jonathan said, "What do you mean, prepare?"

Joe said, "You have to go into the Tonto."

"The what?"

"The forest. To hide out."

Jesse said, "I know a lot of good hiding places out there."

Jonathan said, "What about your leg?"

"My leg is fine."

Jonathan was stunned. "This is crazy. We can't run away into the forest."

Joe said, "Just until Bill gets back."

Jonathan said, "What makes you think they won't find us in the wilderness?"

"Son, the Tonto National Forest covers almost three million acres. Hell, Robert Fisher went out there and they never did find him."

"Who's Robert Fisher?"

"A guy from Scottsdale, killed his wife and kids back in 2001. The guy turned psycho, cut their heads off. Well, not the wife. He shot her, then he burned his house down. The kids were ten and twelve years old."

"That's cold."

"Yeah. Bastard made the FBI's Top Ten list, right next to Osama Bin Laden. They found his car and his dog near some cave in the woods. They came in with dogs and helicopters, searched everywhere. People called in hundreds of tips. It was a real media circus."

"Kind of like this is turning out to be."

"Yeah. That's why we need to get a handle on this before it spins out of control."

Jonathan said, "I agree. I want you to take me into town right now. Turn me over to the police."

Joe said, "The sheriff."

"Whatever. Turn me in."

"You think you'll get there alive?"

"Dammit!"

"Calm down, son."

"How did everything get so screwed up?"

"Well, that's what happens when you're dealing with the Feds."

"I don't believe that guy's a Fed. He's a killer."

"A man can be both."

"You're nuts."

"Come on inside." He took Jonathan by the arm and led him to the living room. "Sit down. Maria, get us some coffee."

Maria said, "Please?"

Joe said, "Please."

"Jesse, come on inside. They're not going anywhere."

Jesse came in and aimed her camera towards Joe and Jonathan, snapping photos as she walked.

Joe said, "Jesse, put that thing down."

Jesse lowered the camera and said, "What?"

"I want you to travel light, just one weapon each. Jesse, how did Jonathan do with the CZ?"

Jesse said, "He got the hang of it."

"Good. Jonathan, you'll carry that. Jesse, leave the Glock here and take the Rascal."

"The youth rifle?" said Jesse.

"Yeah. I've packed rations for you but if you're out there for any length of time you'll want some fresh meat. That little gun is perfect for small game, and it's light."

"But how does it shoot? I mean, it's a kid's gun."

"It shoots straight enough. Chelsea's taken a lot of squirrels with it."

Maria said, "I know she has. Then I have to skin and clean and cook them. She has all the fun and I do all the work."

Jonathan said, "You eat squirrels? People actually eat squirrels?"

They all looked at Jonathan.

Jonathan said, "Never mind."

At six o'clock, Joe called Neela. This time Joe had Jesse put it on speaker.

Neela said, "I'm glad you called. Have you seen any police

around there?"

Joe said, "No, why?"

"Somebody phoned in a tip, said they saw Starker up in Young."

"There's no way. He's under wraps. It must have been Roberts."

"That's what I think. Anyway, you guys are going to be flooded with LEO. They're probably flying in as we speak."

"You're right."

"It's time for phase two."

"I'm way ahead of you."

"Call tomorrow, 6 AM."

"You got it, Honey."

Joe hung up and turned to Jesse. "Get your things."

JOE SAID, "Did you saddle the horses like I told you?"

Jesse said, "They're ready."

"Okay. Listen up, you two. Jonathan, I'm giving you a compass and a topo map."

Jonathan said, "Topo map?"

Jesse said, "Topographical. It shows where the mountains and rivers and things are."

"Wouldn't a GPS device be easier?"

Joe said, "A GPS can be tracked."

"But I've never read a topo map."

"Here, look." He spread the map out on the table. "You see these contour lines, they show the elevation of the land features."

"Oh, yeah. I've seen these before. I just didn't remember the term."

"Good. Jesse, I want you to see this, too."

Jesse leaned in close.

"Here's Lost Camp Canyon."

Jesse said, "That's our fishing spot, by the waterfalls."

"Near there, yeah. You know the escarpment west of there, here on Lost Camp Mountain, that's where I want you to camp. There's lots of places you can stay out of sight and have a little shade. No-body camps out around there but people like to fish north of there and screw around by the falls, so stay up in the escarpment during the day. You can get fresh water from the creek early in the morn-ing and late in the day."

Jonathan said, "Is the water safe to drink?"

Jesse said, "We use water filters. In case of giardia. Hey Papa, may I borrow your camera?"

"The GoPro? Sure."

Maria said, "Jesse, when you get there, you'll want to disin-fect that leg. I put some alcohol in your pack. Pour some on your wound, then dab it with Neosporin and dress it. Try to keep it dry."

"It's fine, Mama."

"Just do it."

"Okay, Mama."

Joe said, "Look, we're going to use the horses, head up here and follow along the ridge, then down to the Haigler here. There is no way they can track you. If they do search the Haigler they'll prob-ably look at Alderwood, maybe as far in as Gordon Canyon. At least at first."

Jonathan said, "If we're coming in from the north, how do we get to the mountain? There's a creek in the way."

"You'll notice I put everything in waterproof bags. You're going to be crossing the creek."

Jesse said, "How long do you want us to stay out there?"

"Just a few days. There's a hand-held short wave in your pack. Call me every day at 7 AM and 8 PM."

Jonathan said, "Why don't we use the cell phones?"

"I put a cell phone in your pack, Jonathan. I left the battery out so they can't track you. You only want to use it as a last resort. I'm only keeping two, one for you and one for me. The feds will be all over my place tomorrow, maybe tonight, and we don't want to give them any leads. The radio in your pack uses the amateur radio band. Just get to a high spot and my big antenna will pull you in. Now, if you can't get ahold of me, don't worry, but if you can't get ahold of me two times in a row, bug out."

Jonathan said, "Bug out? Where?"

Jesse said, "Gisela."

Joe said, "Right."

Jonathan said, "What's a Gisela?"

Jesse said, "It's a town. Our family has emergency plans, for bugging out. Gisela is where we meet up."

Jonathan said, "Well I don't even know where that is."

Joe said, "Look." He took a marker, drew a circle around Lost Camp Mountain and said, "This is your base camp." He drew a circle around Gisela. "And here is your destination." He drew a line from the base camp, ran it along Haigler Creek to the Tonto Creek, and down along the Tonto to Gisela.

Maria said, "Okay, now get that map off my table and finish your dinner so I can make it look like it's only the two of us here."

Joe said, "That's my girl."

Maria said, "You're going to get it."

"I'm counting on it."

Jesse said, "Get a room."

JONATHAN SAT BEHIND JESSE on her horse, his arms wrapped around her as Joe led them though the darkness. Their backpacks were tied onto Joe's horse. They rode north for a while, following a low ridge, then headed west through open country along the edge of a thick pine forest.

Joe said, "Those woods between us and the Big Ridge Trail would be a good place to hide out if you needed to. There's plenty of game in there, too."

Jonathan said, "How can he see where he's going?"

"Papa knows every inch of the Tonto. He grew up here."

Joe said, "Hell, the horses know every inch of the Tonto. I'm just along for the ride. Listen, you two should try to stay away from any large predators. They can become desperate in drought conditions, attack prey they wouldn't ordinarily go near."

Jonathan said, "No problem."

"What brought that to mind is I can smell mountain lion."

"I wondered what that was."

"One of those big kitties marked his territory. Anyway, be careful where you camp. That escarpment might be home to a mountain lion or a bear. Use your judgment. Look for signs. And if you start any fires, keep them small and out of sight, like in a recess or small cave or something, and only build a fire if you're cooking something you've caught or shot."

Jonathan said, "We have to find our own food?"

"No, you don't have to find your own food. I've packed enough food to last you for five days. But I know my Jesse, and once she gets a look at those native browns in the Haigler, there'll be fresh fish on the menu. Now, the safest time to cook food is when any hikers downstream at Hell's Gate are cooking, too. If you smell them cooking their catch, you go ahead and cook yours. Then put the fire out quickly."

Jesse said, "I just might shoot some rabbit."

Jonathan said, "Won't the hikers hear the shots?"

Joe said, "That's why I packed sub-sonics."

Jonathan said, "Sub-sonics?"

"That loud crack you hear when you fire a .22 is the sound of the bullet breaking the sound barrier. Breaking it two times, really. Once speeding up and once slowing down. Sub-sonic ammo is designed to travel below the speed of sound. The loudest thing you'll hear is the gun's mechanism operating."

Jesse said, "I thought you weren't supposed to use subsonic ammo in rifles."

"I think they'll work just fine in that little bolt action Savage. Oh, there it is."

Joe turned and headed into a canyon and they were now moving in a southwest direction. They slowed down as the horses carefully worked their way past boulders, loose gravel, and thick brush.

Jonathan thought he heard rushing water in the distance. The farther they rode the louder the sound got until they came upon a series of deep, quiet pools of water. The sound of rushing water Jonathan had heard was coming from downstream. They dismounted from their horses.

Joe said, "Make camp here. You don't want to cross the Haigler in the dark. You'd have to sleep in wet clothes. Get up early tomorrow, cross the creek, and follow the canyon up a little ways on the other side. If you circle around to the north you'll find some overhangs and shallow caves. Jonathan?"

"Yes?"

"I'm counting on you to take care of my Jesse."

"I will, Sir."

"Hide when you can, but if the cops find you, get down on the ground, face down, and stretch out your hands. Don't give them a reason to shoot you."

"I won't, sir, you can be sure of that."

"They think you killed one of their own, and they're not going to give you the benefit of the doubt." He sighed and said, "You take care of that leg, Jesse."

Jesse said, "Papa?" and threw her arms around his neck.

Joe said, "I love you, Jesse," climbed back on his horse and started back up the canyon, leading Jesse's horse behind him. A moment later he disappeared into the darkness.

TWENTY

JONATHAN TRIED TO FALL ASLEEP, but every time he started to doze off he would hear an animal scurrying in the bushes—sometimes in the distance, sometimes close by—and he would wake with a start. Whenever that happened, he looked over at Jesse. She was always fast asleep. This went on for several hours until he thought he noticed the eastern sky start to lighten and gave up on getting any sleep. Pretty soon he saw some feathery pink hints of clouds against the blue, and decided it was time to get started. "Jesse, wake up," he said close to her ear. "It's morning."

Jesse opened her eyes and looked around. "We need more light. Let's eat something and let the sun rise a little higher." She untied the straps on her backpack and dug out a gallon size baggy. She tossed it to Jonathan. She said, "Here. I need to pee," and walked away towards some trees.

Jonathan opened the baggie and pulled out a power bar. He was eating it when Jessie returned. Jessie dug out a bar and the two of them ate in silence. When they were finished, Jessie slid a plastic water bottle out of a pocket on the side of the pack, and shared it with Jonathan.

When breakfast was over, Jesse took the camera out of her backpack, hanging it around her neck with a strap, pulled out an empty baggie, and handed it to Jonathan. "Put your pistol in here until we get to the other side. It's time to go."

"It doesn't look very deep."

"It's not. There hasn't been any rain for a while. When it rains these pools turn wild. Muddy and wild. But we'd better not talk in case somebody is camping nearby."

Jesse stepped gingerly into the edge of the creek, feeling the rocky bottom with her feet. A few more steps and she sank into the deep pool, swimming quickly but quietly across. By the time she reached the opposite bank, she had drifted downstream a little. She turned around and motioned for Jonathan to follow.

Jonathan stood at the bank's edge staring at the water.

Jesse motioned Come on with her hand.

Jonathan didn't move.

She whispered, "Hurry up."

Jonathan still didn't move.

"Now."

Jonathan stepped into the shallow water and eased into the cool, deep pool.

By the time he reached the opposite bank, Jesse had removed her backpack and was taking pictures of him with the GoPro. She set the camera down on a boulder and reached out to him, helping him climb out of the water. She opened his backpack and retrieved the pistol. She pulled it out of the baggie and handed it to him, saying, "Let's get away from the creek."

Jonathan strapped the pistol back onto his belt and followed Jesse upwards through the canyon. It was rough and rocky, with pine trees, thorny brush, and loose granite. Jesse seemed unaffected by the climb, taking pictures the whole time. When they reached higher ground, Jesse veered to the right and headed west, upwards across open country. She followed the rounded contour of the peak of the mountain for a short distance, and led them down into a secluded area between a peak to the west and an escarpment to the east. The rocky face of the escarpment jutted up and out over the area like a canopy, providing cover and shade. Under the canopy were several shallow caves. Jesse walked over to the shaded area, dropped her backpack and said, "Honey, I'm home."

He said, "Where the heck are we?"

Jesse motioned with her hand. "This is Lost Camp Mountain. We just climbed out of Lost Camp Canyon."

"Appropriately named," he said, dropping his backpack next to hers. "Let's have a look at your leg."

"Masher."

"You made a joke. Really, let's have a look."

"I can take care of it."

"If I let you get gangrene your Mama is going to shoot me. Where's the first aid kit?"

"It's in your backpack."

Jonathan dug the first aid kit out of his backpack, along with a towel and plastic pint bottle. Wrapped around the bottle was a note. It read: Tequila. Use sparingly. Love, Mama. He took Jesse's leg in his hand and unwrapped the dressing.

Jesse said, "How's it look?"

"It's healing nicely." He poured tequila over the wound.

"It doesn't hurt much at all."

"You just need to keep it clean and you'll be fine." He dabbed her leg dry with the towel, squeezed out a line of Neosporin on the wound, and taped a bandage on it. He said, "There," and set her foot back down.

"Thank you."

"So, where do we go from here?"

"Nowhere. This is where we hole up."

"For how long?"

"Until Neela says it's safe."

"They won't find us here?"

"They might, but it will take them a while. If it rains, they won't be able to track us to the river."

"You think it's going to rain?"

"We're due for the Monsoon rains."

"Monsoon. Mark talked about that."

"The seasonal change in the prevailing winds. In the winter our weather comes in from the west. This time of year we get storms up from Mexico. Sometimes it rains every night."

"Well I haven't seen any rain yet, just this humidity. I thought it was supposed to be a dry heat?"

"It is, up until the— "

"Monsoon."

"Right. Hey, let's stash our gear and have a look around."

After they secured their gear in the largest of the caves, Jesse lead the way out from under the overhang. She was carrying the rifle and a small day pack. She handed the pack to Jonathan and stopped at the edge of the shade.

"We're going to scout the area for other people. We'll hike along the ridge of the mountain parallel to Haigler Creek and stay hidden in the trees. Now remember, we're not in a hurry. Try not to make any sound and be careful where you step. If we stay quiet we'll hear any hikers or fisherman. They make a lot of noise. What I worry about are hunters. Some of those old boys are stealthy. The point is, we don't want to be seen or heard."

Jonathan nodded. Jesse walked out of their hiding place and turned west.

Jonathan said, "But shouldn't we check if— "

Jesse stopped and turned around. She put her finger to her lips, turned back, and continued walking. There wasn't any trail, but Jesse seemed to know where they were going. Travel was rough; the terrain was steep, and the ground was covered with jagged rocks, pine cones and fallen branches. Jonathan started to sweat. Every once in a while a breeze would blow and Jonathan would shiver while the entire forest would come to life in a chorus of swaying branches. When the wind subsided, it became quiet again, except for the trickling of distant Haigler creek and the chatter of wakening birds and squirrels. At one point Jesse pointed the rifle barrel at some animal droppings and whispered, "Black bear."

They walked for about an hour before Jesse stopped and motioned towards Jonathan's pack. Jonathan removed the pack and handed it to Jesse, who reached in and took out a bottle of water. She handed it to Jonathan but he refused to take it. Jesse took a swig of water and handed it back to Jonathan, who then took a drink. Jesse handed the pack to Jonathan. He put the water bottle away, and the two of them marched on.

About a half an hour later, Jesse lead them close to the edge of the mountain overlooking the creek. They peeked out from behind a tree. Jesse leaned in close to Jonathan's ear. "Leo Canyon," she said. "Remind me to tell you about it. We're getting close to Hells Gate, so we have to be extra careful." Jonathan nodded.

They hiked for another hour-and-a-half when Jesse stopped next to a tree and pointed north. Leaning in she said, "Tonto Creek. Hells Gate is a little ways up stream."

"Now what?" Jonathan said.

"We wait." She propped the rifle against a rock, sat down and motioned for the pack. They had a drink of water and ate some Peanut M&Ms. Jonathan had a look at Jesse's wound and when he determined it wasn't getting infected he gave her a "thumbs up". They lounged there for a while, listening to the Tonto and Haigler creeks merging together in the distance below. Above them they heard a squirrel arguing with a jay. It was a beautiful day.

After a while Jesse stood up, shouldered the rifle, and started back towards their camp. Jonathan stumbled to his feet, sliding his arms into the backpack shoulder straps, and hurried to catch up to Jesse.

"I thought we were supposed to be quiet," he said.

"There's nobody camping at Hells Gate. They'd be up by now and we would have heard them. That doesn't mean that there won't be anybody coming in from up along the Tonto, but most of those people will head on back up the Tonto, or camp out overnight at Hells Gate before they hike on up the Haigler. We're good for the rest of the day from here to our campsite."

"Those are the only two ways in?" he said.

"There's always a chance somebody might come up the Smoky Hollow Trail, but we would have seen the dust from their four wheelers from miles away, and they'd be headed to Hells Gate anyway to splash in the pools. Hikers and people on horseback coming in from the north tend to stay on the north side of Haigler Creek. Now we need to get back and watch for any hikers or fishermen moving in from upstream on the Haigler. That's probably the direction the police will be coming from, by the way."

"That's what I was wondering about," he said. "When we were leaving the camp I wanted to ask you why we didn't look in that direction."

"They're not going to start out looking way out here. When they were looking for Fisher, they searched the local campsites and spelunking caves for him. They'll search those places before they decide to fan out."

"Why wouldn't they look here?"

"Because they don't know I'm helping you. All they do know is you're a guy from the suburbs. You're not going to go solo hiking in the Hellsgate Wilderness. If they do figure out that we've gone this way, they won't know where to look. Even with dogs they won't have our scent anywhere near the direction we went. The only thing we have to worry about for a while is being spotted by hikers, horseman, hunters, and fishermen."

"What about aircraft and drones?"

"They won't see us."

"You know they search with infrared sensors, don't you?"

"You think they'll be able to detect us in this heat, under that granite roof?"

"I suppose not."

By the time they got back to camp the sun was high in the sky and the clouds were starting to gather over the Tonto Rim to the north. The air seemed extra thick with humidity and Jonathan was having trouble breathing. Happy to be back under shade of the overhang, he sat down and poked around in the larger backpack.

Jesse said, "What's for lunch?"

"Salami and canned cheese on crackers."

"I've got some self-heating dinners in my pack. They're actually pretty good. We'll wait until dark to do any cooking, but I don't think anybody will be camping close by. They'll be upstream at Alderwood or way down at Hells Gate."

After lunch Jonathan and Jesse spread their padded ground cloths out under the overhang and fell asleep on them. About three o'clock Jonathan woke up covered with sweat. He looked around and Jesse was gone. He bolted to his feet and looked outside the cave. There was nobody there. A moment later Jesse appeared from around the escarpment.

"Where were you?"

"I was setting up our kaibo."

"Our what?"

"Kaibo. Outhouse."

He stared at her.

"I dug a hole to use." She tossed him a roll of toilet paper. "It's behind a tree on the next hill over."

"Come to think of it," he said, as he headed for the next hill over.

When Jonathan got back, they sat in silence for a while. Finally Jonathan said, "So what is the story behind Leo Canyon?"

"Oh, yeah. I didn't want to talk back there. It's named after Leo, the famous MGM lion."

"They named a canyon in Arizona after a Hollywood lion?"

"They did indeed. It was back in the 1920s. MGM wanted to fly Leo from San Diego to New York. As a publicity stunt. So they built this special cage on the back of the plane with controls on it. This way the pilot could pull a lever and give Leo some milk. Anyway, this guy's flying this old-fashioned airplane, the kind Lindbergh flew across the Atlantic in, and with the cage and the lion and the extra fuel, he can't make it over the Mogollon Rim. There's too much weight. So they crashed into that canyon. Years later the Forest Service named the canyon after Leo."

"Did the lion die in the crash?"

"No, neither Leo nor the pilot was seriously injured. The pilot hiked out and got help. Poor Leo was stuck there for a week before they could find him and haul him out of there. When they did it was a big event up in Payson. They let the kids out of school and everything."

Later, when the shadows were long, Jesse opened two bags of Chicken Pasta Italiana self-heating meals. She put the meal bags inside the heater bags and poured in the heating liquids. Ten minutes later, the food was hot, ready to eat.

When they finished their dinner, Jesse said, "Are you still hungry? We've got all kinds of canned and dehydrated stuff."

"No, thank you. This Arizona weather is killing my appetite."

"I know what you mean."

IT WAS LATE AFTERNOON by the time Joe heard the commotion. He walked out onto the porch and saw his dogs menacing two men in a government sedan. He said, "Diablo, leave it," and the dogs sat quietly. The men carefully exited the car and walked up to the porch. They showed him their badges.

One of the men said, "Joseph Conrad?"

"Yes?"

We're with the F.B.I. Have you seen this man?" He showed him a printout of Jonathan's photo.

"Yes, I have."

"You have? Where did you last see him?"

"On TV."

"You haven't seen him in person?"

"No, I have not."

"Do you mind if I search your property?"

"Do you have a search warrant?"

"Sir, in an emergency situation a search warrant is not necessary in order to protect public safety."

Joe looked around. "I'm afraid I don't understand what the emergency is."

"Sir, every one of your neighbors has cooperated with us so far. Is there any particular reason you won't?"

"You mean other than the fourth amendment to the Constitution?"

"Sir, is Jonathan Starker holding you against your will?"

Joe laughed. "No, it appears you are."

Maria walked out onto the porch with her rifle in her hands.

"Sir, we can have a swat team down here in ten minutes. Do you really want that?"

Joe said, "Maria, go back inside. Gentlemen, I will grant you permission to search the house this one time."

The men entered the house and asked Maria for her rifle. When she refused, Joe asked her for it and she gave it to him. He unloaded it and set it down on the couch. The men asked for Joe's handgun and he set it on the couch next to the rifle. The men looked angry but didn't push any farther.

The men went through every room and searched closets, under beds, and in showers. One of the men asked what the door in the back of the kitchen went to.

Joe said, "I'll let you in there, but there's something I need to show you first so you don't shit your pants. He walked into his bedroom and came out with a file full of papers. He laid the file down on the kitchen table and opened it, spreading the papers out. There were licenses and permits for the weapons in the basement. The men looked the papers over, exchanging glances and shaking their heads.

Joe said, "Seen enough?"

"Yeah."

Joe unlocked the door and led them into the room, saying as he walked down the steps, "Don't touch anything."

When they reached the basement, the men were stunned. One of them said, "You have paperwork for all of these?"

"What did I just show you?"

"Why do you need all these weapons?"

"That's none of your damn business. Everything here is legal, I have no criminal record, and there is no fugitive hiding here. Now get the hell out of my home."

One of the men smirked and said, "All right, Grandpa," and they headed back up the stairs. They left the house and wandered around the property, looking through the stable and in storage buildings before driving away.

ROBERTS DROVE TO PAYSON and parked around the back of the Majestic Mountain Inn. The only motel in Star Valley had been full so they had driven a few miles farther down the 260 and ended up here. When he entered the room, Valdo was lying in a bubbling hot tub.

Roberts said, "Are you comfortable?"

"Screw you."

"You'd like that." He looked at the bed. It was king size and the wall next to it was covered in mirror. "I told you to get two beds."

"This was all they had available. You're sleeping on the sofa."

"Hey, I paid for this room."

"Too bad. So what's going on back at the ranch?"

"Meanwhile?"

"What?"

"Never mind. I didn't see anybody leave. The Feds came around but they didn't find Starker. He must have a good hiding place under the floor boards or something."

"He could've snuck out. That place is surrounded by trees."

"Nah, I think he's still there. I also think somebody is feeding them information, may be the guy who works for Phoenix P.D."

"So?"

"We need something stronger to flush them out. If I tell the Feds about the girl, put them on her heels, and they hear about it, you know they'll bolt."

"So how you gonna grab them before the Feds do?"

"Let's wait a day or two for things to quiet down around Young, then we'll make our move."

JESSE SAID, "It's almost eight. We should call Papa." She picked up the walkie-talkie and said, "We need to get to that peak." She pointed to a high point a short distance away. "There." She put a battery in the radio and they walked to the peak. At eight o'clock she squeezed the call button and said, "Hello, Papa?"

"Hello, Jesse. How are you doing?"

"We're fine. Do you have any news?"

"Well, we had a visitor today."

"The same as before?"

"No, someone new. An official visitor."

"Oh, no. How did Mama take it?"

"Everything went fine."

"Good. Did you talk to Neela?"

"Yes, we talked this morning and again just before you called. She's getting antsy. She said she's going to do some deeper investigating."

"Tell her to be careful."

"She knows, Honey. Look, um …"

"What?"

"It's about Tyler."

"Did Neela bring him his motorcycle?"

"Yes, she did, only …"

"What is it, Papa?"

"Tyler's dead. Somebody shot him."

"Oh my God."

"I know, Sweetheart. I'm so sorry."

"You be careful, Papa."

"You too. I'll talk to you tomorrow."

"Tell Mama I love her."

"I will."

Jesse removed the battery.

Jonathan said, "Tyler?"

"I don't want to talk about it."

They walked back to the cave in silence.

TWENTY-ONE

JONATHAN WAS DREAMING he heard a child scream when he realized the scream was real. He woke with a start and heard it again. He shook Jesse awake and said, "What was that?"

"What?" She rubbed her eyes and said, "What time is it?"

There was another scream.

Jesse said, "Oh, that. That's a mountain lion."

"I thought lions roared?"

"Not mountain lions. They scream."

"Do you think they're close?"

"Hard to tell. I didn't see any scat or paw prints near the cave, otherwise we wouldn't have camped here."

Jonathan was soaked in sweat. He said, "Why is it so warm?"

"You're in Arizona."

"No, I mean, it's the middle of the night and I'm still sweating."

"If it would just rain, it would cool down at night, but as it is, the cloud cover holds in the heat. Go to sleep." She turned away and buried her head in her sleeping bag.

"Good night."

"Good night."

* * *

JONATHAN WOKE UP to Jesse's whisper, "Wakey wakey." He looked around and saw it was still dark out with just a hint of sunrise.

He said, "What's going on?"

"Let's go fishing. I don't feel like eating beef jerky and trail mix for breakfast."

They took turns visiting the kaibo before setting off for the creek. When they reached the bank, Jesse carefully unwound a few yards of line from a drop line rig onto the ground. She held the line a few feet from the end, swinging it around in a circle over her head and tossing the weighted lure towards the stream. It landed about half way across. She started winding the line back onto the rig. Jonathan saw the fuzzy lure meandering back towards them like a bug swimming through the water. When the lure reached the shore, Jesse let some line out again and cast it back out. After several attempts, she finally caught the attention of a large brown trout. It followed the lure, and Jesse wound the line quicker, increasing the speed. The trout closed in on it and struck. Jesse jerked the line, setting the hook in the fish's jaw. The fish made a run away from the shore, and Jesse let out some line while keeping tension on the it, then slowly wound it in. They repeated their routine, the trout running and Jesse winding, until she had worked it close to the shore.

She said, "Get the net."

Jonathan picked up the net, took a step towards the stream and froze.

"Get it."

The trout flipped over and escaped the hook, swimming away at top speed.

"That was breakfast."

"I'm sorry."

"That's okay." She handed the drop line to Jonathan. "You do it.

I'll handle the net."

"I'll try."

With Jesse taking photos, Jonathan let out some line and spun the weight around in a circle. The circle was too wide and the line caught on a tree. It took him fifteen minutes to untangle it. He tried it again and this time succeeded in casting the line, but managed to cast it too far and get it caught on a stump on the far bank. After a few pulls he popped the line clear and wound it back in. The third time he cast it perfectly. This time a rainbow trout noticed the lure and struck. Jonathan wound the line and pulled it towards shore where Jesse netted it. She unhooked it from the line and tied it to a stringer cord, setting it in the water. Jonathan cast out again and this time he caught a large brown trout.

Jesse gutted and scaled their catch and they headed back to camp. On the way they ran across a small rattlesnake. Jonathan almost stepped on it.

Jesse snapped a picture of it and said, "Don't move." She walked wide around Jonathan and the snake and disappeared around the corner. He stood there watching the snake rattle its tail, waiting for what seemed a long time but was probably just a minute or two until Jesse came back carrying her rifle. She eased slowly up to Jonathan and lowered the barrel of the rifle until it was lined up with the head of the snake. She squeezed the trigger. The snake's head exploded and its body writhed on the ground. Jesse pulled the knife she had cleaned the fish with out of its sheath and cut the pulpy head off the snake. She kicked the head into a bush and picked up the body. It was still twitching.

When they got back to camp, Jonathan made a fire while Jesse skinned the snake. They placed the snake next to the fish on a folding grill and slid the grill over the fire. They cooked and ate their catch and there were no leftovers.

By the time they had finished their breakfast, the sun was up and the temperature was rising, so they moved into the shade in the back of the cave. They lay down on their sleeping bags and dozed off.

VALDO AND ROBERTS returned to Young and found a spot where they could park and watch the ranch house through binoculars. Roberts opened his phone and punched in a phone number. "Hi, it's me ... Yeah ... Yeah, here's what I need you to do. I need you to put out the word that Starker has an accomplice ... Yeah, he's being helped ... Right ... The accomplice is a woman, and they're hiding out at the woman's parents house up in Young ... No, no names, just what I told you. Can you do that? Great."

Valdo said, "Why didn't you do that in the first place? You wasted a lot of time making the cops think Starker was up here."

"I didn't realize before they were getting inside information. Now that the search has died down, we can feed them some bullshit, they'll get tipped off, and they'll bolt. That's when we grab them."

"You think they're still there?"

"Positive."

"I think they're already gone. I would be."

"Well we can't all be as smart as a bar bouncer."

JOE GOT A CALL on his short wave radio. It was Harry, a friend of his in Oregon. Harry had gotten a call from Neela, who told him to have Joe call her. Joe put a battery in the phone and punched the speed dial number.

"Joe?"

"Neela. How did you know about Harry?"

"It's my job to know about things. Look, Joe, I heard some talk about the case. The buzz is they know about Jesse."

"Oh, Jeez. Roberts must have tipped them off."

"Well here's the weird part. I can't confirm it with my sources in law enforcement. Either this is the most tight lipped they've ever been or they don't know themselves, which means it could be a set-up."

"We can't take any chances. Maria and I are going to have to leave. When Jesse can't get ahold of us, she'll know to leave, too. We worked it out before they left. In any bug-out situation they're to meet us in Gisela."

"I'm not 100% on this information."

"It doesn't matter. They've been out there long enough."

"All right, Joe. You be careful."

"Thanks, Neela."

They grabbed their bags and headed out the door.

On the way out of town, Joe pulled into his neighbor's driveway. The Stevens were the Conrads' friends going back for generations, and could be trusted to keep their mouths shut.

Joe knocked on the door and Karl Stevens answered. "Oh, hi, Joe."

"Hi, Karl. We're going to be gone for a few days. Would you mind tending to the animals?" Karl had a key to the house and the dogs knew him.

"No, not at all. Do you know when you'll be coming back?"

"I'm not sure yet. I'll call if it's going to be more than two days. And Karl, if anybody comes snooping around, don't tell them where we are."

"That'll be easy. I don't know where you're going."

"Yeah, that's right. Very good then."

"You be careful, Joe."

"Thanks, Karl."

VALDO AND ROBERTS WAITED an hour before the old couple left in their pickup truck. When they stopped down the street, Valdo got out of the car and moved in close, scooting tree-by-tree until he was squatting down in the driveway right behind the truck. He peeked over the tailgate and dropped back down. Satisfied, he moved stealthily back to the car.

Roberts said, "Man, you are really nimble."

"Shut up."

"No, I mean it. A guy your size, you move like a ballerina. Jeez. That hot tub must have done you some good, huh? By the way, are they in the truck?"

"No."

"Shit. I thought for sure they'd sneak out with grandpa. They must still be in the house."

"Unless they already left."

"I don't know. But I do know we can find out now. Let's check out the ranch."

Valdo pulled into the driveway and up to the house. The dogs appeared almost instantly, barking and snarling. Valdo calmly reached back and retrieved his Pelican case. He removed his Ruger MKII and screwed on the suppressor, rolled his window down a crack, aimed the weapon at the largest dog and squeezed the trigger. The dog fell to the ground without even a yelp. He repeated the action, killing the other two dogs before stepping out of the car. They walked up to the front door and Valdo shot the lockset. The door wouldn't budge. He shot it four more times before they were able to go inside.

They turned the house upside down but couldn't find any clues about where Starker and the Conrad girl had gone, so they helped themselves to beers and sat down in the living room.

Roberts said, "That's some gun collection, huh?"

Valdo said, "We're lucky they didn't stay here and stand their ground."

"Hell, they're lucky. The ATF would have torched this place. So where do we look for them?"

Valdo was leafing through a large photo album on the coffee

table. Roberts leaned over as he turned the page and came upon old wedding photos. Roberts said, "Is that interesting?"

Valdo kept turning the pages. He turned one of the pages back and looked closely at one of the photos. He said, "Do you have that guy's phone?"

"Who?"

"The mechanic."

"Yeah, why?"

"Are there any pictures on it?"

Roberts went out to the car and came back with the phone. He opened the phone and navigated to the gallery where he found pictures of cars and airplanes and aerial photographs. He kept flipping the photos with his thumb until he came upon a photo of the girl. He flipped to the next one and it was the mechanic and the girl in the woods. The next one showed them holding fishing gear and a string of fish. Roberts read the caption, "Lost Camp Canyon".

Valdo pointed to a photograph in the album. It was the girl, but about ten years old, holding a string of fish. Below the photograph was a caption, hand-crafted out of green card stock. The caption was, "Lost Camp Canyon."

Roberts went back into the office he had just trashed and shuffled through the papers on the floor. He found a map and brought it back to the living room, spreading it out on the coffee table. They looked through the map and found nothing useful, so they flipped the map over and Roberts said, "There." It was Lost Camp Canyon.

Valdo shook his head in agreement and said, "On that river. That's a long way from here."

"Not really. Look at the scale."

"This line, is that a road?"

"That's a fire control road."

"You think my car would make it?"

"We'll find out. Tomorrow morning."

"Why not go now?"

"Did you see those clouds out there? Those are thunderheads. I don't want to get stuck in the middle of a lightening storm. We'll go first thing, catch them off guard. In the meantime, we need to leave. It could get real busy around here."

"In a minute." Valdo went into the basement and came out with an armful of guns.

Roberts grabbed the map and the photo album and followed him to the car.

TWENTY-TWO

JONATHAN HAD BEEN in and out of sleep for an hour or two when he heard the voices. Jesse sat up. She must have heard them, too. There were people down by the creek. Jesse tiptoed out of the cave and Jonathan followed. They worked their way down the canyon, slipping behind rocks and bushes until they had a clear view of Haigler Creek. Three young men were wading downstream, floating their back packs in front of them. They were laughing and joking as they stumbled and slipped along the wet rocks. Jonathan and Jesse tried to stay as quiet as they could until the hikers had passed.

The sun rose higher and the shadow from the overhang moved slowly across the cave, and they moved their ground cloths along with it. Around mid-day Jonathan looked though his backpack and found a stick of Genoa salami. In her bag Jesse found a box of melba toast and powdered orange drink. Jesse poured the orange drink into a quart water bottle, and lunch was served.

After lunch Jonathan said, "I haven't looked at your bullet wound lately."

"Oh, please. It's healed."

He knew she was right but he wanted to anyway. He enjoyed taking care of her instead of being the dependent one. "Let me have a look."

"I told you it's healed."

"Maria will kill me if I don't."

"No."

"Just one last time. Kind of like a follow-up appointment. If it's healed I won't bother you again, I promise."

"Okay. One last time."

Jonathan brought out the first aid kit and the tequila, and carefully unwrapped the bandage on her leg.

Jesse grabbed the bottle and said, "Hell, I'm bored. I can't stand being stuck in this cave." She unscrewed the lid on the bottle of orange drink and turned the tequila bottle upside down over the mouth of the bottle. The tequila poured in with a chug-chug-chug sound. She put the lid back on the bottle and shook it, opened the drink spout, and squeezed a stream of mixed drink into her mouth. She coughed and handed the bottle to Jonathan.

Jonathan said, "No, thank you."

"Why not? There's nothing else to do. Maybe it will take our minds off this awful humidity." She raised her arms, exposing dark rings of sweat running down her shirt.

"I don't drink."

"I don't either. I mean I drank a lot when I was in college, but not much anymore." She held the bottle out again. "Come on, just this once?"

"No thank you."

"Suit yourself."

Jonathan said, "Oh, what the hell," and grabbed the bottle. He took a small squirt and made a face. "Why do people like this crap?"

"It's better with real orange juice."

Jonathan took another squirt—a generous amount. He sat back and in a moment felt relaxed for the first time since he left California. They passed the bottle back and forth and after a while the orange drink cocktail tasted pretty good. Finally when Jonathan squeezed the bottle, nothing came out. He tilted the bottle back and managed to coax a few more ounces. He tossed the bottle aside and said, "I guess we drank it all," turned to Jesse and said, "May I ask you something?"

"Sure, anything."

"Why did you leave the television station? Were you fired?"

Jesse laughed. "No, I wasn't fired. I quit."

"So why'd you quit?"

"I got into journalism because I wanted to make a difference in the world. I thought I could do that by exposing corruption and revealing the truth."

He nodded in agreement. "Revealing the truth."

"Speaking truth to power."

He raised his fist. "Truth to power."

Jesse looked sad. There was a long pause until Jonathan said, "So did you?"

"What?"

"Expose corruption and all that?"

"I tried to, but I found out the news media isn't interested in the truth. All they're interested in is their ratings and their narrative."

"Narrative?"

"I don't want to talk about it."

"Okay."

After a long period of silence, Jesse reached into her shirt and fiddled with her bra. She pulled the bra through her left sleeve and tossed it towards the corner of the cave, where it landed next to Jonathan.

Jonathan said, "Feel better?"

"A little."

She leaned back against the granite wall and said, "Let's have fish again tomorrow."

"Absolutely. I hadn't eaten fresh trout since ..."

"You've had it before?"

"Yeah. I used to go fishing with my dad."

Jesse smiled. "Tell me about your dad."

"Is that the journalist asking?"

"No. No. Well, yes. But I really am interested. He used to take you fishing?"

"Yeah."

"Where?"

"All over. The first time I remember was at a place called Laguna Lake in Fullerton. I caught a blue gill about this big." He held out his hand with his thumb and forefinger stretched apart. "When I got older we used to go to Huntington Beach. Sometimes we'd go surf fishing, but most of the time we'd fish off the pier."

"Did you ever catch anything?"

"Oh, yeah. Mostly sand dabs at the beach. My friend, Michael, caught this huge halibut off the pier. We had to use a gaff on the end of a rope to land it."

"Did you ever fish anywhere else?"

"We went deep sea fishing a few times. I got seasick but we caught some bonita and barracuda."

"How about river fishing? Is that where you caught the trout?"

Jonathan fell silent.

Jesse said, "What's the matter?"

"I was just thinking."

"About what?"

"River fishing."

"Which river?"

"The Kern."

"Did you catch a lot of fish there?"

"A few."

"Is that where you lost your father?"

Jonathan's eyes welled up. He said, "Yes."

"What happened?"

Jonathan looked down and held his chin in his hand.

Jesse said, "Are you okay?"

"Yes. It's just that I've never told anyone about my dad."

"We can talk about something else."

"No, I want to tell you. I feel I can tell you anything."

Jesse's eyes welled up.

Jonathan said, "It was in the summer. I was twelve. We were camped out next to the Kern, doing some trout fishing. It was really hot out—like here—so we decided to go swimming." He looked around and couldn't find a towel so he dabbed his eyes with her bra. "The Kern isn't like this little creek. It's a lot bigger, and strong. But where we were camped it was slow because the river was shallow and really wide. At first it was awesome. The water was so cool and we were floating along having a great time. But the river got narrower and started running faster. We could hear the rapids up ahead and my dad said to get out, but we couldn't. The bank was muddy and we couldn't get a foothold. We tried to grab some reeds growing up near the bank, but when we grabbed them they just pulled out of the mud. It got even faster but we were helpless against it. We could see the rapids, and just before we got to them we saw a tree growing out of the river near the shore. We managed to grab hold of it, but the force of the water was pulling on us, pulling us down. My head was underwater and I was holding on with my fingertips dug into the bark. I don't know how but I managed to pull myself back and wedge myself between the flow of the river and the tree, so that the pressure was pinning me against it. Once I did that, I was able to climb up the trunk out of the water. I sat down on a branch and when I looked back at the river, I saw my dad being pulled under. He was looking up at me from underwater as he was swept away. I saw him bounce off a boulder and there was blood in the water. Then he was gone."

Jesse sat next to Jonathan and held him in her arms. She said, "That's why you're afraid of the water."

He shook his head yes.

Jonathan gathered himself, wiping his eyes and clearing his throat. Changing the subject, he said, "I never did get a look at your wound."

Jesse said, "I guess you'll have to do it without the tequila."

"Yeah, well you said it was healed. I just have to make sure."

Jonathan stood up to move over so he could face Jesse and look at her leg. He felt dizzy and wondered if he had too much to drink. He carefully removed the bandage and looked closely at the wound. It was healing nicely and he didn't think it needed the bandage any more.

After he finished inspecting it he held on to Jesse's leg. He caressed her leg next to the scar and said, "I think it's healed." He continued caressing her leg, moving a little higher.

Jesse's voice sounded different. "Are you sure?"

He moved his hand up to her knee. "Yeah, I think your leg looks ... very nice."

She stood up and said, "Um, I have an idea. Come on." She took Jonathan by the hand and led him to the creek. When they got there, she took his hands in hers and stepped backwards into the water. "Let's go swimming."

"What, what if somebody sees us?"

"Anybody coming in from upstream would have passed this way already. Besides, if we're quiet, we'll hear if anybody approaches."

"I don't know."

"Look, I'm hot and sweaty, and the water is clean and cool. If we're going to enjoy it we have to do it now."

He stood motionless.

"Come on. It's okay."

Jonathan stepped into the water.

She said, "Oh, wait," and pulled a baggie out of her pocket.

Jonathan removed the holster from his belt and sealed it up in the bag. The two of them slipped into the cold water, Jonathan carrying the bag over his head. Jesse drifted next to him, close enough for him to feel her breath on his ear when she said, "Are you okay?"

It was then Jonathan realized he had been so distracted by her he forgot to panic about the water. His face flushed as he said, "Yeah, I'm okay."

As they drifted downstream, the canyon narrowed and the cliffs grew in height, blocking the sun. The swimmers stopped in a shallow pool just above a small waterfall a few feet high. Jesse climbed out onto a narrow ledge. Jonathan followed her around the falls where he stashed his gun behind a tree. They slid down into a deep pool carved out of the bedrock. The water splashed down the waterfall and bubbled into the pool.

Jonathan said, "Jacuzzi!" as the two of them swam under the fall.

Jesse sighed. "Oh, I needed this." She closed her eyes and let the waterfall pour down over her head.

Jonathan drifted over next to her. When she opened her eyes he was looking into them. Jonathan inched closer to her until their bodies were touching. Jesse's skin got goose bumps, and Jonathan noticed a change in her expression. He wasn't sure what to do. He felt an intense desire to kiss her, but he didn't know what her reaction would be. They stood there, not moving, eyes locked, water flowing down over them and splashing around their bodies in a boil. Finally Jonathan couldn't hold back any longer. He put his arms around her and pulled her close to him. Her body felt hot in the midst of the cold stream. He pressed his lips onto hers. This was the moment he was anticipating—and dreading. How would she respond? Would she laugh? Would she kick his ass? Soon he had his answer. She wrapped her arms around him and kissed him back. She touched his face tenderly and they kissed again, intensely this time as he held her tight against him.

Light flashed around them.

Jesse stopped and looked up. "Lightning." Thunder rumbled in the distance.

Jonathan said, "Dammit."

They climbed out of the pool. He picked up his gun and they worked their way back to camp where they spread out their ground cloths as far into the cave as they could. They sat in silence as lightning flashed and rumbled through the valleys. The storm moved closer, the lightning flashing so close it seemed to crack like a whip, before passing over them and fading to the west. At one point, huge rain drops fell, but only a few and for only a moment. They evaporated as soon as they landed, and the air, already hot, became heavy with steam. A long time passed before Jesse said, "Do you want something to eat?"

"Sure."

Jesse poked around in her backpack and fished out some self-heating meals—beef stroganoff. After she got the meals started, she dug a dry shirt out of her pack, turned away from Jonathan, and changed. When the meals were ready they ate in silence.

After dinner they tried to raise Joe on the radio. There was no answer. Jonathan said, "What do you think it means?"

"I don't know. We'll try again in the morning."

When they got back, Jesse sat down next to Jonathan. She leaned back and rested her back against his chest.

Jonathan said, "You know, if I hadn't run into your truck, we never would have met."

"That's true." She grabbed his hand and said, "Jonathan, I have a confession to make."

"Yeah, I heard about you Catholics."

"Jonathan, listen."

"Okay, confess your sins, my child."

"I lied to you. You could have gone to the police right away, but I told you not to because I wanted the story."

"I know."

"What do you mean, you know."

"I know we could have turned ourselves in, I know you lied to me, and I know you did it to get a good story."

She looked stunned.

"Why did you let me lie to you?"

"I was afraid."

"Afraid of what?"

He struggled to find the words. "Not being with you. If I had turned myself in, that would have been the end of it. I never would have had this time with you."

She turned and pressed her lips to his and they shared a deep, tender kiss, lingering with their lips barely touching until Jonathan said, "And I never would have seen you in a wet t-shirt."

"You're damn right." She turned around and leaned back against him. After a moment she said, "So, you want trout again for breakfast?"

"Sure."

When Jonathan woke up the next morning, the sky was overcast, slivers of rising sun glowing through thick dark clouds. Jesse was still asleep. He spent a few minutes looking at her before gently kissing her cheek. She woke up and smiled, saying, "Good morning."

"Are we going fishing?"

"What time is it?" She looked around. "Oh, it's still early."

"Yes. It looks as if we might get another storm, too."

"We'd better hurry."

They gathered their fishing gear and trekked down to the creek. She unwound half the monofilament from the drop line and wound it onto a pine twig, attaching a lure and a weight to it. She gave the line to Jonathan and said, "Now we can catch breakfast twice as fast."

He said, "What do we do if we can't contact your dad? Are we leaving?"

"Papa said if we had to leave Lost Camp Mountain, we should head west to the Tonto, then south to Gisela. We have friends there."

"You don't think they'll be watching the people you know?"

"They can't watch everybody."

"Gisela it is, then. Are we taking the same route along the ridge?"

"We can't. If they know we're here they'll have all kinds of aircraft. We're going to have to stay covered."

"You don't mean …"

"The creek."

"Crap."

"It's narrow, it's surrounded by high canyon walls, and it's covered with trees. We'll be safe from aircraft. And the water will help cover our tracks."

"What about infrared?"

"Half the time we'll be chilled from the water. I think we'll be okay."

VALDO TOOK FOREST ROAD 129 northwest out of Young. The going was rough and the old car kept bottoming out, but he drove slowly and kept moving forward towards Lost Camp Canyon. Roberts was the navigator, opening up the map every once in a while to make sure they were on the right trail.

Roberts said, "I wasn't going to say anything, but you're starting to reek."

"I haven't had time to get to a dry cleaner. But what do you care? You're not my lover."

"Oh jeez, there's a mental image I didn't need. Why didn't you bring some clothes you could wash or throw away? I mean, look at you. We're in the middle of nowhere and you're wearing a suit."

"I like to look like a professional."

"Yeah, a professional idiot."

They drove down FR 129 for seven and a half miles and turned

west on Forest Road 133. There the road deteriorated, with deep
ruts caused by runoff cutting through the sand. The Crown Victo-
ria got stuck several times, and each time Valdo was able to get it
unstuck by using "fake" posi-traction: pressing down on the parking brake pedal just enough to encourage the non-spinning wheel
to turn and pull them out of the sand. A hundred yards in they got
so stuck he couldn't coax the car out of the rut. They stepped out of
the car and Valdo opened the trunk. He said, "We need something
to put under the tire."

"Well hurry up."

Valdo removed the upholstered sheet of hardboard covering the
spare tire, brought it out to the left rear tire and said, "We gotta dig
the dirt out first."

Roberts said, "Wait a minute." He was looking off in the distance. The sun was rising and Valdo had to shade his eyes with his
hand to see the cloud of dust approaching. Pretty soon he heard an
engine and could make out a utility quad vehicle coming their way.
Roberts stood in the road, holding up his wallet with the badge exposed. The rider stopped in front of him. Roberts said, "ATF agent.
I'm afraid I'm going to have to commandeer your vehicle."

The rider was a teenager, 15 years old at most. He said, "You're
kidding."

"No I am not, son. We need that ATV for official business."

"My dad will kill me."

"How would your dad feel if you got arrested?"

"Arrested? For what?"

"Don't you know? This forest service road is prohibited for motor vehicles."

"You're driving on it."

"We're here on official business. Now get off that vehicle before
I put you under arrest."

The boy stepped off the ATV and Roberts grabbed him, turned
him around and handcuffed him to the car door.

The boy said, "Hey, what are you doing?"

Roberts said, "I need to make sure you don't tip off the fugitives we're looking for."

"I won't tell anyone, I promise."

Roberts sat down on the ATV and said to Valdo, "Come on."

Valdo shook his head as he sat down behind Roberts. Roberts put it in gear and drove forward. The boy said, "Hey, aren't you going to leave me some water?" but Roberts and Valdo just drove away.

Six miles in they came upon a turnoff, little more than a sandy wash. Valdo said, "Are you sure this is it?"

"Look at the map. It has to be."

"That don't look like no trail. It looks like a gully."

"This is it. Trust me."

They drove through scrub oak and manzanita bush, the ATV struggling to carry the two men as they gained altitude. The trail passed across a wide sandy area, then narrowed and wound back and forth around short granite outcroppings. They kept rolling along until Roberts stopped and shut the engine off.

"Why are we stopping?"

"You see that?"

"What?"

"See?" He pointed to a spot on the map. "If they're up here, we don't want to spook them, so now we go on foot."

Valdo said, "I'll go. You stay here and keep watch." He didn't want Roberts screwing things up again. He got off the ATV and started hiking up the hill, moving behind trees and bushes, being careful to stay covered as much as possible.

He reached the top of the hill and looked around, but didn't see any one. He looked down and saw two sets of footprints, a large set and a small set. The footprints led toward an outcropping to the west. He followed the footprints until he came upon a small cave. Inside the cave he found two backpacks, two sleeping bags on ground cloths, and various other camping supplies, but no people. He headed back toward the trail and looked around some more. The footprints turned north down a canyon. He crept from bush to bush down the canyon, and at the bottom of the canyon he saw someone fishing in the creek. He moved closer and saw it was Starker, no more than fifty feet away. He reached into his coat and slowly retrieved his .45, bringing the barrel in line with Starker's body. He was about to squeeze the trigger when he felt something brush his leg. He looked down and there, slithering past his leg, was a large rattlesnake. He stayed as still as he could, waiting, sweat running down his face, until the snake had moved on down the trail.

When he looked back up, Starker was gone.

He ran down to the creek, sliding and staggering through the loose granite, looking up stream and down. On the creek bank was a drop line. Next to it a stringer was hanging in the water. He pulled on the stringer and on the end was a fish. He threw the fish back in and hiked up the canyon. At the top, he signaled for Roberts, who drove the rest of the way up.

Valdo and Roberts went through the camping gear, turning out the pockets on the back packs, holding them upside down and shaking the contents out. Everything was inside ziplock bags. They opened the bags and dumped out the contents: freeze dried food, first aid supplies, socks, shirts and a map. Valdo picked up the map and Roberts snatched it from his hands.

Roberts said, "Yeah, like you know how to read a map." He spread it out on the ground and said, "Gisela. That's where they're heading."

"All we have to do is cut them off."

"Yep. Look, they're going along the river."

"How do you know? Maybe they'll double back when we leave."

"Oh, no they won't." He opened a utility box on the side of the ATV and looked inside. He slammed it shut and opened the one on the other side, pulling out an orange stick the size of a large pen. He said, "Flare gun," and walked down the canyon towards the creek. Valdo didn't mention the snake. When Roberts got to the creek, he aimed the flare gun at a tree hanging over the creek downstream and pulled the trigger. A streak of red light shot from the end of the gun and flew in an arch, landing in the tree. The tree crackled and a small flame started in its branches. The flame grew larger and spread, first to the other branches, then to the surrounding trees and bushes. He said, "That will keep them moving downstream."

"How do we know they aren't hiding upstream?"

"Because every law enforcement agent in the state is looking for them upstream."

Roberts opened the map back up and traced the marker line along Haigler Creek to where it merged with the Tonto Creek. "There," he said. "We'll cut them off at Smoky Hollow."

TWENTY-THREE

Neela drove down to the scene of the truck crash. The truck was gone but there was still debris strewn about. She got out of her car and walked to the bridge. There was a sign that said Santa Rosa Canal. She walked along the shoreline and found seven spent .45 rounds. They were shiny—fresh, recently fired.

She crossed the bridge and walked along the opposite side. Finding nothing helpful, she returned to her car and drove to Tumbleweed Road. Along the way she smiled and waved at a group of children playing in a field.

At Tumbleweed Road, she cruised down the access road until she came upon the large pipe Jesse had described. She got out and searched the ground up and down the canal. She looked over the edge where the concrete was cracked. She hiked through the brush to Houser Road, crossed it, and searched the other side.

She retraced her steps back to the canal, searching every inch of ground, inspecting the crack again. She drove back to the bridge and searched there over and over before getting back in her car. She drove over the bridge and turned on Houser Rd. She waved at the children again, and was about to turn on Tumbleweed Rd. before she turned around and came back. She walked out into the field and approached the children. They appeared to be 6-10 years old.

One of the older boys held an iPhone in his hand.

"Hi, Honey."

"Hi."

"Can you tell me where you found that phone?"

A small girl said, "He didn't find it. I did."

The boy said, "You shut up. This is my phone," and shoved the girl, who started to cry.

Neela said, "That's a nice phone. I'd like to buy it. How much do you want for it?"

The boy said, "Ten bucks," and started to laugh.

Neela pulled a ten dollar bill out of her wallet and handed it to him. He threw the phone to her and said, "Boy are you stupid. That phone doesn't even work."

Neela took out a twenty and handed it to the little girl. "Here you are, Sweety."

The boy said, "That's not fair."

Neela said, "Life's not fair." She pulled her coat open and showed the boy her handgun. She said, "Don't let me hear about you picking on her again," and walked back to her car.

She drove down to Jimmy Kerr Blvd and took that to Arizola Road in Casa Grande, where she turned right and drove up to the Walmart. She bought a battery for the iPhone and tried to turn it on, but apparently it was water damaged.

She picked up her own cell phone and called her cousin at the Phoenix Police Department.

"Logan?"

"Oh, hi, Neela. How ya doing?"

"Fine. Look, Logan, I need your help with something but I can't tell you what it is."

"This sounds like one of Uncle Bill's cases."

"Yes, it is. So you can't share this with anybody."

"Okay, no problem. Look, I'm in the middle of something right now. Can I call you this evening?"

"No. It can't wait."

"I'm sorry, Neela, but I'm in the middle of a meeting."

"Excuse yourself and leave. Now."

"I can't do that."

"Now. This is a matter of life and death."

"Okay. Do you want me to come over to Uncle Bill's house?"

"No. I'm coming over to your house. Hurry."

"Okay."

Neela drove out to Queen Creek and waited for Logan to get home. She didn't have to wait long. Inside the house, she was beginning to tell him about the murder when he interrupted.

"—You know where he is?"

"Yes, but that's not important."

"The hell it's not. Do you have any idea how much trouble you've gotten me in just by telling me this?"

"He's with Jesse."

"He kidnapped her?"

"No, she's hiding him."

"Omygawd. Jesse is hiding a killer?"

"He's not a killer. And inside this phone is proof. Now you can get all hysterical over this and get Jesse killed or you can calmly retrieve the data on this phone and put the bad guys behind bars."

TWENTY-FOUR

JONATHAN FOLLOWED RIGHT BEHIND JESSE along the edge of the creek past the pool and waterfall. He whispered, "Man, I got lucky."

Jesse said, "It wasn't luck. You were looking around, being alert."

Jonathan laughed. "Being paranoid."

"Exhibiting zanshin."

"Exhibiting what?"

"Situation awareness."

"Listen."

There was a crackling sound.

"Look."

A fire was growing among the trees upstream.

Jonathan said, "I guess breakfast will have to wait."

They picked up their speed, easing their way along the rocks, fighting through fallen tree branches and thick brush. The fire seemed to keep up with them, but at least it wasn't gaining on them.

They reached a section of the creek where the walls towered above them and there was no ledge to walk, only deep pools of water to float in. This seemed to act as a natural fire break, although a breeze was carrying smoke their way.

Jonathan said, "My throat hurts. Can we drink this water?"

"Without a filter? I don't think that's a good idea."

The sky to the east turned from gray to a sickly black color, lighted with flashes of lightening. Thunder rumbled down the gorge. The air became so thick it was hard to breathe.

Jonathan said, "Look at that," pointing at the muddy water flowing down the creek.

Jesse said, "Ah, shit."

"What's the matter?"

"It's raining upstream. We have to get out of the creek before we get caught in a flash flood."

"Get out and go where?"

"That's just it. We're getting close to the Tonto. If those guys figure out where we're going, they could try to out flank us by coming in at Smoky Hollow. They could be waiting for us around the next turn. Dammit, this is not good."

Jonathan grabbed her by the arm and looked into her eyes, saying, "We'll be fine."

ROBERTS AND VALDO rode back down to FR 133 and turned right, continuing two more miles to the Smoky Hollow trail head, turned right, and worked their way north towards the confluence of the Haigler and Tonto creeks. Roberts lost track of the trail and it took him a while to find it again before they could resume their trek. They bounced along, climbing higher until the trail became too primitive to drive on. They got off and continued on foot. They hiked up to a ridge, and when they got to the top they looked down at the creeks. Roberts said, "Hell's Gate."

Valdo said, "Why do they call it that?"

"I don't know." His phone chimed. He looked at it and said, "I missed a call. Hey, I've got a bar." He thumbed the screen to return the call and put the phone up to his ear. A man answered.

"Hello?"

Roberts said, "Yeah, it's me."

"Where've you been? I've been trying to call you."

"I'm here. What's up?"

Valdo interrupted. "Hey Roberts."

Roberts waved him off. "Not now."

The man said, "You need to hear this now."

Roberts said, "No, not you. What were you going to tell me?"

"They've got a video."

"They've got a what?"

"A video. You know, of that Maricopa thing."

"I'm not following you."

"The PI brought a video to the FBI. They've got you and your friend on video."

Valdo interrupted again. "I can see them."

Roberts waved Valdo off and said into the phone, "What are you talking about?"

The man said, "The truck driver. They recorded the whole thing."

Valdo grabbed Roberts by the shirt and pointed towards the creeks. "Listen to me. They're right there."

Roberts said, "Shut the hell up, you stupid son of a whore," and walked away from Valdo. He put the phone back to his ear and said, "Who has a video?" but the phone exploded in his hand. He felt his ear. It was covered in blood. He turned and realized he was looking down the barrel of Valdo's .45.

He saw a flash.

JONATHAN SAID, Did you hear that?"

Jesse said, "Gunfire. It sounded like a .45 ACP."

"How can you tell?"

"I can tell. It came from up there." She pointed to the ridge atop Smoky Hollow, where there was a man half running, half sliding down the hill towards them.

Jonathan said, "Let's get out of here. Uh, which way?"

"We can't go towards Gisela. It's too wide open here. We'll go up the Tonto. It gets narrow and steep. That guy's too big and clumsy to follow us through Hell's Gate."

They scurried towards the confluence, splashing and stumbling, and turned north around the bend at Tonto Creek. Jonathan looked back, but Jesse yanked on his arm and said, "Come on." At first the Tonto deepened and they had to wade, then it narrowed and they had to scramble over loose gravel.

Jonathan looked back again and said, "He's right behind us."

They forged ahead, the canyon walls closing in, rising to a thousand feet on either side, the banks disappearing, the creek flowing faster as it filled the deep pools in their path.

There were in Hell's Gate.

They swam hard against the current, and were almost through the pools when the rain started and the water turned muddy. The rain stung their faces, coming at them head on as it was funneled though the canyon by the howling wind. A lightning bolt struck a tree at the top of the canyon; thunder boomed, echoing across the mountain tops, becoming fainter with every repetition. The sky flashed again and again, as jagged bolts streaked across the clouds. The air was pungent with the smell of ozone and burning pine trees, and smoke filled the canyon until they couldn't see the trail. They stopped.

Jonathan said, "Which way?"

A wall of muddy water burst down onto them, throwing them backwards down the creek. The flood was pushing rocks and tree branches along with them. Jonathan felt himself being pulled underwater as the angry brown water engulfed him. It seemed like a lifetime but eventually he was able to climb up onto a ledge just above the water. He was disoriented and struggled to get his bearings, but when he did, he discovered he was alone. He looked up stream but he couldn't find Jesse. He looked down stream and there she was on the opposite bank. Valdo had his arm around her and was threatening her with his pistol. Jonathan reached into the plastic bag and took his pistol out of the holster. He kept his eyes on Valdo, and Valdo was looking back at him. Jonathan held the pistol with both hands, lined up the iron sights and stopped. He couldn't aim through the smoke and rain at this distance. He had to move closer, but the walls of Hells Gate went straight up.

He would have to swim.

He put the pistol in the holster and jumped into the raging torrent. He was immediately sucked underwater. Down the Tonto he bounced, smashing into boulders as he went. He pushed off the creek bottom and gasped for breath. A young pine tree came roaring towards him, and he jumped aside quickly enough to avoid the trunk and branches, but the trunk rammed into a boulder, spun around and scraped his stomach with its roots. He started to bleed. He became dizzy and his legs buckled. Lower and lower he slid to the bottom of the rocky pool. He was reliving it all, the canal in Eloy, the Kern River. His nightmare had become real. He was going to drown.

Jonathan faded, his sight graying out the way it did in the canal. He was a brief moment away from death, with only one thought keeping him alive.

He had to save Jesse.

Gathering his strength, he pushed himself to the surface and swam to the side, scratching his way up the slippery bank. Turning around, he saw he was directly across the Tonto from Valdo. Thank God, he hadn't killed Jesse. He was using her as bait so he could get both of them. Jonathan took the pistol out of the bag and aimed with both hands.

No good.

Valdo was using Jesse as a shield. Jonathan closed his eyes, his mind focusing on the video game, Deadly Combat, let out a sigh, opened his eyes, raised the pistol, and fired.

TWENTY-FIVE

JESSE SAW A FLASH from across Tonto Creek before she heard the crack from the CZ52. She looked up at Valdo and saw him smile with a smugness which faded into a look of confusion.

This was her chance.

Jesse spun around, breaking Valdo's grip. Another flash, and Valdo dropped to the ground. She sprinted towards Haigler Creek, stumbling over the rocks, turning her head long enough to see Valdo lying face down on the bank, red trickling from his chest, mixing with the rain, flowing down to the Tonto.

Jesse scrambled, climbing and picking her way over the boulders until she came to the confluence and stopped. She looked across the creek and there was Jonathan. He had followed along the east side of the creek. She cupped her hands and shouted, hoping he could hear her. "Come on over."

Jonathan yelled back, "No."

"It's okay. We can go to Gisela."

"I want to go back."

"What?"

"I want to turn myself in."

"What?"

Jonathan waved his arm, motioning towards himself and shouting, "You come over here."

Jesse walked back and forth until she found a narrow point and crossed over, slipping twice along the way. She sat down to catch her breath and said,

"What did you say?"

"I want to go back."

"You want to go back? Why?"

"This is crazy. We can't keep running."

"Jonathan—"

"I want to turn myself in."

Jesse sighed. "All right." She looked around and said, "Well, we can't go back up Haigler Creek, and we can't hike up Tonto Creek. Why don't we go to Gisela and turn ourselves in there?"

Jonathan hesitated, thinking. "You know, Esposito didn't walk all this way. If we trace his footsteps, we'll find his car."

"We might also find Agent Roberts waiting for us."

Jonathan held up his pistol and said, "I'm ready for him."

"Well, look at you!"

They walked, stumbled, and waded across Haigler Creek and climbed up Smoky Hollow. On the other of the peak they found Roberts lying in the mud, his head shattered. The remnants of a cell phone—shards of circuit board and plastic—lay next to him in the blood. They didn't stop to look but kept walking down the mountain. Half way down they found the ATV. Jonathan opened a utility box and found a bottle of water which he handed to Jesse. He found another bottle and took that one for himself. After they had emptied the bottles, Jonathan said, "Well, let's go on back."

Jesse said, "I want to drive."

"Be my guest. I'm too tired to drive."

Jesse mounted the ATV and Jonathan climbed on behind her.

At the bottom of the hill Jesse turned east, and about two hours later they came upon Esposito's car. It was parked next to a white

SUV, and a law enforcement officer was standing between the vehicles talking to a teenage boy. Closer now, they could see the markings on the SUV. It was a Gila County Sheriff's vehicle. The deputy drew his sidearm and Jesse braked. She put her hands in the air and said to Jonathan, "Get off slowly. And don't tell them anything."

Jonathan stepped off, followed by Jesse. The rain was heavy now, and they both lay down in the mud with their hands behind their heads. The deputy hurried over, keeping them covered as he scurried forward saying, "Is that them?"

The boy said, "No, I've never seen them before. But that's my Dad's quad."

Jesse said, "Officer, you should know he has a firearm. It's on his belt."

The deputy holstered his own sidearm and said, "Don't move," as he grabbed Jonathan's left wrist and dropped down, putting his knee onto Jonathan's back. He pulled his wrists back one at a time, putting hand cuffs on them before removing Jonathan's pistol from the holster, standing up and redrawing his own firearm. He said to Jesse, "Don't you move, I mean it." He went to his vehicle and came back with a second pair of handcuffs. He put them on Jesse. He backed up and said, "On your feet." They stood up and he walked them back to his vehicle, shoving Jonathan into the back seat. He started to shove Jesse but stopped, a shocked look on his face. He said, "Jesse?" Jesse didn't say anything. "What's going on, Jesse? What are you doing with this man? Do you know he's a fugitive?" but Jesse kept her mouth shut. The deputy carefully guided her into the SUV.

The boy said, "Can I go now?"

"No. Get on your quad and follow me to the substation." The deputy climbed in the driver's seat and headed towards Young. As they started down the forest road, he said to them, "You have the right to remain silent …"

* * *

WHEN THEY ARRIVED IN YOUNG, Jonathan was separated from Jesse and locked in small holding cell. He asked but they wouldn't tell him where Jesse was. After an hour, a man came into the cell with him, the deputy standing by keeping watch. The man said, "I'm Doctor Lewis. How are you feeling?"

"Okay, I guess."

Doctor Lewis pulled Jonathan's shirt up and said, "How did you get this wound?"

"A tree crashed into me."

"You're kidding. Where did that happen?"

"In Hell's Gate."

The doctor nodded his head, impressed. He pushed in on Jonathan's stomach in several places. Jonathan winced at one spot and the doctor spent more time prodding that area, saying, "Have you experienced any nausea?"

"No."

"Any blood in your urine?"

"No."

Jonathan said, "How bad is it?"

"Well, you won't be doing any crunches for a while, but you'll live." After he had washed, disinfected, and wrapped the gash, he said, "Keep it clean and change the dressing daily. Do you need anything for the pain?"

"No."

"Are you allergic to any medications?"

"No."

"I'm writing a script for some antibiotics. I'll have the deputy administer them." He turned to leave but Jonathan stopped him. Jonathan shook his hand and said, "Thank you."

"Your welcome."

Jonathan overheard the conversation in the next room. The deputy said, "Do I need to call for a medevac, or can he wait for the ride down the hill tomorrow?"

"The gash is superficial. He has abdominal contusions, but they're not deep. He's in remarkable physical condition, and that's probably what saved him from serious injury."

The deputy came back to the cell and told Jonathan he could make a phone call. Jonathan called his mother. His mother said, "Oh thank God, you're alive. Are you okay?"

"I'm fine, Mom."

"Oh, Jonathan, what in the world is going on?"

"Wait until I get home, Mom. I'll tell you everything."

She started to cry. "I'm so sorry, I should have driven you to Phoenix."

"It's not your fault, Mom."

She sobbed.

"It's okay, Mom. Everything is going to be fine. I have to go now, Mom."

"Wait. Debrah Schwartz wants to know where you are, to tell the lawyers."

"I already have an attorney."

"You do?"

"Yes, Mom. Look, I really have to go."

"You take care of yourself, Jonathan."

"I will, Mom. I love you."

"I love you too."

The doctor came back the next morning to change the dressings. He said, "How'd you sleep?"

"I didn't."

"Are you experiencing any new or increased pain or nausea?"

"No, I'm just worried."

"You should be." When he had finished, he held his hand out to Jonathan and said, "Good luck."

Jonathan shook his hand and the doctor left. A moment later, he heard him say, "He's ready."

A U.S. Marshal came into the cell, shackled Jonathan's hands and feet, and led him out of the building. It was cooler outside than it had been since Jonathan had first entered Arizona. A thin fog hung over the ground and a fine mist floated down from a small patch of clouds. The marshal guided Jonathan into the back seat of a black Ford Explorer. They drove south, the paved road turning to gravel, and were soon climbing along a road that wound high into the forest. When they reached the peak, it was shrouded in thick, dark clouds. As they headed down the other side, they were greeted by sheets of rain. A bolt of lightening shot down from the clouds, hitting the narrow roadway next to the SUV with a snap. Another bolt struck, then another, and another. Lightening flashed in the clouds and all around them. It was so frequent Jonathan said to the marshal, "This is quite a light show."

The marshal said, "Shut up, I'm trying to keep us on the road."

Jonathan kept quiet the rest of the way.

A thousand feet down, they came out of the cloudburst and Jonathan had a breathtaking view. He could look out and see thick streaks of rain falling on the desert thousands of feet below, or look up and around and see magnificent thunderhead clouds, billowy white and gray, lighting up, smashing bolts of lightening onto the mountain.

They arrived at the Florence Correctional Institute where he was processed—a humiliating experience—and put in a jail cell. Neely came to see him the first day. She said, "Did you say anything to anybody?"

"No."

She shook her head in approval. "Bill is on his way home. You just need to sit tight. He'll take care of everything."

"How is Jesse?"

"Jesse is fine. They really didn't have anything to hold her on."

"Oh, thank God."

"Jonathan, I have to tell you something." She fidgeted in her seat.

"Just say it."

"I let them think Jesse was your hostage."

"My hostage?"

"Yes."

"Good. Very good."

"Are you being sarcastic?"

"Not at all. I think it's brilliant. It kept her out of jail."

"So you're okay with it?"

"Of course. I wish I had thought of it myself. Maybe she never would have been arrested."

"No no, you just keep your mouth shut. This is how it works, Jonathan. You say nothing and they have nothing to use against you. Other than the evidence."

"Fine. How long do I have to stay in here?"

"I don't know. There are a lot of people who want you prosecuted."

Jonathan dropped his head.

"Hang in there. Bill will take care of you. It may be a while but you'll get out. And don't worry, there's no way you're going to prison."

"What do you call this?"

"This is a medium-security facility the Marshal Service is using to hold you until the government decides what they want to do with you."

Jonathan shrugged.

"Hey, this is just temporary, I promise. Okay?"

"Okay."

"So, have you talked to your mother?"

"Yes. She was relieved to hear from me."

"I'll bet. What did you tell her?"

"I told her I was innocent and that I was being treated well."

"That's all?"

"I didn't give any details."

"Good boy."

"Hey, is there any chance I could talk to Jesse?"

"No. You kidnapped her, remember?"

"Oh, yeah. Tell her I miss her."

TWENTY-SIX

Back in Chandler, Jesse brought Uncle Bill his dinner while Neela tapped on her laptop. She sat down next to his recliner. After he had finished eating, Jesse said to him, "So why can't I talk to Jonathan?"

Bill said, "This is a complicated game, Princess. Our first priority is to keep you out of it. As far as they're concerned, you were his hostage."

"You're lying to them?"

"Oh, no. I never told them that. That idea started with the deputy who captured you. He said you alerted him to the pistol Jonathan was carrying."

"And from that he figures I was kidnapped?"

"Well, it may be a little creative thinking on his part. You know, he's a friend of Joe's. He might have assumed you couldn't possibly be an accomplice, or he could be trying to help you out. Anyway, he got the ball rolling and I just stayed out of the way."

"Can you at least give Jonathan a message for me?"

"How bad do you want me to get him out of this mess?"

"More than anything."

"Then trust me. Let me do what I do. Okay?"

"Okay." She hugged him and he kissed her on the forehead. He lay back and fell asleep.

Neela said, "Let him rest. He just got through a twelve hour flight. And a heart attack."

"I know. So where's Kotryna?"

"Back in Lithuania. She decided she didn't want to be saddled with an invalid."

"He's not an invalid, he just needs to stay on his meds."

"Well, the way she sees it he spoiled her honeymoon."

Jesse slammed her fist down on the table. "That bitch!"

"Shh, keep it down. Bill doesn't know yet. I want him to get a good night's sleep before I break it to him."

Whispering, Jesse said, "What a bitch."

"That's better."

"So what's going on with Jonathan's case? You said you found his iPhone and Logan retrieved the video. Isn't that enough to spring him?"

"Spring him? You've been watching too many movies."

"You didn't answer my question."

"They're being stubborn. They've got an alphabet soup of law enforcement agencies eager to tear into him."

"But he's innocent."

"Well, not exactly."

"What the hell does that mean?"

"Don't you raise your voice with me."

"What do you mean, he's not innocent?"

"Well, let's go down the list. Driving without a license. Stealing the truck, that's grand theft auto— "

"He had to steal it. His life was in danger."

"—the truck and its cargo, that involves interstate transportation, a federal crime. So that's 20 years. Failing to stop at the railroad crossing. That's a crime. Then there's damage to the train and the cars he hit. One woman is claiming whiplash. That's a civil matter, but hitting the cars and the train, those were done while committing a felony."

"A felony?"

"Stealing the truck and its cargo, remember. Then he ran into Eduardo's flatbed, another collision involving the semi."

"They found his truck?"

"Well, yeah, it was right there below the bridge. Anyway, that makes two instances of leaving the scene of an accident."

"Everything you mentioned was out of his control. He was fleeing for his life. You know that."

"I'm not the one you have to convince. Speaking of fleeing, how about evading arrest? Another felony. Oh, and he killed that goon up in Hell's Gate. Or so you say. They haven't found the body."

"Are you kidding me?"

"No. A bear might have dragged him off. Or a cougar. I don't think coyotes would have had the strength. Anyway, they did find Roberts. Ballistics determined he wasn't killed with the CZ52 Jonathan was carrying. But if Esposito's corpse shows up, that's a homicide."

"Is that everything?"

"No. They suspect he hit a street sign on Sunshine Blvd, but they don't have any evidence. Oh, and then there's impeding an investigation, leaving the scene of an accident, aiding and abetting. Those are for you. Or would be, if you weren't his hostage."

"Yeah. So I'm a victim and he sits in jail. I don't like it."

"Jonathan said it was a great idea."

"He did?"

"Yes he did."

"Well, I still don't like it. He could get hurt in jail."

"He's a pretty tough guy. Did I tell you about his hair?"

"What about his hair?"

"When I cut his hair I saw huge chunks of scalp missing. He must have hurt himself in the wreck."

"He did have some blood on him."

"Here's the thing. I asked him what happened and he blew it off like it was nothing. You know it must have hurt like hell. He's tougher than you give him credit for."

Jesse thought for a moment and said, "You never did answer my question."

"What question was that?"

"About the video exonerating him. Jeez, why are you being such a jerk?"

"Sweetheart, you need to let Bill and me do what we know how to do. You're not our co-council. Which is why you can't see the video, by the way."

She glared at Neela. "Let's try this again. You have his video?"

"What about it?"

"Did it show Mark being murdered."

"Yes it did."

"And you handed it over to the FBI?"

"Some of it."

"Some of it?"

"A couple still shots."

"Showing the murder?"

"Yes."

"And they're keeping him locked up anyway."

"Jesse, you've never dealt with the federal government before. They're in some deep shit and they know it. This was a federal agent who was involved in a murder. That's an embarrassment. They're going to do everything in their power to avoid admitting guilt."

"But you have him on video."

"Wow."

"Wow what?"

"You know, for a reporter, you don't dig very deep below the surface."

"What are you talking about?"

"Think. What was in that truck?"

"Oh yeah. Papa said it could have been a gun walking operation."

"See, you've been so focused on getting Jonathan out of jail, you forgot to look at the big picture. There hasn't been any public admission by the FBI that the video exists. There's been nothing in the news. At all. They're hoping they can still keep this thing from spinning out of control. Jonathan is their leverage. The video is ours. It's a game of poker."

"Oh my God, you've made duplicates, haven't you?"

"I'm insulted you would even ask me that."

"Good. So what's next?"

"We give them another still shot. A close-up of Roberts."

"While Jonathan sits in jail."

"You seem to have a one track mind." She looked up from the laptop and said, "Just what happened between you two up there in the woods?"

Jesse blushed and said, "Shut up."

Neela's phone rang and she went to another room to talk, leaving her laptop open on the table. Jesse slid behind it and scanned the notes Neela was writing, storing names in her memory. She skimmed through the directories until she came upon one labeled JS iPhone and opened it. It contained several photo and video files. She grabbed the thumb drive attached to her keychain, plugged it into the USB port, and began downloading the media files onto it. The last file was large and was taking a long time to transfer. She heard Neela walking down the hall as she pulled the thumb drive out and navigated back to the file Neela had been working on.

JONATHAN WAS SITTING IN HIS CELL reading a Vince Flynn novel when the guard said, "You have a visitor."

"Who is it?" Neela wasn't scheduled to see him that day.

"How should I know. Hands."

The guard handcuffed him and led him out of the main cell block to the visitors center where he sat Jonathan down in a cubicle behind a thick pane of glass. Jessie was sitting on the other side of the glass, looking worried. She picked up the phone, pointed to it, and pointed to the phone on his side. He picked it up and said, "Hi."

"Hi."

"You're not supposed to be here."

"I know. How are you holding up?"

"I'm okay."

"Yeah?"

"I've been keeping to myself. I guess they think I'm important. They have me under extra security."

"That's good. Look, we don't have much time. Tell me everything you remember, from the moment you got in the truck in California to the instant you ran into us by the bridge."

"I already told you what happened."

"I need details. Everything." She picked up a pen and a tablet.

Jonathan said, "Okay," and for the next 45 minutes he talked and she wrote.

A guard came and said, "Time's up." Jesse pressed her hand onto her side of the glass and Jonathan pressed his to the other. As they were leaving, Jonathan saw her say, "Goodbye." He said, "Goodbye," and walked off with the guard.

TWENTY-SEVEN

"What the hell is this?" Neela was pissed.

Jesse looked at the laptop Neela was holding, the browser opened to her blog page. She viewed the headline:

FROM MOVIES TO MURDER.

Beneath the headline was a photo of the shootout between Mark and Esposito. Jesse said, "That is great resolution. I'm going to look into those iPhones."

That made Neela angrier. "You won't think it's so funny when the feds come and take you away. What were you thinking?"

"You're the one who said this was a poker game. I'm playing my hand."

Neela paced back and forth, mumbling. Jesse said, "Speak up, I can't hear you."

"I said you are a spoiled little shit, and I'm not going to visit you in prison."

"I'm not going to prison."

Neela grabbed Jesse by the shoulders and said, "You can't toy with these people, Jesse. They will crush you."

"Look at the photo."

"I've seen the photo."

"Look closely. At everything."

"I know what's in it."

"Look at what's not in it."

Neela held up the laptop and stared at the screen. "You can't see Roberts."

"No. I cropped the photo."

Neela scanned the article. "You didn't mention his name either. You just said there was another man."

Jesse smiled. "This made the Drudge Report. He put his siren up. Now they know we mean business."

"Oh God, what am I going to tell Bill?"

"Tell him the truth. He won't be angry with me for long."

"No, he won't. Hell, he's crazy enough to get a kick out of it."

"Did you, did you tell him about Kotryna?"

"Yes, I told him this morning."

"How did he take it."

"He already figured it out when she didn't come with him on the plane."

"Well, he's not stupid."

"No. But I think I'll wait a few days before I tell him about your blog article." Neela's phone rang. She looked at the screen and rolled her eyes. "The feds have noticed your article. I really don't know what they're going to do now."

"They're not going to do anything to me."

"Don't be so sure. Why don't you go home and get some rest. You're probably going to need it."

"What about Uncle Bill?"

"I got things under control around here. Go home. And cool it with the publishing for a while."

* * *

THE NEXT MORNING Jesse got a call from Bill.

"How are you doing, Princess?"

"I'm fine, but I'm not the one who just got out of the hospital. How are you doing?"

Bill said in a British accent, "Ah, It's just a flesh wound."

Jesse giggled.

"Listen, Honey, I just got off the phone with the AG's office."

"Neela told you?"

"No, she didn't. I found out by myself. You think I'm too old to browse the Interwebs?"

"I don't think you're old."

"Tell that to my heart. Anyway, they wanted to lock you up, but I talked them out of it."

"Thank you."

"Don't thank me yet. They've got a judge on their side. She's demanded that you cease publishing anything about this case."

"What about the first amendment?"

"That's what I said. There is no way her order will pass constitutional muster. But the wheels turn slowly. If you defy this judge, she will have you arrested and it will take a long time to get you out."

"They can't stop me."

"They're going to try real hard. They're cutting you off from your source."

"What does that mean?"

"She's issued a restraining order. Two, in fact."

"I don't follow."

"You are forbidden from contacting Jonathan, and he is forbidden from contacting you."

"Are you kidding me?"

"No, I am not."

"What's her name? The judge."

"Don't do it, Princess."

* * *

A WEEK LATER NEELA DROVE TO JESSE'S APARTMENT and pounded on the door. A woman from the next apartment opened her door and said, "What's wrong?" Neela glared at her and she went back inside.

Jesse opened the door and Neela stormed into the apartment.

"I thought I told you to cool it with the publishing."

"Jonathan's still in jail. I had to increase the pressure. To get things moving."

"Well, things are moving. Federal marshals are on their way over here to pick you up. You just had to name Judge Reinburg, didn't you?"

Jesse was arrested and sent to the detention center in Florence where she was put in administrative segregation. She was denied access to computers and kept from contact with anyone besides Neela and Bill.

TWENTY-EIGHT

Neela got the phone call from Bill at three in the morning and hurried over to his house. He greeted her with a cup of coffee and said, "It seems our Jesse has the government on the ropes."

"O-kay?" She took the coffee and followed Bill over to the living room. She sat down on the sofa, took a sip and said, "Go on."

"I don't know how she did it. She's been isolated for a week."

"Did what? Tell me."

"She posted another article. This one mentions the guns. Alludes to them."

"WordPress."

"What?"

"She publishes her blog in WordPress. You can write an article and schedule it to be automatically published in the future."

"Damn, that girl's smart."

She took another sip. "Yeah, we'll see how smart this move is."

Later that week, Bill called Neela over for a progress report. Bill said, "That last article struck the judiciary hard and they are furious with us for defying a judge. I don't know if I can get a fair hearing for any of my clients now."

"They do stick together, don't they?"

"They think they're gods, and an attack against one god is an attack on all."

"You'd better push back your cases until this blows over. You can use your heart attack as a pretext."

"You're right. I'll do that. So what else is going on?"

"This is turning into a war between old school and new media. The alphabet networks are tearing into Jesse."

"Indeed. They have too much invested in their early portrayal of Jonathan to change course now."

"A lot of the new media is on our side. And Jonathan's fans have started a hashtag movement."

"What is it?"

"It's a coordinated Twitter conversation."

"I know what a hashtag is. What is the hashtag they're using?"

"#FreeGeo."

"Who is Geo?"

"A character in his story."

"FreeGeo. I like it. Do you think it will help?"

"It will help keep the issue on the front page."

"Good. Look, I'm feeling a lot better today. I'd like to get back to work."

"Okay, but on a limited schedule. And you tell me if you get tired."

"I will."

Neela kept Bill informed of developments in Jesse's and Jonathan's cases. Not much happened for several days, but one morning when she came to Bill's house he greeted her with a hug and a smile. She said, "You're certainly in a good mood."

"My contacts in the AG's office tell me they're about to crack. They're going nuts over that hashtag movement."

"Yes, it's incredible. Jonathan has fans all over the world. They're spray painting #FreeGeo on walls from England to Russia."

"Well, the PR is killing them. Big bad government picking on a comic book hero." He laughed a little before turning serious. "Now they're really at their most dangerous, you know. A wounded animal."

"I know they're desperate. My deep contacts tell me they're attempting to shut down Jesse's blog."

"Can they do that?"

"They can try. They went after the domain, but it's registered in Hong Kong, out of their reach."

"Good."

"They also attempted a Denial of Service attack, sending waves of requests for the blog, hoping to overwhelm the web servers, but it's hosted on a Content Delivery Network with servers all over the world. When one server goes down, another takes up the slack and the blog keeps chugging along."

"I sense Logan's hand in this."

"Absolutely."

JESSE'S BLOG HAMMERED AWAY with a new revelation every week. First it was a photo of Agent Roberts, next it was a closeup of his badge, then it was a series of still shots spanning the entire shooting. Finally she published the video and the public outcry was too much. The charge against her—contempt of court—was dropped and she was released from jail.

The first thing Jesse did when she got home was take a shower—alone. She had missed this, the privacy of her refuge. She turned the water on as hot as she could stand it and sat on the shower seat, soaking until she ran out of hot water. She dried off and called Uncle Bill.

"Hi Princess. Did you get home okay?"

"Yes, Uncle Bill. Thank you."

"You're welcome, Sweetheart. Are you hungry? If you're out of food you can come over here, I'll fix you something."

"No thanks. Neela stopped at In N Out, picked up some burgers."

"Okay. Do you need to talk?"

Jesse choked up. "Yes."

"Come on over, then."

Jesse drove to Uncle Bill's house. They sat in the living room for a long time without talking. Uncle Bill stood up and poured himself a Scotch in a short glass. Jesse said, "Are you supposed to be drinking?"

"If I stop now my body won't know what to do. You want something?"

"A glass of wine would be nice. No, a shot of tequila, with ice."

He brought her drink over and set it on the coffee table, saying, "Since when did you start drinking hard liquor?"

She said, "Recently," and took a sip.

"Your folks are driving down tomorrow." He swigged half the glass. "They were furious with me for not getting you out sooner. Your father was really pissed, the ugly son of a bitch."

Jesse giggled. "What does that make you?"

"I'm the handsome twin."

Jesse smiled but a tear rolled down her cheek."

"What's the matter, Sweetheart? Did something happen to you in jail?"

"No. I just want you to get Jonathan out."

Uncle Bill hugged her, holding her head against his shoulder. "I'm trying, but they won't budge. Judge Reinburg took your defiance personally. If it weren't for your blog and Jonathan's fans, you'd still be in there, too." He held her a few inches away from him and looked her in the eyes. "Oh boy. This is more than a feeling of responsibility, isn't it?"

She shook her head yes.

"Let me get you another shot."

* * *

ONE MORNING FIVE MONTHS LATER Jesse got a call from Neela. Jesse said, "Tell me something good."

"The State of Arizona is dropping all charges, as are the counties."

"Thank God."

"Don't get excited yet."

"What do you mean? Aren't they going to release him?"

"Not the Feds."

"Damn Judge Reinberg."

"It's not just her, Honey. Who knows know high up in the government this goes. They're still in damage control mode."

"How long can they hold him? Shouldn't he get a trial?"

"Oh, no, you don't want a trial. If he's tried by a judge, well, you might get a friend of Judge Reinberg. And if it's a jury, anything can happen."

"So he's just going to rot out in Florence?"

"That's the other news. He's been transferred to Riverside. The county prosecutor says he wants a crack at him. Of course it's bullshit. I think he's just playing along with the feds."

"And they okay-ed the transfer? Just like that?"

"Just like that. I guess they're trying to make things miserable for Bill and me."

"And me. I'm flying out there to see him."

"You can't. You know that."

"But I thought—"

"Nothing's changed with the restraining orders."

* * *

JONATHAN WAS SITTING IN HIS JAIL CELL sketching a storyboard for his next novel. He decided to take a break and catch up on the news, and when he turned the newspaper over, he couldn't believe his eyes. There on the front page was the headline:

FEDERAL GUNWALKING MURDERS.

Under the headline was a photograph of an AK47 on the ground. It was the picture Jesse had taken by the canal. Beneath that were smaller photographs of the truck and Agent Roberts' badge. The byline was Jessenia Conrad. Jonathan read that story and other stories related to it. Jesse had spilled the beans—all of it. Within a week all charges against him were dropped by everyone and he was released from jail.

Jonathan's ordeal made him an international celebrity and the exposure made West Wave I a blockbuster success, setting new records for attendance. Debrah kept him busy with signings and important social events. She scheduled them all in Los Angeles.

Judge Reinburg kept the restraining orders on them for almost a year.

TWENTY-NINE

FOUR MONTHS LATER, Jesse was sitting at her desk behind three 24 inch monitors when the receptionist buzzed her.

"You have a visitor."

"Who is it?"

"Jonathan Starker."

"Send him in."

Jonathan entered the office wearing denim clothes and leather boots. He was holding a motorcycle helmet.

Jesse said, "Well hi, stranger," stood up, and threw her arms around him. "It's so good to see you."

He said, "You too. I was in the neighborhood and thought I'd stop by."

"Oh yeah, West Con II." She grabbed the helmet from his hand. "You rode out?"

"Yes. I really hate flying."

She laughed. "I know you do." She hugged him again.

He said, "Are you busy?"

"I'm always busy."

"I was wondering if you wanted to go get some lunch."

"Sure." She looked down at the skirt she was wearing and said,

"Why don't I drive?" She set his helmet down on her desk and followed Jonathan out of the office.

JESSE TOOK A SIP OF ICED TEA and said, "I really wanted to thank you for giving me that exclusive on your iPhone video. That story put my news service in the national spotlight."

"Thank me? That saved our butts. By the way, I have your blog set as the home page on my browser."

She smiled.

"And those pictures you took of the guns." He laughed. "Those were kryptonite. Ten minutes after you published those everyone backed off."

"They sure did."

"How in the world did you get them?"

"You're not going to believe it. There I was, relaxing in my apartment, drinking my morning coffee, browsing the news, well, basically just sitting there in my underwear."

"Wait, wait. I'm forming a mental picture. Thong or granny panties?"

"Bikini."

"Even better."

"Anyway, there's a knock on the door so I put a robe on and open the door just a crack, and there's Albrecht standing there."

"Albrecht. From the saloon?"

"Yeah. Any way, there he is, and he says—in that thick German accent of his—he says Ms. Conrad, may I come in, please? He was so formal, I have to laugh. So I let him in and he's complimenting the apartment and apologizing for bothering me and he opens this box he's carrying and what do you think is in the box?"

"Your camera?"

"Yes! My camera, my phone, my snubby. They're all there in the box, cleaned up and in perfect working order."

"Wow. How do you suppose he found them?"

"He must have gone diving in the canal."

"Well, why not? We did."

"Yes, we did. Hey, Jonathan, there's something I always wanted to ask you. Did you jump into the canal on purpose?"

"What do you think?"

"I think you just fell in. Fell in and took me with you."

He shook his head and smiled. "That's pretty much how it happened."

They both laughed.

He said, "Have you gone on any more adventures?"

"Unfortunately, no. I went from being a one girl operation to a national news organization. I have six reporters, and stringers in almost every state. I hardly ever get out of the office."

Jonathan stammered. "So, are, are you … seeing anyone?"

"Who has time?"

"Oh. Good." He looked relieved.

"But I know you are. You made the cover of People Magazine, you and what's-her-name, the French pop star."

"Bridget."

"Yeah, her. You know, I never buy those gossip rags, I really hate them."

"Yes, so do I."

"But I had to buy that issue. It was staring me in the face, you and Bridget."

"Actually, we were never really going together. Deb set that up. For the publicity. I, I kind of got steamrolled into it. Anyway, that's all in the past."

"Really. What happened?"

"We broke up."

"We?"

"I did. I told her I didn't want to see her anymore."

"I'm shocked. She seems like a real catch."

"She's a wonderful girl."

"Wonderful? She seems perfect."

"She's not perfect."

"No? She's rich, she's famous, she's beautiful. Don't you think she's beautiful?"

"She's very attractive."

"Attractive? She's gorgeous. Tell me, Jonathan, just between you and me, are those real?"

"Jesse—"

"I know, a gentleman never tells. But aside from her obvious, um, qualities, you said in the interview you thought she was intelligent?"

"Yes."

"And witty?"

"She is."

"So, let's go down the list. She's rich, famous, gorgeous, intelligent, and witty. Sounds perfect to me."

"She's not perfect."

"Really? With all that going for her, what kind of defect could she possibly have to make you break up with her?"

"She's not you."

Jesse's eyes welled up.

He said, "All the time I spent with her, every moment together, in the back of my mind I was comparing her to you. I love you, Jesse."

The waitress arrived and said, "Would you like to order now?"

Jesse wiped her eyes with her napkin and said, "I haven't even looked at the menu."

Jonathan said, "Me neither."

The waitress said, "I'll give you two a little more time."

Jesse said, "Wait."

"What is it, dear?"

"Do you serve trout?"

A NOTE FROM JEFFREY YOCHIM

I hope you enjoyed reading Collateral Crimes. The good news is the story doesn't end here. Find out what happens next to Jonathan and Jesse.

Sign up for the Jeffrey Yochim Reading List at
JeffreyYochim.com

ABOUT THE AUTHOR

Jeffrey Yochim earned a living driving trucks and handling freight for thirty years in California and Arizona before becoming an award-winning web designer. Shifting vocational gears once again, he has produced his exciting debut novel, Collateral Crimes.

Today he lives with his family in Arizona.